WHISKEY ON THE WARDS

This book is for those selfless fools who tirelessly dedicate their lives to Medicine. Remember to take care of yourselves.

Also by Jeffrey Brichta

Safety Nation

WHISKEY ON THE WARDS

JEFFREY BRICHTA

PRESENT

The horse hated me. The feeling was mutual. It hadn't helped me win Anne back, and now I was stuck with it. I had to drag it through the city like a fool. It glared at me with its huge brown eyes, and tried to shake itself free. I pulled the reins.

Rain started to fall. Scattered drops quickly turned into a drizzle. It felt like someone spitting at me. I rubbed my sleeve across my face. Then, I realized my clothes were flecked with horse shit. Perfect.

My left hand snapped back again. I yanked the reins as hard as I could. There was a grunt and a mistimed step, and then the clopping hooves resumed their usual pace.

As the two of us trundled along the sidewalk, people gave us a wide clearance. A couple, holding each other tightly beneath a single umbrella, walked by without noticing me, a man in a dirty tuxedo pulling a horse.

My chest became heavy when I saw them. If only I hadn't screwed up everything. But it was Anne's fault, too. I had done this for her. It was what she wanted. I felt bile rise in the back of my throat.

The rain fell harder. Soon, I was caught in a downpour. A fat bolt of lightning cracked overhead. The horse jerked hard on the reins, and they slipped through my wet fingers.

I turned around, shouting, "Hey!" at the animal, as if it could understand me. It cried and darted across four lanes of traffic. Cars screeched to a halt as the horse galloped away.

It reached the other side and kept running. At least it wasn't my problem any longer. The guy who rented the horse to me shouldn't have taken a bribe if he expected to get it back.

I put my hands in my pockets and slogged back to my car. I started the ignition and wasted no time speeding home.

The key rattled, stuck, and rattled again in the rusty lock. An unsettled feeling fluttered in my stomach. I didn't want my neighbors to see me like this. I couldn't survive the embarrassment. I muscled the door open and propelled myself inside the dark apartment.

The tuxedo was stifling. I tore at the bow tie. I flung the wretched thing on the floor. I breathed deeply a few times, trying to slow my heart rate. That usually worked, but this time it didn't help.

I headed for the kitchen. A wedge of light from the refrigerator door brightened my surroundings. I rummaged inside and came away with a can of beer. I cracked it open and guzzled the contents. I grabbed another and drank it as I walked to the bedroom.

In the bedroom, I tried to remove my wet shirt, but it clung to my body. My fingers were cold and numb, and they kept slipping over the buttons. Frustrated, I pulled the fabric in opposite directions. At first I was met with resistance, but then I thought of Anne's horrid face and the shirt was suddenly in two pieces.

Anne had no right to treat me like that. She had wanted a grand romantic gesture. Why would she turn me down when I rode up on a horse, ready to sweep her away? And how could she choose that other guy after all we'd been through?

I went back to the kitchen and reopened the refrigerator. I downed another beer. Then, my eyes were drawn to a bag of IV fluid. How long had this thing been sitting here? I couldn't remember.

The plastic bag squished in my hand. The soft light gave it a ghostly appearance. The letters on the front read: K+ Cl-. My grip tightened and the sides of the bag swelled. It could help me feel nothing at all.

I went to the bathroom. The fluttering sensation in my stomach grew stronger. I ripped the drawers out and turned them over. The contents littered the floor, and I sifted through them haphazardly. I had to find the damn thing and get this over with before I changed my mind.

My fingertips rolled over a small cylindrical object. I picked up the syringe. My head buzzed from the alcohol. I had to do it now.

The wind had shifted outside. Rain pattered against the bedroom windows. The sound became louder as the storm strengthened. Thunder rumbled nearby.

I pulled my belt free and tightened it around my left arm. The buckle pinched my skin. I winced as a bolt of pain ran up my arm. My left hand blanched, and a fat vein in my arm distinguished itself. I picked up the syringe with my right hand, and jabbed it into the bag of fluid. I should have done this before putting the tourniquet on my arm, it would have been easier.

I drew the plunger back, and the syringe filled with clear liquid. How much should I use? I paused and stared at it. It was three-quarters full. My left hand tingled. Not wanting to waste any more time, I pulled the syringe out of the bag. A tiny geyser of fluid shot into the air, like a blowout after striking oil.

The tip of the needle hovered over the vein. I took a few deep breaths. I plunged the needle into my skin. I missed the vein.

Damn.

I maneuvered the needle, trying to hit the vein, but to no avail. As I continued to dig around inside my arm, the needle was met with gritty resistance. Pain radiated up my arm. I pulled the needle out. I had to start over.

I missed again.

Heroin addicts did this all the time. My knowledge of anatomy surpassed theirs, so I should have had no trouble. Why was this so difficult?

I clenched my jaw and swung the needle around. Blood flashed into the needle. At last, success! The hard part was over.

I let the needle go and reached for my cell phone. My thumb hovered over the buttons. Should I call Brad? No, he was probably busy. Who then? Anne? No. Mom? She wouldn't understand. After a moment of contemplation, I dialed 9-1-1.

The phone started to ring, and I let it drop to the floor. I pushed the plunger and injected all the liquid. I removed the belt and waited.

I thought it was supposed to work faster than this. Had I used enough?

Suddenly, a tearing pain ripped through my chest. My heart danced like a bag of worms. I doubled over. I tried to breathe but could only gasp. My face was on fire. The muscles in my body went loose and I fell.

The room spun around me. Sweat poured down my face. I clutched my chest. I was burning up from the inside. Shit, shit, shit. This was a mistake.

The soft blue light of my cell phone glowed in front of me. I heard a distant female voice. "Nine-one-one, what's your emergency? Hello? Is anyone there?"

I reached for the phone, and choked out a few words. After that, everything went black.

Jeffrey Brichta

AUGUST
(ONE YEAR EARLIER)
FAMILY MEDICINE

My heart jumped with excitement. After two years of constant exams, endless labs, boring professors, and tortuously long nights of studying, my clinical rotations were about to begin.

In medical school, the first two years are spent solely in the classroom, packing students' brains full of facts. Remembering even half that information is impossible. Students learn the theory of patient care, but don't get to interact with any real patients.

The third and fourth years, however, are comprised of clinical rotations. Students spend one month in every specialty, caring for real patients and treating real illnesses. I was ready to get out of the classroom and experience the real thing.

I sat in a large, empty waiting room. I was early, and the only staff member here was the secretary. I had impressed no one with my punctuality.

My first rotation was Family Medicine. It was a good starting point, because it would afford me the most variety of cases. It also had a reputation for being laid-back. My classmates who started in more difficult fields bemoaned my good luck.

A girl about my age stepped through the front door. Jet black hair spilled over her shoulders. She had beautiful dark eyes, and a figure that would satisfy any superficial male. Like me, she wore a waist-length white lab coat. My eyes noticed her left hand as it swept by her waist. A gaudy ring too large for her was attached to her fourth finger. Damn.

She noticed me and sat in the chair opposite mine. "First day?" she asked.

"Yeah. The doctor's not here yet. The secretary told me to wait."

"Which program are you from?"

"Med school."

"I'm a PA student. I guess that's why I haven't seen you around."

"Guess not."

"I'm Laura," she said with an outstretched hand.

I shook her hand and introduced myself.

The waiting room door swung open, and an intense-looking woman appeared. She directed us to follow her to the back office. Her name was Jan. She was the office manager. She went over the office safety regulations and privacy policy. I feigned interest in her drivel.

When she finished, she told Laura she would be working with Dr. Cole, and I'd be with Dr. Steinway. Once everything was settled, Jan led us to two adjacent hallways. The first belonged to Cole. Laura remained there and wished me luck. Jan deposited me in the second hallway like a disinterested parent leaving a child at school.

A woman in purple scrubs emerged from one of the exam rooms. She dropped a thin manila folder into a holder affixed to the door. She walked over to a computer mounted on the wall and typed something. When she finally saw me, she asked, "Are you Dr. Steinway's new student?"

"Yes."

"Well, he usually shows up late, so if you want to get started with the patient, go right ahead."

"Oh . . . okay," I said hesitantly. I had hoped for a little direction from my preceptor before jumping right in. On the other hand, I wouldn't want him to think I was lazy.

The chart held two sheets of paper. One had a bunch of uninteresting insurance information. The other was a form that had the patient's vital signs and Chief Complaint, "back pain," written at the top.

I looked at the woman in scrubs. "Get the history and physical?" I asked.

She nodded.

This was it. My first patient. I sucked in air and gathered my courage. I entered the room.

Johnson was a middle-aged man with a red face and a bulbous nose. He sat in a chair next to the examination table. I shook his hand.

"Hello, Mr. Johnson. I'm a medical student working with Dr. Steinway. Is it all right if I get started with you?"

"A student? Uh-oh!" he said in a faux-concerned tone. "Yeah, no problem."

I sat on a rolling stool. "So, what brings you in today?"

"Here for a follow-up," he said, patting his thigh. "Broke my femur a couple of days ago."

His femur? He wore blue jeans with no evidence of any braces, wraps, or a cast. The femur is hard to break, and takes a long time to heal. Perplexed, I glanced back at the words "back pain" in the chart.

"Oh. Well. How are you doing? Is it all healed?"

Johnson slapped his knee hard and unleashed a boisterous cackle. "No, no. Just kiddin'. Actually, I had this tweak in my back, and was hopin' Dr. Steinway could take a look at it."

Not finding his joke as funny as he did, I took the history and moved on to the physical exam. I took notes intermittently, writing in the inadequately small space allotted on the form. When

I finished, I decided this was a case of acute muscle strain. I finished writing my note, but left the Assessment and Plan sections blank. I assumed I would discuss those with Steinway.

"All right, Mr. Johnson, I'll go talk with Dr. Steinway. He should come in, in a few minutes," I said, exiting.

In the hallway, I found a man staring intently at the computer. He had thick, curly black hair, and a protuberant belly that hung well over his brown belt. His jaw moved up and down furiously on a piece of gum. He picked up a sixty-four ounce soda and took a long sip.

I thought he would acknowledge me, but he remained engrossed in the pale light of the computer monitor. He must have known I was here, because I was standing next to him. It seemed like he was waiting for me to speak first.

"Hello, Dr. Steinway. My name is—"

"Go ahead," he interrupted.

"Excuse me?"

"Present the patient."

A heaviness dropped on my shoulders. Apparently, Steinway was unconcerned with trivial matters like the name of his medical student. I opened the manila folder and began to read.

"Mr. Johnson is here today complaining of—"

"Age?"

"Uh, fifty-two."

"Fiftyyy-twoooo," he said, drawing out the words.

"Sorry?"

"Fifty-two year ollld . . ."

"Oh, ah, right. A fifty-two year old white male, um, presents with a, uh, Chief Complaint of low back pain. It started two days ago, and, um, hasn't gotten better. He doesn't have any significant medical history and—"

"Stop."

Steinway took another sip from his giant soda. When he spoke again, his tone was severe. He had yet to make eye contact with me. "You're already getting into the Past Medical History, but you gotta finish the History of Present Illness first."

"Oh, sorry," I said, feeling heavier still.

My eyes dropped back to the chart. I spoke more slowly, hoping this would prevent me from stumbling over mistakes.

"Um, Mr. Johnson, err, sorry, the patient has been having the pain for two days. It, uh, hasn't, uh, gotten any better or worse since then. He took some Tylenol and that didn't help. So now he's, um, here."

I looked back up at Steinway. His paraffin face transitioned perfectly from his beige shirt. He said nothing, which I took as a good sign. My gaze drifted back down to the page, and I continued. "Past Medical History is not significant for, uh, well, anything. He did have–"

"Review of systems."

"What?"

"You can't do Past Medical History yet. You have to do Review of Systems first."

He had grown annoyed. I hesitated, uncertain how to continue. I couldn't remember the specific order of the patient presentation.

My underarms were wet. My trembling hands shook the chart. I sucked in a deep breath and tried to settle myself. "Okay . . . Review of Systems," I said limply. "Positive for back pain, and, uh–"

Steinway snatched the chart from my hands. I reflexively reached for it, and he shot me an irritated look. Steinway muttered something under his breath as he perused the note I had written.

"Woo, doctor, you've gotta do something about this handwriting," he said.

Without another word, he entered the exam room. I stood outside, not sure if I should remain or follow him. I swallowed hard and entered the room. I hoped this was what he wanted.

The exam room was tackily decorated, cluttered from floor to ceiling with sports memorabilia. Steinway sat on the rolling stool, and I stood by the door. It became apparent that Steinway and Johnson were old friends. Johnson recalled the riveting tale of how he had tricked me earlier, and Steinway vented his frustrations of dealing with incompetent students. While they talked, I felt myself melting in the corner.

Steinway performed a history and physical exam. He jotted down some notes, filled out the Assessment and Plan sections, and gave Johnson some advice concerning the usage of Ibuprofen, ice, heat, and rest. Afterward, he returned to his computer.

The following minutes were filled with silence. Icy-hot nausea percolated in my stomach. Steinway gnashed his gum. Through his teeth, he said, "Always start with age, race, sex, and Chief Complaint. Got it?"

"Got it."

"Now, do the next one."

Rooms Two and Three had manila folders stuffed into their chart holders. I approached Room Two and extracted the impossibly thick chart. I hoped this one would go better.

With my second patient, I was more methodical. I organized everything perfectly. It took longer than it should have, but the note was impeccably written. No doubt, Steinway approve.

When I presented it to him, he was quick to find a dozen flaws. With an exasperated sigh, he grabbed the chart from my hands, and proceeded into the room as before.

As with the first patient, Steinway did not discuss the Assessment and Plan with me. He hurriedly returned to the game of Solitaire on his computer. Would we actually get to discuss these patients, or was I simply acting as free labor for him? What was I supposed to be learning from all this?

The morning went on in that manner. I saw a patient, I was treated like an idiot, and the key points of the case were not discussed. With each passing minute, my spirits flagged further.

As Steinway wrapped up the last case for the morning, I quickly checked my watch. It was a quarter 'til one. Steinway's tardiness and his ability to jabber incessantly with patients about sports put us behind schedule.

"Follow me," Steinway said when we exited the exam room.

I followed him to the rear of the office, trying not to stare at the large sweat stain on the back of his shirt. He took me to a small alcove. Steinway looked me in the eye for the first time. His words were laced with venom. "What the *hell* are you doing?"

I started to shake again. "What do you mean?"

"Why are you presenting so badly?"

"I-I don't know. I don't have much experience, I guess."

"I think three months is long enough to be better than this."

"Three months?"

"You're all over the place. You're giving the surgical history before the medical history, the medications in the HPI, and the physical exams are far from complete. You have to be one of the *worst* students I have ever seen."

"I'm sorry, Dr. Steinway. I'm trying to do better. I'm just having trouble since it's my first rotation."

"I don't know what they taught you in school, but you sure as hell better kick it up a notch. I've never seen anyone do this badly after three months."

"Um, Dr. Steinway, this is my first month."

"What do you mean first month?"

"This is my first rotation. My first day."

There was a dense pause followed by, " . . . oh." Steinway's face contorted. A black aura swirled around him. "Well, you still need a lot of work."

He stomped down the hallway and out of sight. I spent the next ten minutes eating lunch, and then resumed my duties of being criticized. The afternoon did go a bit more smoothly, as I now expected my hard work to be berated.

The last patient of the day was a morbidly obese woman named Thomas. When I entered the exam room, I was assaulted by a foul smell. It came from her. I paused, feeling my nose sting. I composed myself and got started.

"Good afternoon, Mrs. Thomas. I'm a medical student working with Dr. Steinway. I'm going to get started with you before he comes in. Is that okay?"

"Yes, of course."

I sat on the rolling stool, and backed as far away as possible. She had lost all interest in taking care of herself. A huge roll of belly fat ballooned outward. Her hair, greasy and matted, couldn't have been washed in weeks. Her clothes were in tatters. Yet, she had a beaming smile, completely oblivious.

"What brings you in today?" I asked.

"I got this damn heartburn."

"When did it start?"

"About six months ago."

"What took you so long to come in?"

"I dunno. I've been busy."

She hadn't been busy with her personal hygiene.

"Describe what it feels like," I said.

"It's this gnawing pain, right here," she said, pointing to a spot just below her sternum.

Internally, I was ecstatic. I knew what was wrong. She had a gastric ulcer. In school we learned to keep an ear open for certain phrases. A gnawing pain in that spot was almost always an ulcer.

I shuffled her to the exam table where she landed with a thump. I was so close, her odor was like a faceful of gas. I had her lay back, and lifted her ratty shirt. A layer of grime caked her abdomen. Despite that, the physical exam was normal.

"Okay, Mrs. Thomas, I'll get Dr. Steinway. Just wait here."

"Thank you," she said pleasantly.

I felt bad for being judgmental. I didn't know her situation, and she had been nice. Nevertheless, my shame didn't stop me from rocketing out of that gas chamber.

Back in the hallway, I went straight for a bottle of hand sanitizer. I pumped the nozzle five times. My hands were doused with slimy green gel. Rubbing them together, gel splattered every direction.

"Whaddaya got?" Steinway asked from his computer.

I opened the chart and read. "Mrs. Thomas is a forty-eight year old white female who presented today with a Chief Complaint of upper epigastric pain. The pain began about six months ago and has progressively worsened. The pain is worse when she eats. It gets better when she take antacids—"

Suddenly, the chart was gone. Steinway had taken it.

"Keep going," he said.

"I'm sorry?"

"Keep presenting."

"Oh, uh, well, antacids make it better. Um, it started six months ago. Uh, her dad, I think, had ulcers? Her medications are Metformin, HCTZ, and, uh, a couple of other things. Her Past Surgical History, oh wait, I mean Past Medical History is positive for diabetes and hypertension. Surgeries . . . uh, I'm not sure. Uh, let me see, there was something else, um . . ."

"Pitiful. Your presentation with the chart was passable, but you were terrible without it."

"Dr. Steinway, how am I supposed to present without the chart?"

"You gotta memorize it. When I was a Resident, they always made me present without a chart. You're just going to have to try harder," he said. He brushed past me and entered the exam room.

I wasn't a Resident yet. I wouldn't be for two more years. That part came after medical school.

I was working my ass off for this guy, and his expectations were unreasonable. I boiled with anger. I waited a few moments until the feeling subsided.

When I returned to the gas chamber, Steinway was regaling Thomas with sports trivia. After that, he told her she had an ulcer and prescribed a medication. He didn't bother to tell me which one.

When Thomas left the office, I looked at a red and white clock that boasted the name of a cholesterol medication. We finished an hour and a half late. I wondered briefly about Laura. She had probably finished on time.

Steinway walked me to the front door. As he let me out of the building, he slapped me on the back and said, "Good job." The resonance of his voice was hollow.

I returned the same empty sentiment with a weak, "Thank you."

The timing of my departure allowed me to perfectly hit rush hour traffic. My car crawled along at ten miles per hour. I thanked Steinway again with a choice expletive.

At my apartment, I tried to absorb the reading assignment Steinway had given me during a brief interlude between patients. The siren song of television was far more appealing. I tossed the assignment aside, and ate dinner while watching TV.

The weeks went on with each day the same as the last. Steinway arrived late, but expected me to be early and see all the patients before him. He told his dull tales of sports fanaticism, consistently got behind schedule, chastised my poor skills, and offered no guidance concerning the management of patients.

One day during the third week, Steinway called out sick. Jan told me I would have to work with Cole for the day. She was a portly woman with a shrill Boston accent and a yellow perm that looked more like plastic than anything resembling human hair.

I relished the chance to have a preceptor who was actually interested in teaching. Unfortunately, things only got worse. Cole was short-tempered, and became angered by the slightest mistake. Her solution to fixing those mistakes was to scream at me as loudly as possible. Unsurprisingly, being yelled at was not the way I learned best.

I was harangued for doing things out of order. I presented the cases in the order that Steinway liked, but it was not the order that Cole preferred. I was yelled at thirty times that day.

Laura was there too, and I saw her flit in and out of exam rooms. She moved too fast for me to keep up with her. She glided around the office, laughed with the staff, and was praised by Cole for her astute diagnoses.

At the end of the day, I caught Laura on the way out of the building. We walked to the parking lot together.

"How did it go?" I asked.

"It was fine," she said as if the day was effortless.

"How do you like working with Dr. Cole?"

"She's a wonderful teacher, don't you think?"

"Eh."

"You like Dr. Steinway better?"

"I wouldn't say like."

"I'm just glad to be here. This is a great rotation."

I felt like we were in parallel universes.

"So, how's your husband?" I asked.

"Oh, um, he's fine," she said diffidently.

"How long have you been married?"

"Two years."

"That's great. Are things going well between you two?"

"Um . . ." she said followed by a long pause, "yeah, they're fine."

"Oh, good. Say, do you have a sister or anything?"

"Uhhh, yeah, she's older. She's married."

"Hey, I was thinking–"

"Well, here's my car. I gotta go. See you later."

She ducked into her car, and hit the gas before buckling her seat belt. I wondered why she left so abruptly.

The next day Steinway returned, and it was back to business as usual. His teenage daughter wrote a sports article that was published in the newspaper. So, when he wasn't indulging in sports trivia, he was showing off his daughter's article to anyone who couldn't get away fast enough.

The days dragged on endlessly. Each patient was more confusing than the last. Each presentation I gave was condemned. He gave me words of encouragement like, "Your diagnostic skills are terrible," and, "Get your act together," and, "This is pathetic."

An hour past closing, I entered the third exam room, ready to see the last patient of the day. This room was also covered from top to bottom with dusty sports memorabilia. Steinway would be better off opening a museum than being a doctor.

McNeely, a thin man in his late thirties, was sitting on the exam table. He looked healthy. Hopefully, this would be fast.

I got started in the usual fashion. His history didn't reveal anything. The physical exam was normal. We chatted a bit, just small-talk, and when I finished, I told him everything looked good. I went to get Steinway.

When we returned, I stood in my usual place in the corner. Steinway repeated everything I had just done. Once he finished, he assaulted McNeely with sports tales: how Steinway caught a famous home run, how Steinway's father had been the physician for a professional basketball team, how great Steinway had been at football in high school, and on and on. Meanwhile, McNeely's eyes glazed over.

"Okay, Bill," Steinway said, "let's get you going."

Steinway looked away to write in the chart. McNeely turned pale. His eyes screwed upward. His back arched. He fell backward, hitting the exam table. All at once, his extremities began to shake. Steinway was up at McNeely's side, trying to turn him to the left. He struggled against McNeely's thrashing.

"Hold him!" Steinway shouted.

I grabbed his shaking legs. It was enough for Steinway to turn McNeely on his side. The shaking continued. It didn't seem like it would stop. Every second on the clock felt like an hour.

At last, his body fell limp. He broke into a sweat, and the smell of urine filled the room.

"All right, set him back down," Steinway said.

We gently laid him on his back. Steinway looked him over. With a tongue blade and pen light, he examined the inside of his mouth. Looking satisfied, he said, "He didn't bite his tongue. Get the MA. Tell her to call an ambulance."

I ran down the woman in purple scrubs and relayed the command. When I returned to the room, McNeely was conscious but confused.

"Is he okay?" I asked.

"He should be fine. Far as I know, he doesn't get seizures. Stay here and watch him."

Steinway stepped out of the room. I was left alone with McNeely, sweaty and having pissed himself. I wondered why he had a seizure. It was probably from Steinway's stories.

~ ~ ~

It was the second to last day. I stepped out of an exam room, happy to escape. The patient, an elderly lady, had a list of things she wanted to discuss. The list stretched to the floor. I tried to get her to only discuss the two most pressing items, but that was impossible. When she was on item twelve, I excused myself from the room.

In the hallway, Steinway conversed with a leggy brunette roughly my own age. She was ridiculously attractive. She wore a business suit and skirt.

"No, sorry, I don't have the time," Steinway said.

"It's going to be interesting. The speaker is coming all the way from New York."

Steinway nodded at me. "Try the kid."

The gorgeous brunette approached me. Her perfume wafted over. Her looks, her smell, her smile, they were intoxicating. She handed me a pamphlet. "We're having a dinner tonight. With a special guest speaker."

A pharmaceutical company logo was printed at the top of the pamphlet. Beneath that was a title, "New Insights into the Diagnosis and Treatment of Osteomyelitis." It sounded as boring as hell, but how could I pass up a free dinner?

"Are you a Resident?" she asked.

"No, a medical student."

"But you'll be a doctor soon."

"In two years."

"That's great. Would you like to come?"

"Yeah, it sounds good."

"You can fill me in on what you learned tomorrow," Steinway said. "Now, get back to work."

"I've just finished one, Dr. Steinway."

"Fine. Start the next one."

I put the chart down beside him. While I started toward the next exam room, Steinway grabbed the drug rep by her arm and pulled her toward his computer. "Here's something you gotta see," he said. "My daughter got an article published in the newspaper . . ."

Steinway let me leave on time so I could make it to the dinner. I didn't have time to go home, so I went to the restaurant wearing my work clothes.

The hostess at the front desk smiled and asked, "How many tonight?"

"Just myself. I'm here for the drug company dinner."

"And which one is that?"

"Um . . ."

"We have three tonight. Do you know the name?"

"Actually, I don't. It was for osteomyelitis if that helps."

She looked at me like I was speaking Portuguese. She told me to wait and vanished for about five minutes. When she returned, she was decidedly less warm. "Follow me."

The hostess escorted me through the steakhouse. It was dark and decorated with deep mahogany. The patrons wore expensive suits and dresses. I felt out of place. We turned right and entered a small dining room. An entire wall was lined with wine bottles.

The leggy brunette from this afternoon stood beside the sign-in sheet. She still looked fantastic. I said hello, and she immediately said hello to the doctor standing behind me. I was invisible.

I took my seat at a table with three doctors. A waiter handed me a pre-arranged menu with chicken, steak, or vegetarian entrees. I ordered steak and a glass of red wine.

This was great. Free dinner and all I had to do was listen to a stupid lecture. I listened to hundreds of lectures in school and never got gourmet food for it. I was moving up in the world.

The room filled to capacity, and the speaker began to discuss osteomyelitis. An ancient doctor at my table was enthralled with the presentation. I was more focused on eating. I hadn't eaten anything this good in years. The speaker droned on, providing some nice background noise.

When he concluded, there was a hearty round of applause. The floor was opened to questions. A few hands went up. The speaker began to answer the questions in turn.

"What are your thoughts on aggressive IV antibiotics only in MRSA osteomyelitis?" the ancient doctor at my table asked.

"That's a tough one," the speaker said. "Of course, I still maintain that there will need to be some degree of surgical debridement. But if you catch it early, IV antibiotics might be enough."

Another hand rose. On the other side of the room, another doctor, a woman as equally ancient as the man at my table, said, "I'm sorry, but you can't possibly suggest you would ever treat a case of osteomyelitis without surgical intervention."

"I take everything on a case by case basis," the speaker said.

"It seems dangerous to even consider antibiotic therapy alone," she said.

"You don't need to do surgery for every case," the ancient man said loudly.

"What are you, crazy? How do you expect to do anything about the necrotic tissue?" the ancient woman shot back.

The ancient man stood up. "I've done it many times!"

The ancient woman stood up. "Name one!"

"In forty-five years of Internal Medicine, I've done it countless times!" he said.

"In fourty-eight years as a surgeon, I know that this disease requires a surgical intervention!" she said.

"You goddamn surgeons always want an excuse to cut something!"

"We have to, because if we don't, you'll kill these patients!"

"You're an idiot!"

"You're full of shit!"

"Please, please, everyone calm down!" the speaker shouted over them.

The insults continued to bounce across the room. The ancient man was red in the face. The ancient woman shook with rage. I couldn't believe what was happening. I struggled to stifle a laugh.

The speaker went on, "We've all had different experiences in our cases. The important thing to remember . . ."

I decided to leave. The two ancient doctors kept yelling, and a few others were getting in on it, too. As I scurried out, I turned back to look for the cute drug rep. She was up front, waving her arms, trying to calm everyone.

I waited in the parking lot, hoping to catch the leggy brunette and strike up a conversation. After thirty minutes passed I figured she wasn't coming, and I went home.

The next day, my last of the rotation, Steinway hadn't bothered to ask me about the dinner. Either he had forgotten or didn't care. I didn't volunteer anything since I had learned nothing.

Once all the patients had been seen, it was time for him to fill out my End of Rotation Evaluation. It ranked me on a scale of one through five concerning various student qualities including knowledge, appearance, patient management, exam skills, courtesy, and more.

Steinway's pen ticked down the list, never straying far from a three. If he thought I did something well, which was seldom, he gave me a four. I'm not sure how I didn't get a five for appearance when I came in every day showered, shaved, and wearing a tie. Did he expect me to wear a tuxedo?

He handed me the evaluation. "You've got a lot of work to do before you'll be any good. Next time, try harder. Do you have any feedback?"

I wasn't sure what to say. I could tell him the truth, that I hated him, and burn a bridge, although his bridge was one I didn't want to cross again, or I could lie and say this rotation had been a good experience. I worked out a compromise.

"I would have liked to spend more time going over the A and P," I said, referring to the Assessment and Plan sections of the medical exam.

Steinway waved his hand dismissively. "I wish I could have, but you know how busy I am. Just look at how late I finish every day."

If he had no intention of teaching, then why did he waste his time with students?

Satisfied that my training with him had reached its conclusion, Steinway made a beeline for his computer. He fired up a game of Solitaire, and took a long drag on his giant soda.

I passed Cole's hallway on my way out. I looked for Laura, hoping to spend a few minutes chatting with her, but she was nowhere in sight. She was probably gone.

When I left the building for the final time, I felt lighter. My shoulders relaxed, and my stride had a spring in it again. I decided not to look back for fear I would be sucked back in like Eurydice.

SEPTEMBER
INTERNAL MEDICINE

Of the six major hospitals in the city, I was about to start at the county hospital. It was notoriously underfunded, overworked, and inundated with the dregs of society. Still, there was something appealing about all that. Being able to care for those who had been tossed aside could be its own reward.

Things got off to a great start. I went to the medical education office to get my ID badge, and they informed me that they had not received my rotation paperwork. The fifty thousand dollars I paid in yearly tuition kept my education running smoothly.

Fortunately, I had the phone number of someone at school who could help. About ten minutes later my paperwork spat through the fax machine. I was then handed a student ID badge and sent on my way.

I was placed on Team Three, scheduled to meet on the sixth floor at 9:00 AM. As I rode the slow elevator up from the basement, my thoughts drifted to what the coming month had in store for me.

This was the so-called "bread and butter" of medicine. Teams of doctors would assemble to pour over the minutiae of labs and physical exam findings for extraordinarily sick patients, and determine the most crucial course of life-saving treatment. At least that's how it was on TV.

The rusty elevator doors groaned open. At the far end of the vinyl-tiled corridor, the ward awaited. It was a hotbed of activity. Nurses huddled together, relaying information, and Residents hurried back and forth with charts under their arms.

I walked down the corridor, feeling self-conscious about my short white coat. It was a symbol of partial knowledge. It declared my status as a student.

The ward was shaped like a cross. Halls spread out in four directions, each labeled with a letter, A through D. Lining each hall were about a dozen rooms. I stood beside the Unit Secretary's desk, unsure what to do next.

"Can I help you?" a gruff voice asked.

The Unit Secretary was a morbidly obese woman in her late forties with numerous gray chin whiskers. She glowered at me intensely.

"I'm looking for Team Three. They meet here, right?"

She threw her thumb toward a man at a nearby desk and said, "Dr. Abbas is on that team."

"Oh, thanks," I said with a strained smile.

Abbas was reading a thick chart. He flipped back and forth between a pair of pages. A discerning scowl was scrawled across his face.

"Dr. Abbas?"

He looked up, the scowl still on his face. He was an Intern, which meant he was in his first year of post-medical school training.

"Is there anything I can help you with?" I asked after I introduced myself.

"Have you done a wards month yet?"

"No."

"Hmm. Well, why don't you see Chavez and write a quick progress note. Then we'll meet back here for rounds at nine." He pushed the encyclopedic chart forward. I was happy to lend Abbas a hand, however, there was one problem.

"I don't know how to write a progress note."

A stunned look passed over his face. One thing I was learning on these rotations was how much I hadn't been taught in the first two years of medical school.

"It's easy. Just write down the vitals and the new labs, ask him how he's feeling, write that down, and copy the rest of my note from yesterday. Also, write down anything important from the consultants' notes."

"Okay."

"Thanks. This will save me a lot of time."

Abbas vanished. I sat in his seat. The chair was still warm. Given his eagerness to hand off this patient, I wondered if this case was toxic.

The chart was a monstrosity. It was a huge gray plastic three-ring binder. There must have been a thousand pages, and they were all from the current hospitalization. The first few pages sat loose, partially torn. They were demographics: age, thirty-four – race, Hispanic – address, homeless – insurance, none – next of kin, unknown – language, Spanish.

The admission note was from forty-two days ago. It was written illegibly. I flipped through the first few progress notes to get a sense of what had been done for Chavez. Each note was labeled at the top by specialty: IM, Pulmonology, Infectious Disease, etc. Each note was more unreadable than the last. The chart went on and on, and his symptoms never changed.

I didn't have time to read all that, so I skipped to yesterday's notes. From what I could tell, Pulmonology had just obtained a sputum sample from Chavez's lungs. Meanwhile, Infectious Disease was awaiting bacterial cultures and recommended switching antibiotics.

Whatever.

I wasn't going to learn anything this way. I flipped the chart closed. It slammed under its own massive weight. The sticker on the front read: 6D-10-1. That was code for floor, hallway, room, and bed number. I headed that direction.

The lights in the room were off, and everyone inside was asleep. A series of curtains divided the room into four squares, creating a small area for each patient. Chavez was in the first bed on the left.

He slept on his right side, with his hands beneath his head. He exhaled raspy breaths. He was emaciated, and couldn't have weighed more than a hundred pounds. His hair was ratty and unclean. His face hadn't been shaved in at least a week. He smelled terrible. Had he not bothered to bathe in the forty-two days he had been here?

It was still early, and he would probably be angry if I woke him. But I couldn't just examine him, could I? No, it would be worse if he was jostled awake with my hands all over him.

"Mr. Chavez?" I called out quietly.

No response.

"Mr. Chavez?" I said more loudly.

He groaned and stirred a bit, but he still slept.

I reached down and patted his calf. "Mr. Chavez," I said in a normal volume.

"Keep it down!" another patient grumbled.

Chavez's eyes fluttered open.

"Mr. Chavez, I'm one of the medical students. How are you feeling today?"

He looked at me, nonplussed.

I didn't speak Spanish, but I knew a few phrases from high school. I would give it my best shot. "Señor Chavez, cómo estás?"

"Mmm, bien," he replied sleepily.

It was a ridiculous question. I had just woken him. How would he have had any time to know how he was feeling today? I pressed on. "Tienes dolor?"

"No."

"Tienes náusea o vómito?"

"No.

"Ah, bien."

There were a few more questions I should have asked him, but I had exhausted my knowledge of medical Spanish. If he wasn't having any pain, nausea, or vomiting, then he was probably okay.

I pulled out my stethoscope. Chavez, well acquainted with this part, tuned out and closed his eyes. His heart thumped steadily. I listened intently for the stutter of an extra heart sound or the whoosh of a murmur. Everything sounded normal. I switched to his back so I could listen to his lungs. "Respire profundo," I said, and he breathed deeply.

I took his pulse. I timed his breaths. To finish the vital signs I needed to measure his blood pressure. But I didn't have a blood pressure cuff. Was I supposed to bring that with me? I never saw doctors carry those things around. I would have to look for one.

"Un momento," I said as I exited the room.

The ward was buzzing. The nurses were finishing their reports, and various monitor-alarms beeped and chimed. Where would I find a blood pressure cuff in this chaos?

A pair of nurses sat in a tiny alcove to my left. They were handing off care of a patient. I felt awkward interrupting them, but there was nothing I had done today that hadn't felt awkward.

"Um, excuse me," I said meekly.

The nurses stopped abruptly. One of them turned her lips down in a snarl.

"I was wondering if you knew where I could find a blood pressure cuff?"

"Ask the CNA," she snapped. She started to turn back to her colleague.

"Um, sorry?"

She turned around again with a look of disgust. "What?"

"Who's the CNA?"

In the same friendly manner as the Unit Secretary, the nurse threw a thumb toward a blonde girl at the other end of the hallway. I thanked her and immediately left. I made a mental note to avoid her for the rest of the rotation.

The CNA was roughly my age. Her long, dirty blonde hair was done up in a ponytail. She wore a pair of black scrub pants and a floral-patterned scrub top. Her physical attributes met all the necessary criteria. She leaned forward against the desk. Her cell phone was in her hands, and her thumbs clicked the buttons furiously. As I approached, I inspected her left hand. A small diamond sat atop a white gold band. Was every cute girl on Earth already taken?

"Hey there, hi. Are you one of the CNAs?" I asked.

She looked up from the phone. "Sure am."

"Oh, great. Maybe you can help me out?"

"I'll try if I can," she said non-commitally.

"Do you know where I can find a blood pressure cuff?"

"Just the cuff? I don't know. But I can show you where the vitals machine is if that helps."

"Yeah, that would be perfect."

She led me to another small alcove where four vital signs machines stood. Their wide set wheels and mass of cords were tangled together. The two of us managed to free one of the machines. I wheeled it down to Chavez's room.

He was breathing more heavily now, likely asleep again. I tried not to wake him as I wrapped the cuff around his bicep and put the oxygen monitor on his finger. The device registered a blood pressure of 128/82 and oxygen saturation of ninety-five percent. I disconnected Chavez from the apparatus, and wheeled it back to the alcove, all while trying to keep those numbers in my mind before they tumbled away.

I passed the CNA and said, "Thanks a lot."

"No problem. I'm Anne, by the way."

I introduced myself.

We smiled at each other for a moment before I returned to the desk where I had left the Chart-from-Hell. Uncertain how to write a progress note, I followed Abbas' format. In the subjective portion I wrote, "Pt feels good, denied N/V." In the objective portion I wrote his vital signs and my physical exam findings. For the Assessment and Plan, I copied Abbas' previous note verbatim. I signed it.

While I had no clue what I had written, if someone were to read my note, they would think I had a firm grasp of medicine. I put the chart back in the rack and checked my watch. I had about thirty minutes left. I decided to go to the cafeteria.

As I left the ward, I walked by Anne again. She was texting on her phone and didn't notice me. She was probably talking to her husband. My stomach gurgled. I would put her out of my mind. It would be easier to concentrate on eating.

~~~

It was now 9:00 AM. After slowly eating a greasy breakfast burrito, I ambled back upstairs. Getting some exercise by taking the stairs seemed like a good way to work off the cholesterol from breakfast, however, I ended up with a cramp in my side. When I got back to the ward, I found Abbas in the Nurses Station.

"Did you get that note done?" he asked.

"Yeah, but I had trouble finding the vitals machine."

"Vitals machine? You don't need to take the vitals."

"I don't?"

"No, you can just copy what's in the Vitals Book. The techs take all the vitals in the morning."

". . . oh."

I felt like an idiot. Leave it to me to botch a task like copying a bunch of numbers.

Abbas pulled a trio of folded papers out of his white coat's inner pocket. He looked them over and shuffled them like playing cards. They were photocopies of progress notes. He made a copy of my note and added it to his collection.

A few minutes later, the next two team members arrived: Sandra and Charles. We performed a round of introductions, and they welcomed me aboard. They said it would be nice to have a medical student on the team, although the value I had was nebulous.

When we finished our introductions, another person wearing a short white coat appeared. His name was Brad. He was also a third year medical student. I felt a bit of a reprieve as I was no longer the only student. I'd have someone to commiserate with if things became too intense.

"Who else are we waiting for?" I asked.

"Smolensky," Charles said. "He's the Attending."

"How is he?"

"He's all right. Kinda chill, which is good."

"Yeah, but next week we got Weismer," Sandra said with a shudder.

"Who's that?" I asked, imagining an asshole of the greatest proportions.

Before anyone could answer, a tall, lanky man appeared. He was completely hairless except for a large blonde mustache. In an unidentifiable eastern European accent he asked, "Are ve ready?"

"Yep, where would you like to start, Dr. Smolensky?" Charles asked.

"Do ve still haf Peterson on top floor?"

"Uh-huh."

"Let's start zere and vork our vay down."

Charles nodded in approval, although I doubted he had much choice. The team climbed the stairs up two flights to the eighth, and top, floor of the hospital. We reconvened in the middle of the ward, which looked identical to the one on the sixth floor. Abbas went to the chart rack and pulled out a chart labeled "Peterson, C." He handed it to Sandra. Abbas withdrew one of his folded papers and began to read from it.

"Mr. Peterson is a seventy-six year old white gentleman who presented two days ago with chest pain and shortness of breath. Workup so far has been negative . . ."

As Abbas spoke, Smolensky looked blankly at the wall. He had either zoned out or was so engrossed he shut off all other stimuli. Abbas rambled on, reciting the contents of his note word for word. Once he finished, Smolensky snapped out of his trance.

"Mmm, yis, vell, let's see 'im."

Team Three crowded around Peterson's bed. Smolensky asked him questions about chest pain and shortness of breath. Peterson didn't understand, and Abbas asked the questions again in clearer English.

Smolensky listened to Peterson's heart and lungs, and gave a cursory look over his abdomen and legs. Satisfied with whatever he had gleaned from the exam, he departed from the room, not saying another word. We hurried out after him.

"Vhy don't you change some zings?" Smolensky said in the hallway.

Abbas nodded and flipped the chart open to the section labeled "Orders." Smolensky instructed him to change doses, to discontinue one medication and start another, and to order a PT/OT consult, whatever that was.

"Good," Smolensky said. "Who do ve haf next?"

It looked like Smolensky wasn't going to explain the changes or teach us anything about the case. Sandra spoke up, stating that her patient, who was down one level, was next on the list. And so, we all trudged downstairs and repeated the process.

Sandra recited her progress note from a photocopy, which made me realize I should have copied the note I had written on Chavez. As she spoke, Smolensky went into his bizarre trance, and when she finished, he reawakened.

In the patient's room, Smolensky spoke and Sandra translated. Smolensky examined them and exited the room without a word. He gave Sandra orders without any explanation. No one questioned him.

Rounds progressed this way for the entire morning. Sandra and Abbas traded off presenting their patients. Charles, who was a year ahead of them in training, was responsible for both of their patients. He interjected with an occasional extra bit of information. When we moved down to the sixth floor, I knew my presentation of Chavez was imminent.

Mimicking what I had seen before, I grabbed the chart. "The medical student saw Mr. Chavez," Abbas said.

The medical student? I have a name. Before I had time to grumble more, Smolensky turned his attention to me for the first time. He looked at me with his pale blue eyes. His mustache somehow seemed bigger. "Go," he said.

I recited my note while Smolensky hypnotized himself. When I finished, we went about the standard routine. I copied the orders he dictated to me and Abbas signed them. As a medical student I was not yet able to sign orders or write prescriptions.

After morning rounds finished, Smolensky told us to call him with new admissions. He departed. Our small team clustered together. Charles took the lead. "All right, good job this morning. Brad, why don't you take the first admission with Sandra?" He looked at me and said, "You can do the second admission with Abbas. Make sure you're back here at seven tomorrow to get started."

Everyone agreed. The Residents went about their day, leaving Brad and myself behind. Brad had arrived late enough to avoid picking up a morning patient. That meant tomorrow he would only have to round on one, while I would have two. Lucky bastard.

We went down to the cafeteria to eat and talk and wait for patients to show up. Brad's admission came in just before 2:00 PM, giving him plenty of time to get it done. Mine rolled in around 3:15 PM.

~~~

The ER was a madhouse. There must have been a hundred people darting about. It was one giant room with a series of curtains dividing it into thirty patient "rooms," which were little more than stalls. Behind one curtain a woman wailed in pain. Behind another, a demented old man called out, "Nurse! Help! Nurse! Help! Nurse! Help!"

I walked down an aisle, looking at the green and white numbered placards over each stall. There, number fifteen. I drew the curtain back and found my patient.

Abbas had sent me a text message a few minutes earlier: "new patient, er 15, reynolds, dvt." I found it strange, yet comforting, that the ER physician had already given us the diagnosis. It wasn't like that in my classes. Somehow, this felt like cheating.

Reynolds was lying on a narrow cot. He had a salt-and-pepper beard, scraggly and long, which complemented his unkempt gray hair. He appeared normal, except for his left leg which was red and swollen. Its diameter was about twice that of his right leg.

"Mr. Reynolds?"

He looked up.

"Hi, I'm one of the med students. I'm here to examine you. Is that all right?"

"Sure, go ahead," he said apathetically.

I gathered his history. He was a smoker who had just returned from a long plane ride. Two days ago his leg became painful and had grown redder. It was a classic DVT story, which meant a blood clot had become trapped in one of the deep veins of his leg. Next, I examined him. His heart, lungs, and abdomen all seemed fine. His leg, however, was quite warm and painful to the touch.

"Don't worry, Mr. Reynolds. We're going to take good care of you. Dr. Abbas will check on you soon."

"Okay. Thanks, doc."

I left and went to a small room designated for doctors writing notes or giving telephone dictations. I began transferring my rough notes into clear sentences on the official admission form. When I was about halfway through writing my note, Abbas arrived.

"Hey, did you see that guy yet?" he asked.

"Yeah, I'm just doing the write-up."

"Throw it in his chart when you're done, and then you can go home."

"Shouldn't we go over it before that?"

"No, it's late. We can talk about it tomorrow."

Abbas wandered down the hallway to find Reynolds. I continued the write-up, but paused when I reached the Assessment and Plan sections. Uncertainty filled me. I wanted to do a good job, but I wasn't sure what to write.

I scribbled, "DVT – treat with Heparin and compression stockings."

That's all I knew. I had no idea what dose of Heparin to use or how often to give it. I felt compelled to add more, but I was clueless what to write. A nervous tingling crept from my stomach to my chest.

Abbas reappeared. He couldn't have been gone longer than five minutes. He must have planned to use my history without gathering his own.

"I'm not sure what to write for the A and P," I said.

He stepped closer and gave my note a cursory glance. "That's fine."

"Are you sure? Shouldn't we–"

"No, no. It's fine. Just go home."

"Okay."

I felt used. Like Smolensky and Steinway, Abbas wasn't interested in teaching. Instead, I was a reconnaissance drone tasked to gather information so they wouldn't have to. How was I supposed to learn anything?

The next day was similar. Chavez was the same. Reynold's leg was still huge and red. Smolensky let me tell their stories, but that was the end of my participation in their care. After rounds concluded, Sandra and Abbas discharged two patients each. They were engaged in the usual pre-call ritual of discharging as many patients as possible.

Tomorrow we would be on-call and have to work overnight. We would be responsible for everyone on the Internal Medicine service, and we would admit all the new patients. So, the more people discharged today, the less to worry about tomorrow.

~~~

The county hospital was in the middle of the ghetto. Barbed wire fences walled off the hospital grounds. Every nearby business was a strip club, a pawn shop, or a carnicería. The entire block was canvassed in graffiti. Iron bars striped every window. Trash decomposed on the street. Gang members congregated on street corners, and bums were sprawled out on bus stop benches. Within the confines of the hospital I felt safe. I only hoped that my car would stay safe, unattended in the parking lot for the next thirty hours.

I walked toward the hospital. The sun peaked over the horizon. My ears heard something peculiar, a rooster's crow. I paused, thinking I must have imagined it, but then I heard it a second time. It was unmistakable. A rooster. In the city. Bizarre.

Rounds went much as they did before. Chavez was unchanged. My third note was copied verbatim from my previous two notes. I scanned back through the chart and found that the other services were doing the same thing. Nobody ever did anything different. Maybe this guy would spend the rest of his life here? I doubted he would mind.

Sandra and Abbas wrote orders. Charles flew through dictation summaries. Smolensky nodded approvingly of everyone's work and vanished without a trace.

Brad and I were instructed to go to the library to "do some reading." I would have preferred to do something else, just to get some kind of experience. Unfortunately, we languished in the library until 4:00 PM. I checked my watch over and over again. The minute hand crept more slowly than I thought possible.

At 4:01 PM, my cell phone lit up with a text message, "new pt, 4b-12-1, george, abd pain."

I jumped out of my chair. Finally, I would get to do something productive. I bounded up to 4B. I found a tall man lying in bed, smiling oddly, and watching television. Each bed had a small TV attached to it by a maneuverable arm.

"Mr. George?"

He looked up. "Yeah."

I gathered his history, but I was constantly fighting against the TV. Either he was distracted and didn't hear my questions, or I couldn't hear him over the program's raucous laughter. I didn't feel confident enough to reach over and turn the TV off. I didn't want this guy to get mad at me.

As I went through George's story, I tried to work out what he suffered from. I had trouble narrowing it down. At least we would be able to do some tests now that he was in the hospital. I got through the bulk of his history and reached the final part, the social history.

"Do you smoke?" I asked.

"No."

"Do you use any illegal drugs?"

"Yeah, man. I use crack."

"Crack? Oh, uh, how much?" I asked, shaken by how forthcoming he had been.

"I dunno. Maybe an eight ball a day."

"An eight ball, okay," I said, writing it down, as if I had any idea what that meant.

"Any other drugs?"

"Just heroin. I tried it a couple times, but I didn't like it."

"Okay. Do you drink alcohol?"

"No way, man, that shit will kill you."

Chuckling, I responded, "That's right, it will."

Except for some diffuse abdominal tenderness, I didn't notice anything abnormal on his physical exam. Although, if there had been an abnormality, I wasn't sure I would be able to discover it.

When I wrapped up, I thanked him. He gave no response. He stared into the blinking void of the TV.

Later, I ran into Abbas and we discussed George. He nodded approvingly when I relayed my findings. He started to walk away, but I stopped him. He turned back with a baffled look on his face. I asked him about our treatment plan.

He answered vaguely. "We'll scan his abdomen, draw some labs, and give him fluids." He then turned and hurried down the hallway, his pager blaring.

With no idea where to find the call room, I returned to the library. I sat down in front of a computer. Just as the relief of sitting entered my joints, my cell phone buzzed again. It read: "new pt, 6c-4-4, ricardo, chest pain."

Couldn't he have waited ten minutes?

I found Ricardo a few minutes later. He was an elderly male, half-asleep on his bed. He didn't speak a word of English. Immediately, my pulse skyrocketed. The one thing I actually had some confidence in doing, the history, would be impossible.

A moment later, a girl no older than twelve popped her head into the quarter section of the room. "Are you the doctor?" she asked in a sweet voice.

"No, I'm a med student. Is this your grandfather?"

"Yes."

"Do you speak Spanish?"

"Uh-huh!"

"Can you translate for me, please?"

"Okay!"

I felt ridiculous, a grown man enlisting the services of a prepubescent girl to translate for her grandfather. So there I was, relaying information back and forth from twenty-six year old to tween to geriatric and back again. I hoped Abbas wouldn't walk in right now. I looked like a fool.

Using a translator was like slogging through mud. And using a translator who didn't know medical terminology made things worse. I constantly rephrased and reworked my questions. Impatience nagged at me. I started to skip the less important parts.

I neglected follow-up questions. I wanted to get this over with. At length, we reached the end, and I moved on to the physical exam.

As I was looking for a pair of latex exam gloves, I felt my cell phone vibrate. I pulled it out of my pocket. The screen read: "new pt, 5a-8-2, dukowman, copd."

Already? I hadn't finished with this one yet!

I went through the exam as quickly as possible. This time I noted a few abnormalities: a whooshing heart murmur and swollen legs bilaterally. I committed each finding to memory. When I finished, I thanked Ricardo and his granddaughter. I left the room and found an open spot in the Nurses Station to write my note.

I got through this one faster than the last. I wrote more quickly and saw a proportional decline in my handwriting's quality. I finally understood why doctors had horrible penmanship. If they took the time to write clearly, they'd work twice as long.

I sped through the admission note. When I reached the Assessment and Plan, I blinked dumbly. The EKG was already done. Cardiac enzymes, already done. Various other labs, already done. What was left?

My cell phone buzzed again. I dreaded looking at it. I slowly removed it, flipped it open, and read the message. Another one. Was Brad getting hit with this many, or were they saving all the work for me?

I leaned back in the chair and rubbed my face. I was exhausted, and I had more work to do. I decided to forgo the final section and move on to seeing the next two patients. I hole-punched the admission note and dropped it in Ricardo's chart. I'd come back and finish it later.

The next two patients were a blur. I worked robotically, asking questions, performing exams, and writing in charts despite having no clue what was wrong with any of them. It was an exercise in futility.

The next time I checked my watch it was 2:43 AM. I had just completed my sixth admission. I staggered out of the patient's room and wobbled back to the Nurses Station. I plopped into a chair, my eyes burning, but afraid to close them for fear of falling asleep.

A man walked up to me. I wearily raised my head and Abbas came into focus. "You see that end-stage renal guy yet?" he asked.

He was all business. The only thought that ever crossed his mind was whether or not I had written his H and P. We had yet to discuss any of the cases.

"Yeah," I gasped.

"Finish writing him up, and then go home."

"Really?" I asked, not believing him.

"We got our six, and we capped. No need to stay any longer."

"Great, thanks."

"Just make sure you start seeing your people by seven."

"All of them?"

He nodded with a stupid grin and clapped me on the shoulder. "Welcome to Medicine, buddy."

His pager blared again. Abbas grabbed a nearby phone and dialed. He deliberated with the person on the other end of the line, and then hung up and dashed away.

I finished my work and headed out, feeling leaden, but happy about the prospect of getting some sleep tonight. When I returned to the parking lot I found my car was still intact.

~~~

The next morning, the patient census was exploding. Sandra and Abbas each had six new patients in addition to all of their old ones. I had trouble waking up and didn't arrive until after seven. Brad looked tired too, but more put together than me.

Abbas told me to present George and Ricardo, and he would take care of the rest. I grabbed the first chart and opened it. I pulled out my admission note and found that I had left the final section blank. Shit! I had forgotten to go back and finish it. I was going to look like an idiot in front of everyone.

Smolensky told me to begin. He clasped his hands behind his back and entered his trance. My voice wavered as I read. My hands shook. My eyes flitted from the paper to Smolensky and back. When I reached the end of what I had written, I fell silent. The silence stretched.

Smolensky's eyes fluttered open. He stared at me with unsettling blue eyes. "So, vat do you vant to do?"

"We started him on Heparin and IV fluids," Abbas said, saving me. He explained the details. Almost as quickly as anxiety had gripped me, it abated. Abbas was good for something after all.

Abbas, Charles, and Smolensky discussed the case. I looked down at the paper in my hands. It was unused, unread by anyone but me.

Once we had rounded on everyone, I helped Abbas tidy up some loose ends. He was disheveled after a night of hard work and no sleep. We finished everything just after noon, and signed out to the new on-call team.

I stepped into the elevator. It was empty. I hit the button for the first floor and closed my eyes. The large metal box started its descent. It jerked to a halt one floor down. Dammit. I wanted to get the hell out of here, not pick up more passengers.

When the elevator doors slid open, a pretty girl stepped in. It was the same girl who had helped me find the vital signs machine a few days ago.

Her face lit up. "Oh, hey! How ya doin'?"

I was surprised she remembered me. "Okay. I just got done with call."

"How'd it go?"

"Not bad. But I'm really tired."

"I don't know how you guys do that."

"Me neither. It was my first time."

"Ooo, you popped your call cherry."

I laughed nervously. My face felt hot. "Guess so."

"And just think, you'd never have done it if I hadn't helped you," she said with a wry smile.

"Yeah, probably not."

"You looked really lost!"

"Well, if I get lost again, I'll call you to help me out," I said boldly.

I quickly felt embarrassed. The silence that followed seemed like an eternity. She probably thought I was a creep. I'd just blown any chance I had with her.

The elevator came to a stop. The doors opened and Anne stepped out. She turned back and said, "You could call me, anyway."

Before I could respond, the doors closed, and the elevator went back up. I didn't care. That was the best thing I'd heard since starting these damn rotations.

~ ~ ~

Friday and Saturday were the same as the others. I had Sunday off, and I slept for half the day. The other half I spent watching TV, too drained to do anything else.

There was a nagging thought in the back of my mind that I needed to study. I tried my best to ignore it. From my chair I could see a stack of books on my desk. I had a test at the end of each rotation, and I had barely passed the first one. If I wanted to do better, I needed to review the material.

I didn't study. I desperately clung to my fleeting day of respite. At one point my parents called me to ask how things were going. It was odd because they didn't call me often. They asked me if I enjoyed seeing real patients. Before I could finish my response, they blurted out that my sister had just given birth. They were calling to let me know how amazing the whole thing was. I couldn't care less.

On Monday morning I went to see Reynolds. He wasn't in his room. An elderly woman occupied his bed. I asked the Unit Secretary to help me find him, and she gave me a look like I had just throttled a baby. With an exasperated sigh, she looked him up in the computer.

"He's gone," she said.

"Gone?"

"They discharged him yesterday."

I was shocked. I didn't think he was ready to go home. Abbas hadn't mentioned anything about a pending discharge. Why didn't they tell me these things?

I moved on, rounding on my other patients who were still in the same places I had left them. I wrote new progress notes and arrived at the usual meeting place. There was a heretofore unseen electricity in the air. The Residents huddled together, fidgeting with nervous energy.

"Hello Team Three," a voice said.

Everyone turned. An impeccably dressed man stood before us. He wore a suit instead of a white coat. He was in his early fifties, thin, average height, and boasted a well-manicured gray beard. A stethoscope hung from the back of his neck.

"Good morning, Dr. Weismer," Charles said.

The two Interns stood at attention like soldiers. Brad and I exchanged a worried look, wondering what was going on. I hadn't seen them so nervous before.

"Where should we start?" Weismer asked.

"How about Stapleton?" Charles suggested.

"Fine, get the chart."

Charles nodded to Sandra who rushed to the Nurses Station. While she was gone, Charles and Weismer reviewed the patient census. I tapped Abbas on the arm. He didn't turn to face me, but leaned slightly to one side.

"What's the deal with this guy?" I asked.

"He's the Residency Program Director," Abbas whispered before returning to full attention.

As the director, Weismer was in charge of all the Internal Medicine Residents. I had envisioned a fat bureaucrat in a corner office somewhere, not someone working in the trenches with the regular doctors.

Sandra returned with the chart, and Weismer escorted us to the patient's room. We found Stapleton and introduced ourselves to her. Weismer told Sandra to begin. Sandra trembled slightly as she gave a succinct retelling of Stapleton's reason for hospitalization, her progress so far, and her current exam findings. All the while, Stapleton looked at us from the bed, silent.

As Sandra read, Weismer studied her, not in a trance as Smolensky would have been. When she finished, Weismer asked Stapleton if he could examine her. She agreed. He deftly examined her and turned back to Sandra.

"What do you think?"

Smolensky never asked for opinions, he just told the Residents what to do. Weismer was altogether different with these bedside rounds and his interest in teaching.

"We need to get more fluid off of her. I was thinking about increasing the dose of Lasix."

"And what about her legs?"

"Her . . . legs?"

"Yes. What are they missing?"

Sandra leaned forward and inspected them as if she had overlooked something minute. She stared at them until Weismer said, "SCDs. Where are they?"

"Oh, I'm not sure."

"Did you order them?"

"I, um, may not have."

"She needs SCDs so she doesn't get clots in her legs, right?" He was referring to cuffs that strap around a patient's calves, periodically compressing and deflating.

"Right."

"Very good. Let's go."

We left the room, and Sandra wrote orders in the chart.

We moved up one floor to see one of Abbas' patients. I wasn't familiar with him. We stood at the bedside and Abbas read from the chart. "This is Mr. Gutierrez, a forty-seven year old Hispanic male who presented with . . ." He recounted the entire hospital course leading up to today.

"Good morning, Mr. Gutierrez, do you mind if I do a quick examination?" Weismer asked.

"I don't mind, but my name's not Gutierrez," he replied.

"I'm sorry?"

"My name is Lee," the polite Asian patient said.

"Oh, well then, I'm very sorry to have bothered you, Mr. Lee," Weismer said with a smile, and then led the team back into the hallway.

"Where's Gutierrez?" Weismer asked sternly.

"Sorry, Dr. Weismer. He's in the same room number, just a different hall."

"And is there a reason why you don't know what your patient looks like?" Weismer asked.

Abbas' eyes widened and he shook his head.

We walked to a different room and found the real Gutierrez. Weismer confirmed who he was twice. Abbas looked at the floor with embarrassment. After completing his examination, Weismer began interrogating Abbas at the bedside. This style of quizzing, nicknamed pimping, was a means of mercilessly asking questions to both assess someone's knowledge, and make them feel like they know nothing at all.

Frazzled, Abbas could hardly answer. I wished I knew more so I could rescue him. I looked at Charles, but he was distant. Sandra looked too afraid to interrupt. The situation concluded with Weismer saying, "Tomorrow, make sure you have the right patient, and you know what you're doing with him."

"Yes, of course," Abbas groveled.

"Now, who's next?"

"Chavez," Charles said.

For over a week, I had written his progress notes on autopilot. I barely examined him. I had no clue what we were doing with him. I couldn't even talk to him. I felt my stomach begin to churn.

As we walked toward Chavez's room, I wiped my sweaty palms on my pants.

"So, how is Mr. Chavez doing today?" Weismer asked in the hallway outside the room.

"Um, he's comfortable in bed in, uh, no acute distress," I said. "He's a thirty-four year old Hispanic male who presented with–"

Weismer held up his hand, silencing me. "It's okay," he said. "I'm already acquainted with Mr. Chavez. I had him on my service last month. Somehow, I'm not surprised he's still here."

"He's been here a long time."

"How's he been?"

"To be honest, sir, I haven't read through his entire chart. But as far as I can tell, he's exactly the same."

"He's a rock," Weismer said with a laugh. "I'll go say hi. You guys don't have to come in."

He entered the dark room. Charles, Sandra, and Abbas used this temporary reprieve to quickly deliberate on how to present the next patients.

A few minutes later, Weismer returned and we moved on. Weismer pimped the Residents on diagnoses and treatments, and he always discovered something they missed. When it came to Brad and I, he was courteous and gave us useful teaching points without being condescending.

When rounds concluded we went about the day as usual. Admissions trickled in. Brad and I alternated between admitting patients and languishing in the library. The times I ventured to the wards, I searched for Anne. Engaged or married, it didn't matter. A girl who was this friendly sent me into blissful stupidity.

I never found her.

Monday, Tuesday, and Wednesday were uneventful. Another night of call came and went. Like my last rotation, it was fresh and confusing at first, but with time it became routine.

Weismer showed Brad and I all sorts of things. We learned to palpate an enlarged spleen, how to test a jiggling belly for ascites, how to differentiate various heart murmurs, and on and on.

I had read about these things in the first two years of school, but had not seen or touched them until now. They were intangibly different than what I had expected. The first two years served the purpose of teaching the mechanism of pathology, and the latter two years were dedicated to learning how to diagnose and treat pathology.

Weismer was much firmer with the Residents, his expectations higher. Although his voice became stern at times, he never yelled or belittled them. Despite his even-handed approach, the anxiety of the Residents never eased when he was around.

On Thursday, I dragged myself to Chavez's room once again. The physical exam was unchanged. The progress notes from all the services were identical. He would live here forever. Perhaps he could be the hospital mascot?

When I exited the room, I saw Anne.

She stood by the Nurses Station, texting on her cell phone, just as she had when I first met her. This time she noticed me. "Hi! Need help finding anything?"

"No, thanks. I haven't seen you around for a few days."

"I was out of town."

"Where'd you go? Anywhere fun?"

"Yeah, we went to San Diego. It was beautiful."

We? She and her husband?

"I'm jealous. I was stuck here with a bunch of sickos," I said.

"So what's your story?" she asked.

"I'm a med student. Third year."

"Ah. How's that going?"

"It's okay. A lot of work and not enough free time."

"That's cool."

There was a protracted pause. Her cell phone vibrated. She started to look down at it to read a new message. To keep her looking at me, I blurted out, "Do you think I could give you a call sometime?"

She resisted looking at the phone. She pocketed it and smiled. It was a smile that made me feel warm inside. "Sure," she said, and we exchanged numbers.

"So, Anne, I have to get going. But I'll see you soon."

"I can't wait."

I glided on a cloud for the rest of the day.

~~~

The next day I was performing a physical exam. She was an elderly lady who came in with a bowel obstruction. It wasn't a particularly exciting case.

I heard a moan come from the adjoining curtained area. Whoever was in there was in serious pain. I tried to ignore it, but my curiosity got the better of me. Even though that person wasn't my patient, I should at least see what was wrong. I peeked around the curtain. "Are you all right?" I asked.

The woman, morbidly obese, did not look well. Her face was ashen, and she clutched her chest. The cardiac monitor hooked to her showed a jumbled mess of green lines. Shit! She was dying!

I flung myself into the hallway. "Somebody call a code!" I shouted.

I raced back into the room. Overhead, the PA system blared out the emergency. The cardiac monitor was beeping wildly. The woman's groans had turned to strained gurgles. I blocked out all these sounds and tried to focus.

I curled one hand over the other and put both on the patient's chest. I pushed down. It was like pushing a rock. I pressed harder, but there was barely any movement. This was a lot harder than on a practice dummy.

I pushed down with all my weight. The woman's bones cracked beneath the force. I rebounded up, and then slammed down. The bones cracked again, but offered less resistance this time. Up again, down again. The crunching minimized and the compressions became easier. I pushed as hard and as fast as possible.

I don't know how much time passed. It seemed like an eternity. My body was starting to feel sluggish. I was out of breath. Still, I kept going.

With a crash, the Code Team burst into the room. I was shoved out of the way, and a burly man in gray scrubs took my spot. His chest compressions were faster and harder than mine.

As I stumbled backward, I looked around the room and saw a slew of new faces. An Attending I didn't know took command. He gave orders calmly and precisely. The team moved with focused energy. It was unlike anything I had seen on TV.

Someone ventilated the patient with a bag-mask. Someone else injected medications into the IV port. A line of people had formed behind the man in the gray scrubs, each ready to take their turn doing chest compressions.

I slowly walked out of the room. I watched the Code Team work from the hallway. After twenty minutes, the team collectively sighed with relief. There were a couple of pats on the back from one team member to the next. The Attending nonchalantly walked out of the room, writing on a clipboard.

"Good job!" someone said beside me. It was Brad.

"What do you mean?"

"You saved her life."

"Me? No, not really. I didn't do anything."

"Sure you did. You did compressions and called the code. If that's not saving her life, then I don't know what is."

"Yeah, thanks."

Sure, she was alive, but I only did what I had to. What anyone would have done. I turned and walked down the hallway to find my next patient.

~~~

Another day of call came and went. Fortune smiled upon us as we happened to be post-call on a Friday. That gave us an extremely rare "golden weekend" where we had two consecutive days off. It was like winning the lottery.

Post-call rounds went quickly. Weismer kept his pimping to a minimum. Sandra was in a daze, Abbas was asleep on his feet, and Charles zoned out. We started, as we always did, with the newest patients. Brad and I each presented the ones we admitted: for Brad, an old man with severe COPD, for me, a middle-aged woman with MRSA cellulitis. Weismer approved of both of our treatment plans.

Brad's second admission was interesting. He was a scraggly male, in his late teens, who was handcuffed to his hospital bed. He groaned and shifted back and forth.

"And what do we have here?" Weismer asked.

"This is Mr. Harland," Brad said. He rattled through the relevant details of the case.

Weismer put his hands on Harland's abdomen and pushed around. Harland groaned louder. He tried to pull away but couldn't. The handcuffs locked him in place. "Did we get imaging yet?" Weismer asked.

"Yes."

"And let me guess," Weismer said, closing his eyes and feigning psychic powers. "The results showed this guy is stuffed with balloons full of drugs."

"That's right!"

Weismer patted Harland on the shoulder. "I hope being a drug mule was worth it. If any of those things pop, you're in big trouble."

"I'd say he's already in big trouble," Brad said, pointing to the handcuffs.

Those were placed by law enforcement, not hospital staff. He was brought in by the police, and they wanted to be sure he didn't go anywhere. Whenever Harland was discharged, the police would immediately take him back.

Harland's groaning settled down. He seemed unaware of us. "Has Surgery been up to see him yet?" Weismer asked.

"No, not yet, but we consulted them," Brad said.

"Okay, let me know when they do. Who's next?"

"That would be Baron. He's in dialysis," Charles said.

Baron was my other new admission. He was a twenty-one year old male transferred from prison. According to the ER report, he had been admitted for weakness, nausea, vomiting, and confusion.

In the Dialysis Department, people sat in rows of recliners with tubes leading out of their bodies and into machines. The tubes were red with blood. The blood passed into the machines, turned round and round, and then went back into the patients.

Baron was in the farthest chair, handcuffed to it. A disinterested Sheriff's Deputy sat nearby, reading a newspaper. Weismer nodded to me, and I presented the case.

"So, what's the diagnosis?" he asked.

"Rhabdomyolysis."

"Good." He turned to Baron and asked, "How are you feeling?"

He opened his eyes lethargically. "I dunno. Tired."

"What were you doing before you passed out?"

"Pushups."

"How many?"

"I dunno. Three hundred?"

"Did you just start your sentence?"

"Yeah."

"Okay, kid. You'll be fine."

We adjourned to the hallway. Weismer chuckled to himself. "We got a two for one deal on criminals last night, huh?"

Brad and I smiled, but the Residents just looked tired. "Anyone know why he developed Rhabdo?" Weismer asked.

"The pushups," I said. "He overdid it. Broke down his own muscles."

"That's right. We see this kind of thing with guys who are fresh to jail. They want to show off how tough they are so they won't become someone's bitch."

Everyone laughed.

Once we settled down, Weismer asked, "Now, who's left?"

We had one patient remaining: Chavez. We traipsed to his ward.

Weismer massaged his temples. "How long has he been here?" he asked.

"This is day seventy-two," I replied. The number was comically high.

"Day seventy-two. Jesus Christ. How is that even possible?"

His question, whether rhetorical or not, fell upon silence. Weismer shot Abbas a fierce look. "Who's the social worker? Go get her."

Abbas attempted to stammer out an answer, but changed his mind and ran down the hallway. Weismer folded his arms over his chest and grumbled. It wasn't that long ago when he laughed about Chavez, as if they were old friends. But it seemed the novelty had eroded.

Abbas returned with the social worker, a stout middle-aged woman with short red hair. Weismer launched into his questions. "What's Chavez's dispo?"

"Nothing," the woman replied.

"Why not? What's the holdup?"

"He has no money, no relatives, no insurance, and *the doctors* are in no hurry to discharge him."

Weismer tried his best to conceal the disgust on his face. He spoke in an even tone, although he was obviously restraining himself. "I would be happy to discharge him if *Social Work* could put some effort into finding a place for him to go."

"Fine," the woman said apathetically. "I'll give him a list of homeless shelters."

Weismer shook his head. "He's got TB and HIV, and he'll be non-compliant with his meds. Unless we want him to infect everybody, he can't go to a shelter."

"Then the only other option is to DC him to the street."

Weismer rested his chin on his hand and contemplated this. Everyone else stood silent and motionless. No one wanted to offer up any suggestions, lest they say the wrong thing. Weismer, perhaps for the first time in his life, looked like he was about to lose his cool. Nobody wanted to be the one to push him over the edge.

"This guy has been wasting a bed for seventy-two days. There's got to be a way to get him out of–" Weismer paused as a new idea popped into his brain. He continued, "Can the hospital pay to taxi him to Mexico?"

The social worker's mouth dropped. "I don't know if we've got enough in the fund. I'll have to check."

"Good!" Weismer said, clapping his hands a single time. "If the hospital can't afford the whole thing, I'll cover the balance."

It was weird how he said it. He sounded jubilant.

"Really? Your own money?"

"Sure. Why not? It's Friday."

The social worker said she'd get to work on it right away. On impulse, I blurted out, "Do you want the taxi to just drop him off at the border?"

I didn't know what I was thinking. Weismer was going to be mad. In my peripheral vision I could see Brad wincing. Weismer smiled. "Of course. There's a first time for everything."

Abbas prepared the discharge paperwork. Chavez had received the finest medical care our country had to offer. Now, with no money and no place to go, he would have no follow-up care and not be able to afford his medications. He would succumb to the diseases so much time, money, and effort was put into treating. What had been the point?

When work wrapped up for the day, I could not help but be excited. The rotation was at an end. Tomorrow, I would take the exam and be free from Internal Medicine. After that, I could do whatever I pleased. And I knew what I would do. I would call Anne.

On the way out, Brad stopped me. "It's been great working with you," he said.

"Yeah, same here."

"You want to, I don't know, hang out sometime?"

"Hang out?"

"You know, grab a beer or something?"

I felt uncomfortable. I didn't understand why Brad had taken an interest in me all of a sudden. "I'm not sure, you know school is so busy," I said.

"Give me your number. I'll call you. We can complain about whatever rotations we're on."

"Yeah, okay, sounds good."

"Great. See ya 'round," Brad said after we exchanged phone numbers.

I was never one to have a lot of friends. Acquaintances were easy to make, but friendships were hard to maintain. Acquaintances said hello and nothing else. Friends always wanted to know what you were up to. I didn't like the attention.

I forgot about Brad. All I could think about was calling Anne. A thousand practice conversations ran through my head. Should I invite her on an extravagant date, or play it casual, like I wasn't too interested? I loved the mystery and anticipation. But more than that, I loved that a girl had given me her phone number.

~~~

It was Saturday night. Earlier, when I called Anne, she didn't recognize my voice. She asked if this was Tony, and if I was fucking with her. I assured her it was really me. After that, her voice brightened. I asked her out for drinks, thinking it would be shorter than a movie and cheaper than dinner if things did not go well. She agreed and chose the place.

The place was called "The Trojan Horse," a tacky faux-Greek restaurant. I seriously doubted that anyone Greek worked here. The restaurant was half-full, but a steady stream of patrons trickled in.

The restaurant was a narrow rectangle. Small booths lined the left wall and the bar stood on the right. The bar was made of rustic wood, scratched and sticky. The bar stools were made of wood, too. The hard maroon leather seats were cracked and stained with age.

I drummed my fingers on the bar. More people filtered in, and the seats quickly filled with customers. I kept my hand firmly planted on the stool to my left. I felt a growing sense of urgency. Anne had better show up soon. I didn't know how much longer I'd be able to save this seat.

She arrived a half-hour late. This was the first time I had seen her in normal clothes. She wore a knee-length black skirt and a plain yellow top. Her hair tumbled over her shoulders and down to her mid-back. I hadn't realized it was so long. As she walked toward me, my eyes went to her left hand again. The ring was still there.

She slid onto the bar stool next to me. "Nice to see you," she murmured. She said it like we had met for a business lunch.

"You, too. You look really nice."

"Thanks," she said, her head craning around as she inspected the room. "Wow, this place is already filling up, huh?"

"Do you come here a lot?"

"Not that often. But it's close to home. So, yeah, I guess I do. Maybe once a week. Not a lot, I guess."

Her babble of contradictions spilled out as she continued to look around the room. She was looking at everything in the restaurant except me. She seemed awfully preoccupied.

"What's good here?" I asked.

"Huh?" she grunted, still searching.

"What's good here?"

Anne's eyes locked onto mine. I finally had her attention. It seemed that whatever she was looking for wasn't here. "Oh, anything's good. I like Fuzzy Navels. That's my drink."

I beckoned the bartender. I ordered one of those for her and a beer for myself. As we drank, we continued with small talk.

"How long have you been working at the hospital?" I asked.

"A couple years."

"You like it?"

"It pays the bills. I'll probably only do it 'til I finish my Bachelor's. After that, I dunno. Maybe become a Nurse Practitioner or a Dental Hygenist. Or get back into acting again. I haven't decided."

She downed half her drink in one gulp. The restaurant was crowded now. The din was near-deafening. Anne and I were almost shouting at each other. She took another gulp and set her empty glass down on the bar. I ordered her another.

"So, you're one of the Interns?" she asked.

"No, I'm a third year med student."

"What's the difference?"

"Well, med school is four years long. The first half is all lectures and stuff. The second half we rotate through all the major specialties, so we can get exposed to everything, and pick which one we want to do. An Intern is someone who already graduated from med school and picked their specialty, and is in their first year of, uh, on the job training."

"So . . ." she looked befuddled.

I simplified it. "They're doctors. I'm not."

"But you will be."

"In a couple years."

Anne had a disinterested look on her face. The conversation was going nowhere.

She was halfway through her second drink. My beer was still half-full. Beads of condensation covered the glass. I would have to drink faster if I wanted to keep up with her.

My eyes wandered over her. Her legs were tanned and smooth, her stomach was flat, and she the swell of her breasts was substantial. My eyes continued to track upward. When my gaze arrived at hers, she asked, "What do you like to do?"

If she had been aware of my ogling her, she did not make it apparent.

I had to think hard to answer the question. The last two years of my life had been non-stop studying. And four years of college prior to that was dedicated to preparing for medical school. And I wasn't exactly a social butterfly in high school. I didn't really do anything.

"I play Tennis," I lied. Then, I added something a little more daring. "And I like hiking and mountain climbing."

I cringed at how ridiculous it sounded. I had never climbed a mountain in my life. She probably thought I was a jackass.

Her face lit up. "Wow! Mountain climbing! What mountains have you climbed?"

"Oh, well, Mt. St. Helen's, Mt. Fuji, and Mt. Rushmore."

"Mt. Rushmore! Really? I had no idea they let people climb that."

"Yeah, sure do. It's one of the hardest."

"That's so cool!"

She placed her hand on my forearm, and I felt great. I wanted more of that feeling.

The date continued on that trajectory, with me confabulating and her fawning. At first, I felt awkward lying so much, but it quickly became natural. My boasts grew more preposterous, but with more alcohol my confidence made up for that.

Midnight came and my stomach was bloated. My mind swirled and my fingertips felt fuzzy. Anne looked to be in similar condition.

"Hey," I said, my tongue feeling loose, "ya wanna get outta here?"

"Sure. Walk me home."

"Where d'ya live?"

"Down the block."

I paid the bar tab. It was far more than I could normally stand, but for my chances with a pretty girl, I didn't mind. I couldn't remember the last time I had been with a girl.

As the two of us lurched down the street, arm in arm, fantasies of us as a loving couple danced in my mind. I desperately wished she was my girlfriend. Looming ahead was the goodnight kiss. Would I do it, or would I chicken out? I ignored the thought as long as I could.

"Okay," she said. "Here we are."

I had only gotten to ignore it for about five minutes.

A few concrete steps led up to a wide brown door. Hers was the middle unit in a long stretch of townhouses. It had a small window to the right of the door, and a second story above. All of the attached houses were dark inside.

She took a couple of steps up and turned around. She reached out with both hands. I hesitated for a moment, and then took her hands in mine. She smiled softly. With her being two steps up, we were now equal in height. This was it, the signal. If I didn't act now, I could forget about her. A girl like her would not give me a second chance.

"Good night," I said, leaning forward.

Our lips met. Hers were soft and moist and full. I held there for two seconds, three, four. Then, worry that I would overstay my welcome pulled me back. As I did, she pulled me toward her. We kissed again. Longer this time. Sloppier, too. I felt a rush of excitement within myself, down below. I pulled back again.

"Do you want to come in?" Anne asked.

I nodded, unable to form words.

Inside, the house was dark and quiet. We only made it as far as the couch before being overcome by passion.

As we fumbled in the dark, my anxiety-riddled brain would not shut off. I was so drunk, so inadequate, I screwed up everything. She sighed with annoyance when I was unable to unhook her bra. Each time I thrusted, instead of enjoying pure pleasure, I only felt incredible pressure on my full bladder. I climaxed too soon.

Anne didn't say anything about the mechanics. I wasn't sure if she had enjoyed it. We kissed a bit longer, with her sitting on my lap. Eventually, the need to relieve myself became too great. I stumbled through the dark hallway and into the bathroom.

When I returned to the living room, a table lamp was on. Anne was pulling on her underwear. "Hey," she said flatly, "if you wanna spend the night, that's cool. But I don't mind if you wanna take off." She looked at me like an unwanted object. I should have gotten out of there.

"I'll stay if it's all right."

She shrugged.

Still reeling, I staggered upstairs, following Anne to her bedroom. In bed, she curled into a ball and turned away from me. I inched forward and wrapped my arm around her. Her body was warm, and I wanted to savor this moment for as long as I could.

She began to snore.

My eyelids felt heavy. I closed my eyes and slept.

OCTOBER
RADIOLOGY

Back home, the leaves were changing from vibrant green to beautiful gold. The trees that lined the main street formed a multicolored tunnel of orange, yellow, and red. The days grew shorter, and soon a chill would be in the air. That, of course, was in my hometown. Where I lived now, the seasons didn't change.

It was always hot here. This was an environment held constant. One season lingered in perpetuity. In winter it would cool down at night, but the days always remained blisteringly hot.

The terrain was nothing but rocks, sand, dust, and the occasional green cactus. In the distance, mountain ranges surrounded the city. People found the barren, rocky landscape enchanting. To me, it was miles of brown dirt.

I remained at the same hospital for my next rotation. This time it would be a month of reviewing X-rays and CT scans. It didn't sound like the most exhilarating rotation, but at least it would be more laid-back than my last two. It would probably be a month-long vacation.

Arriving first thing in the morning, I meandered through the labyrinthine basement of the hospital. Tucked within the deepest recess of the building, past the kitchen utility and beyond the morgue, was the Radiology Department.

The Reading Room was dark. I waited for my eyes to adjust as the door closed behind me. There were half a dozen large cubicles, three on either side with a narrow aisle in between. Each cubicle was dimly lit by the soft glow of computer screens.

I was supposed to meet with an Attending, Dr. Az, but I had no idea which cubicle he was in. I tried the first one on the right.

The man in the cubicle, staring at a pair of screens, replied without shifting his gaze. "Az is at the end on the left."

I thanked him and walked down the aisle. I knocked on the padded wall of the cubicle and stuck my head in. "Dr. Az?" A man in his early forties looked up from his own array of screens. He watched me, waiting for me to say something else. "I'm your medical student for the month."

"What year are you?"

"Third year."

"Come in. Have a seat."

He gave a backward nod of his head. A metal folding chair stood in the corner of the cubicle. I sat down and shifted several times until I got comfortable.

From here I could see Az's dual screens and the back of his head. He returned to studying a pair of X-rays. Each screen contained an image of a chest, one taken from the back and the other from the side. He clicked various spots on either image, zooming in, measuring, and changing the brightness.

A few minutes passed. "Any questions?" he asked without looking at me.

Having entered in the middle of the case, I felt a singular emptiness in my brain. "No," I said.

Az picked up a small white device, like a remote control, pressed a button on the side, and began to speak rapidly. "Patientisatwentyfouryearoldmalewhopresentedwithsuddennewon setrightsidedchestpainPAandlateralviewradiographsreveal . . ."

He continued speaking at breakneck speed. Occasionally, he stopped to double-check something, and then he continued his dictation.

While he blathered on, memory overtook me. I drifted back to my date with Anne. Sunday morning, I awoke with a pounding headache. I reached across the bed to find the rumpled sheets vacated but still warm. I craned my neck to identify the source of a soft rustling. Anne stood by her dresser, pulling on a pair of jeans.

"Morning," I said with a smile that went unreturned.

"Your clothes are still downstairs."

"I guess I need those," I said. I stretched my arms above my head. The muscles pulled tight. I yawned.

Light spilled into the bedroom. The curtains were made of wispy white fabric, more for decoration than utility. Sunlight caressed her skin and illuminated her tussled hair. I enjoyed this candid look, out of bed but before making herself up for the world. I always found women most beautiful when they looked like this.

I rubbed my bulging eyes. My temples throbbed. My mouth was dry and my bladder full again. "Do you have any Aspirin?" I asked.

"I have something to do. Would you mind getting out of here?"

"Oh . . . sure."

I crawled out of bed, and felt cold as I stood naked. Anne put her hair into a ponytail. She turned to leave the room, and gave me an irritated look. She pulled the bedroom door open and bounded down the stairs.

In the living room, I dressed quickly. I tried to engage her in conversation, but to no avail. She unceremoniously hurried me out the front door as soon as I was fully clothed. There was no goodbye kiss. There was no goodbye.

At home, I showered and watched TV. Around bedtime I called Anne, but there was no answer. A nervous feeling crept over me. I called again. No answer. This time I left a message.

And now I sat in a cubicle, shrouded in darkness, being ignored by another Attending. I checked my cell phone. No calls. No text messages. I snapped the phone closed and slipped it back into my pocket.

"Nofurtherevaluationrequiredatthistimethisdictationcompleted byAzMDateighteleven AMenddictation."

Az set the dictation device down. A few clicks of his computer mouse closed the current case and opened the next one. The morning went on in this uneventful manner. Az only acknowledged my presence at the end of every case with a simple, "Any questions?"

My reply was always the same. "No."

At noon, my stomach bellowed. I clutched at my belly with both hands, hoping to silence it. Az took no notice. He wrapped up his current case and looked at his watch. "It's noon. Why don't you go home?" he said.

I couldn't believe my ears.

"Are you sure, Dr. Az?" I sputtered, wondering if this was a trick.

"I only have two more cases left, anyway. Go home and do some reading."

"Okay. Thank you."

After how the last two rotations went, I didn't want to decline an offer to go home early, although I had no intention of studying.

I hurried out of Reading Room. Before I left the hospital I went up to the wards to see if I could find Anne. I glimpsed Abbas standing at attention while an Attending screamed at him. I didn't find Anne.

That night I sat in my apartment, lights off, TV on. The room was cast in a pale blue glow. My body melted into the recliner. I sat there nearly twelve hours. I kept my cell phone on the armrest of my chair, an inch from my hand. It lay silent throughout the evening.

I felt pangs of guilt. I should have been studying instead of rotting my brain with television. Reading even a single chapter would have been a more productive use of my time, but fatigue overwhelmed me.

I picked up the cell phone. The tiny screen on the front was still dark. Should I try to call her again? A million possibilities ran through my brain all at once. I decided not to risk it. I set the phone back down and went to bed.

~~~

The next day, Az studied X-rays, CTs, and MRIs while I languished in the corner. If it wasn't so goddamn dark in here, at least I could have been reading something. Why was it so dark anyway? They were looking at computer screens, not films.

Az asked me if I had any questions, and I answered, "No." He let me go home again at noon. We had our routine down.

This time I resolved to get some actual work done. After returning home I sat at my desk, and opened a book to a random page. My mind continued to wander despite how hard I tried to focus. I ruminated about Anne. I alternated between reading pages and checking my phone. It took me several hours to read a single chapter.

Wednesday, Thursday, and Friday continued identically. I only worked four hours every morning, if you could consider what I did to be work. I hardly got any studying done. I called Anne and left several messages with no replies. I wondered what had gone wrong.

The weekend passed uneventfully. No one called me. I lurked inside my apartment watching TV, trying to keep my mind off what I would otherwise be dwelling on.

The following week was more of the same with one exception. On Friday, while maintaining a fixed gaze on his bank of computer screens, Az told me, "Good luck. It was nice working with you."

He explained that his partner from his radiology group would be my preceptor for the next two weeks. I thanked him and left, unaware of what was to come.

That night, I found myself restless. My leg jittered while I sat on the edge of my recliner. The TV flashed endlessly. With nothing to do, my thoughts kept drifting back to Anne. I had to do something to get my mind off her.

I wandered for a while. I passed the downtown shops, and rolled in and out of each. I soon found myself in a coffee shop filled with artistic folks. The girl at the counter was taking orders and making drinks simultaneously.

"Can I get a cappuccino?" I asked.

"Sure, hon," she said with a wink.

Before she winked at me, I hadn't really noticed her. But now I realized I liked her. She wasn't the kind of girl I would normally be attracted to. She had long hair done up in dreadlocks, tattoos, and several piercings. I didn't know what it was, but she was different. Maybe she thought I was cute, too.

She turned away and started to brew the coffee. I watched her as she worked. She didn't have a ring on her finger. My stomach growled queasily, and my heart rate jumped. Despite my nerves, I knew I couldn't pass up this chance. She handed me the coffee.

"What are you doing after work?" I asked.

"Just heading home."

"Would you, uh, like to get a drink with me?"

"No thanks, hon."

"It might be fun. What do you say?"

"Sorry, but I have a boyfriend."

"Oh, I see."

I walked out of the coffee shop feeling like my legs were filled with lead. I threw the coffee into the first trash can I found.

~~~

Monday morning I strolled in fifteen minutes late. In the chair where Az had sat was an ancient man, one hundred years old from the look of him. The light of the computer screens reflected off his bald head. His dark eyes shifted toward me.

"Oh, erm, hi," I said and introduced myself.

He continued to stare. I waited a few beats for a response. My blood turned to ice. I stumbled over my words, trying to fill the void, trying to shift his burning gaze away from me.

"I was, uh, working, um, with Dr. Az last week. And, uh, well . . ."

"Sit down," he grumbled.

I walked past him, feeling his eyes follow me to the chair in the corner. After I sat down he turned back to the computer screen.

"Pull your chair up," he said.

"I'm sorry?"

"Pull your chair up next to me. You can't see anything from back there."

I felt like I was in high school detention. As soon as I sat next to the Attending, who had yet to reveal his name, he pointed to a structure on the screen. "What is that?" he asked.

"Um, I'm not, uh . . ."

"It's a tracheostomy tube."

"Okay."

"What is this?" he asked, pointing to something else.

"It's, err, the aorta?"

"Close. Aortic knuckle. And this?"

"I'm not sure."

"Come on, think."

I strained for a few moments, pretending to be deep in thought, but had no clue. He tired of waiting. "The diaphragm. Come on, kid," he said gruffly.

I felt myself shrinking in my chair. The nameless Attending picked up the dictation device. He didn't speak in such a rapid-fire manner as Az, but he was still pretty quick. He also verbalized punctuation, saying "comma" and "period," which was incredibly strange.

When he finished the dictation he opened the next case, a CT scan of the abdomen. He looked around, zooming in and out, measuring, and inverting the black and white. When he was satisfied, he resumed the pimping session.

"Name this structure."

"The gallbladder," I said proudly, knowing I had gotten one right.

"Good. And this?"

The mouse hovered over a whisper-thin vessel. A few options were in my head: common bile duct, hepatic duct, and cystic duct. Which was it? It wasn't laid out neatly like in an anatomy text book. I ventured a guess. "Common bile duct?"

"No. Cystic duct. This?"

"Descending aorta."

"Right. And this?"

"No clue."

"Vertebral artery."

My fatigue grew as he quizzed me relentlessly. Eventually, the old man paused to dictate his findings on the case. I sneaked a glance at my watch. Forty-five minutes had crawled by. At this rate, the next two weeks were going to be the longest of my life. When he finished, we proceeded to the next case.

He kept me engaged, but it was painful. His growls of disdain with every wrong answer dragged me down. This must have been the style of training he was subjected to when he was a medical student in the 1800s.

After more agonizing hours, the Attending finally said, "I guess it's about lunch time. Why don't you get out of here?"

"What time do you want me back?"

"First thing tomorrow morning."

I was surprised. I figured he would keep me for a twelve hour shift. I suppose all that pimping had really slowed him down.

Regardless of his intent, I was not about to stay one minute longer. I scrambled out of there.

As I slipped out he called after me. "Hey, wait."

I turned back. The old man, with jowls like a Basset Hound, scowled. "Make sure you're on time tomorrow," he said.

"I will."

"And study. I expect you to do better."

I darted away. I had spent four hours in a dimly lit interrogation room with an old man whose name I didn't know. We had another nine days together. Wonderful.

At home I poured over my anatomy atlas. I felt like whatever I studied wouldn't be the right material. At least I wasn't distracted by thoughts of Anne.

~~~

Tuesday morning I arrived ten minutes early. I walked quietly into the Reading Room and sneaked toward the cubicle. I hoped to have a seat and await the old man's arrival. How surprised he would be to find me waiting for him! I turned the corner and my gaze met his. Damn. What time did he get here, anyway?

He said nothing, only returned to an X-ray of a shattered forearm. The bones were splintered into a million pieces. I pulled the familiar chair out of the corner and sat.

The old man started his dictation. I edged forward in my chair, and my eyes scanned the ID badge that hung from his shirt. I could barely discern the photo of his face in the dim lighting. Beneath the photo was his name, but I couldn't make it out. I leaned toward him to get a better look.

I sensed something was wrong. I looked up and saw the old man staring down at me. I sat bolt upright. My shoulders tensed. I prepared for his wrath.

"Do you know how to read a chest film?" he asked.

"I think so."

"How?"

"Look at the lungs and heart and um . . ."

"No, no," he groaned. "What's the process, in order, for looking at it?"

"I don't know."

"Here," he said as he pulled up the next case. Each of his screens was filled with an image of the patient's chest from different angles. With a skeletal finger he pointed to the image on the left. "This is the PA view. Posterior-Anterior. And this," he swung his finger to the right image, "is a lateral view, taken from the patient's right side."

I knew that, but I didn't dare tell him.

"The key to reading any film is consistency. Doesn't matter if it's a CT or an X-ray. Just as long as you're consistent in *how* you read it, you won't miss anything."

"What order do you use?"

"First, I look at the bones. I move from top to bottom and left to right. Then the lungs, the diaphragm, the heart and aorta, the mediastinum, and then all the spaces in between. Now, let's practice."

And we did practice. Seven times. It was grueling, but being methodical helped me catch a number of abnormalities I would have otherwise missed. The old man was right. Consistency was the key.

Once again, when noon rolled around, the ancient Attending released me. Before I left, he told me we would work on CT scans tomorrow. I left feeling today went more smoothly than yesterday. Even so, I still didn't know his name.

Wednesday was better still. I had spent the previous night studying images in my anatomy book from the same point of view as a CT scan. So, when the old man quizzed me, I got a lot of answers right. He grumbled less, and I felt a little smarter. By the end of the day he told me to "keep reading," and I detected a hint of affection in his voice.

By the end of the week he had cut back on the pimping. I was getting the majority of his questions right. He turned to other topics such as the physics behind MRIs. Apparently, the giant magnet in the machine turned all the electrons in the body one way or the other, or something. I didn't quite get it, so he took me on a field trip to the MRI suite.

The machine looked like a giant roll of toilet paper with a bed in the middle. All pieces of metal had to be carefully stowed before entering the room. Once we were inside, the old man handed me a metal chain.

"Don't let go. Understand?"

"Got it."

I gripped the chain at one end. The other end was instantly pulled toward the machine. It levitated in the air as if by magic. I took a step toward the machine, then another. The closer I got, the harder the chain was pulled by an invisible hand.

"Not too close," the old man said.

I handed back the chain. He shoved it into his pocket and escorted me back to the Reading Room. I had a big, dumb grin on my face. That was one of the coolest things I had ever seen.

The weekend and the following week passed quickly. I had all but given up on learning the Attending's name. I tried listening to the end of his dictations, but he always said his employee ID number instead of his name. And at this point, I couldn't ask him, because I'd worked with him for two weeks.

We reached the final day. The Attending had me reading X-rays and CTs and MRIs to him. He nodded approvingly. After a few hours of this, noon came for the last time.

"Okay, kid, any questions before I let you go?"

"Just one," I ventured. "Why is it we're always done at noon?"

"If we leave at noon that gives us enough time to play eighteen holes."

He grinned wryly and guffawed. It was weird hearing him laugh for the first time. I smiled and extended my hand. He shook it.

"It's been a pleasure," I said.

"Good job, kid. Keep reading."

I gave him a quick nod and headed home. I never did ask his name. His signature on my evaluation was completely illegible. It didn't matter. He would always be the old man to me.

NOVEMBER
OB/GYN

Not knowing where to find the stairs, I took the elevator up to the second floor. I looked around the vacant lobby. Beyond a desk and small waiting room was a pair of locked tan metal doors. An intercom was positioned on the wall to the right. I pressed the button, and a female voice responded. "Yes?"

"I'm a medical student. I'm supposed to start today."

I heard a hard snap as the magnetic lock released. I pulled one of the heavy doors open and entered the ward. It was calm. I had half-expected doctors soaked in amniotic fluid, mothers wailing in pain, and babies shooting across the room.

The ward was oval, with the Nurses Station at the south end, and patient rooms around the perimeter. A monitor-alarm chimed in the distance. The Nurses Station was a wide blue desk with an array of computer screens and charts scattered haphazardly. Two nurses, middle-aged and obese, chattered away.

"I'm looking for Dr. Brookstone," I said.

Both nurses looked at me. For a moment they had a look of dutiful attention, but then they saw my short white coat. They returned to their conversation.

"I'm supposed to work with Dr. Brookstone. Do you know where I can find him?"

Between tidbits of gossip, one nurse said, "I think he's in surgery, you'll have to wait."

A couple of chairs stood empty on the other side of the desk. I sat down and wondered if I should try to look busy. The nurses made no such attempt. I decided not to bother.

To my left, one of the computer screens showed a series of eight rectangles, and within each were two lines tracing up and down, from left to right. I tried to dust off the cobwebs from my long forgotten OB/GYN class. One of the boxes started flashing white, and a monitor-alarm shrieked. I spun in my chair, looking at the nurses.

They remained engrossed in their mindless chatter. Was someone in distress? Was a baby dying? Shouldn't somebody see what was going on?

I heard a click, and the alarm ceased. A third nurse had canceled it. She sauntered into the station and engaged with the others.

Thirty minutes passed. Twice more a blaring alarm sounded, and both times a nurse silenced it without checking to see what was the problem. The longer time stretched on, the more awkward I felt sitting there.

I opened my cell phone and pretended to send text messages. I didn't have any friends to text with, but it looked like I was doing something. When I grew tired of that, I read through one of the charts.

"Hey, Dr. Brookstone," a nurse said.

A short, thin man with a bushy mustache entered the ward. Like a reflex, I shot out of my chair and straightened my white coat. Brookstone entered the station, opened a chart, and wrote furiously on one of the blank notes inside. He hadn't noticed me.

I waited anxiously for him to finish. As he closed the chart, I said, "Excuse me, Dr. Brookstone? Hi, I'm your med student for the month."

"Nice to meetcha. C'mon, we hafta do rounds."

I followed him to one of the patient rooms. A teenage girl, covered in acne and cradling a teddy bear, lay in the bed. Brookstone launched into Spanish. I couldn't understand what he said. He kept his hands folded neatly behind his back, and he rocked on his feet. She smiled, and I hoped he said something reassuring to her.

We exited the room. "What do you wanna go into?" he asked.

This was the eternal question every medical student was asked. "I don't know yet," I said. "Something with a lot of variety like ER or IM or FP."

"IM? So you're one of those, huh?"

"One of what?"

"It's too bad you don't want to be a surgeon like me."

A surgeon like him? I was not aware that obstetricians were surgeons. What did they do other than deliver babies?

Before I could ask, Brookstone ducked into the next room where he tended to another acne-covered teenager. As we went from room to room, there was little variety to the patients. None of them spoke English. Many were in the country illegally.

Brookstone told me I was lucky to have gotten this rotation. Normally, a student on an OB/GYN rotation stands back and does nothing. However, his service treated students like full members of team. I would be expected to do everything.

As we made our way around the oval, we saw about half the women on the ward. As exciting as his promise to "do everything" had been, I found myself bored. We did no physical exams, and everything was conducted in a language I didn't understand.

When rounds ended, we found ourselves back at the Nurses Station. "Next thing we gotta do is getcha changed. No sense messin' up your nice clothes," Brookstone said.

He showed me to the physicians' locker room, just outside the ward. I pulled on a set of blue scrubs and threw my white coat on. I glimpsed myself in the mirror. I looked like a real doctor. I returned to the ward, taking large strides.

I found controlled chaos. An alarm blared. Nurses scrambled into a patient's room. I peered inside and saw Brookstone adorned in a surgical gown and leggings. He was positioned at the foot of the bed, between the patient's open legs, hands held outward. "Hurry and gown up," he said.

I turned my palms up and frowned.

"In the bottom cabinet to your right."

I pulled open the cabinet and took out the surgical leggings. I tried to yank them on, but found the thick material unrelenting. Meanwhile, Brookstone was telling the patient to push. I didn't have much time. If I wanted to participate in the delivery, I would have to hurry.

I hopped, and my feet slid farther into the leggings. I hopped again, and my shoes finally slid into place. I pulled the rest of the material up to my waist. I hurried to the bedside.

Brookstone didn't look at me. "There's a gown and gloves on the table. Do you know how to put them on?"

I ran to the table. Meanwhile, the baby's head was emerging. Brookstone's fingers wrapped around it. I had to move faster!

I grappled with the gown. One of the nurses helped me. I got it on, but it was a mess. Now, the gloves. There was a specific way to put them on in order to maintain sterility. I flipped open the sterile paper wrapping the gloves. As I put the first one on, I turned back and saw Brookstone holding the baby's full head in his hands. I was missing my chance!

I scrambled to put on the second glove. "You're doing it wrong," the nurse said.

I didn't care. I had to hurry. I got it on and raced to Brookstone's side.

The baby was halfway out. The mother gave a final push, and the baby slid out with slippery ease. Blood and amniotic fluid splattered onto the floor. It splashed against my legs. It was surprisingly warm.

The nurse clamped the umbilical cord, and Brookstone instructed the baby's father to cut it. He severed it with a look of bored familiarity on his face. With his task completed, he returned to a recliner across the room.

Brookstone placed the baby on the mother's chest. She stroked its face with stars in her eyes. After a few moments, it was whisked to the other side of the room so vital signs could be taken, antibiotic eye drops given, and an array of tests carried out.

"You'll get the next one. C'mon let's grab some breakfast," Brookstone said.

After eating, we continued to round on the patients. One at a time they went into active labor, and Brookstone delivered their babies. I stood at the bedside, dressed and sterile, and not doing anything.

Despite his promise, Brookstone wouldn't let me help. Each delivery was "complicated" and I was relegated to watching. With the third, he let me deliver the placenta. I pulled on the severed umbilical cord, and pressed hard on the woman's bulging abdomen. It was not intuitive. With enough pulling and pressing, the placenta's death grip on the uterus loosened. It slithered out like a mangled jellyfish.

For the rest of the afternoon, I delivered placentas. I didn't have the chance to deliver any babies. At the end of the day, I thanked Brookstone for all of the great teaching points he had given me, most of which I had instantly forgotten.

~~~

The following morning, the atmosphere on the ward was palpably different. Instead of lounging and ignoring monitors, the nurses moved around busily. I wondered what had changed.

A short, bald doctor wearing purple scrubs stomped around the hallway. In an effeminate voice, he shouted some orders at one of the nurses. "Medical student, right?" he asked me.

"Yes," I said offering my right hand. "I'm–"

"You're five minutes late. Let's go."

Without stopping, he continued past the station, and up the opposite side of the oval hallway. I had actually been five minutes early, but I didn't say anything. I hurried after him.

He walked with a wide gait, and his arms swung exaggeratedly at his sides. Despite being a good five inches shorter than me, he was larger than life. His ID badge swung back and forth with the rhythm of his movements. The name printed on it was "Ravmani."

He veered into one of the rooms. He immediately launched into a rapid-fire discussion with the patient. She was fourteen years old, and this was her first pregnancy. First-timers often took forever to deliver, and she would most likely be the last one of the day.

During rounds, Ravmani did all the talking, and all of it was in Spanish. A couple of times he did some physical exam maneuvers, placing his hands on the patients' abdomens, and determining the positions of the fetuses.

"Feel this," he said.

I put my hands close to his. Ravmani pushed into the patient's swollen abdomen with his left hand, then relaxed it, then pushed with his right. "Do you feel that?" he asked.

I felt lumpy resistance. It could have been the fetus, but it didn't seem to have a definite human shape. I nodded.

"What position?"

"Uh, position?"

"The position of the fetus. Which way is it?"

"I'm not sure."

Ravmani scowled. "Here, feel this," he said. He moved my hands with his own through a series of four motions. He told me which part was the head and which was the butt.

"It's Left Occiput Anterior. So, everything's fine."

The patient had a flat look on her face. She didn't know what we were saying, but she could tell Ravmani was not happy with me. She was probably thinking, "I hope the kid doesn't deliver my baby."

Ravmani and I walked back to the Nurses Station. He launched into a tirade. "Is there a *reason* why you don't know Leopold's Maneuvers yet?"

I wasn't sure how to respond, but Ravmani wasn't interested in my response. "You're already way behind. When you're on my service you need to keep up with the material."

He reached into the lowest desk drawer and removed a huge tome. He dropped it onto the desk with a bang. The book's pages were tattered, and its binding came out in strings.

"I expect you to finish this by the end of the rotation. And to know it. The other thing when you're on my service—" Ravmani grabbed the chart rack and swung it on its wheels to face me. "—is you'll need to know every detail of every patient. If you don't know them backward and forward, then you forget about doing anything."

Ravmani told me he had to take care of "other business," and would be off the ward for a while. In the meantime, I was to sit at the Nurses Station and study the book and charts. Anything less than one hundred percent retention would be unacceptable.

Ravmani was worse than Steinway. With Steinway there was indifference. He didn't give a shit if I was there or not. Ravmani intended to put me to work, and if I wasn't up to his standards there would be hell to pay.

I flopped into a chair and opened the book. The first page flew out and slid across the desk. I turned to the first chapter. My eyes scanned the words, but my brain registered nothing.

At noon I ate lunch. The cafeteria served better food than I was used to. This rotation found me in a nicer part of town in a private hospital.

After I ate, I went outside for a walk. The sun shined brightly. The air was hot. The city burned with waves of heat reflecting off the concrete. The landscape was mostly dirt and rocks. Small patches of grass were scorched brown. I only walked for a few minutes before the heat forced me inside.

I returned to the ward and found Ravmani looking over a chart. When he saw me, he narrowed his eyes. "Why aren't you reading? Where were you?"

"Lunch."

"Lunch? In the cafeteria?"

"Yes."

"No, no, no. You can't eat in the cafeteria. You have to eat here. There's no telling when these patients are going to deliver. You can't leave."

"But Dr. Ravmani, you left for at least an hour."

"*This isn't about me!* It's different when you're the Attending. Now, we need to get to work. Come on."

Ravmani and I performed a second set of rounds. With a few of the patients, he performed an induction, where he inserted a weird, pronged device into their cervix. This broke their water and made labor begin. When we finished rounding the second time, Ravmani instructed me to continue reading until someone was ready to deliver.

I poured all my energy into focusing on the book. It was dense with technical information. The occasional picture piqued my interest, but mostly it contained jargon and diagrams of who-knows-what.

A nurse trotted over to the station. She threw her thumb back like a hitchhiker and said, "Arredondo's delivering."

She was one of the older patients, a twenty-seven year old on her third child. She would deliver quickly. Another nurse hoisted herself out of her chair, and the two of them marched down the hallway. I dropped the ancient book and followed them.

The only people in the room were the nurses, the patient, who was already pushing, and me. Fear washed over me. Where was Ravmani? There was no way I could deliver this baby on my own. What if he walked in on me trying to do it? He'd probably smash my head open. Uncertain what to do, I stalled for time by suiting up.

While I pulled on the leggings, my foot stuck. I hopped on one foot while trying to jam the other into place. Suddenly, my center of gravity was off. I flailed as I careened backward. I hit the floor. The nurses managed to restrain their laughter. The patient was oblivious.

I ripped off the leggings, and pulled a fresh pair out of the cabinet. Ravmani arrived and appeared jubilant. "Let's deliver a baby!" he sang.

He slipped on his leggings in a few seconds. He already wore his cap and mask. He fluidly moved to the bedside, and began to put on his sterile gown and gloves. Meanwhile, I struggled to get my gear on correctly.

"Hurry up and get over here, or you can forget about helping!"

I threw on a mask and cap. Next, the gown. It required two people to be put on in a sterile fashion. I handed the main tie to the nurse and began to turn counter-clockwise. "Wrong way!" Ravmani shouted. "You don't turn that way! The other way! Goddammit, *don't you know anything?!*"

I stopped. I was trembling. My breathing was shallow. I slowly turned the other direction, with the nurse guiding me. Once I had turned around, I grabbed the main tie and tied myself up. I took my position beside Ravmani.

"Have you done this yet?" he asked.

"No."

"Did you watch Brookstone do any yesterday?"

"Yes, a few."

"Good. Stand here, and get ready."

Ravmani took a large step back, letting me move into the open space between the patient's legs. My breaths were even faster now. My whole body felt hot. My trembling became shuddering. I extended my open hands toward the woman's vagina. The nurses were holding her legs back as far as possible. Ravmani gave her instructions in Spanish.

Ravmani inspected the fetal monitor. He looked at me again. "What the hell are you doing?"

"What?"

"Put your fingers in there!"

He grabbed my right hand and shoved it into the patient's vagina. It didn't go far. It was met by the fetus' skull. Ravmani told me to move my index finger around, to stretch the vagina, and make room for the baby.

The vagina didn't stretch much, and I wondered how much good this really did. But I wasn't about to argue. I continued forcing my finger around to no avail. Meanwhile, Ravmani barked orders at everyone.

The fetus drew closer. I could see a wet, matted clump of hair on its head. I removed my fingers and positioned my hands like a baseball player ready to catch the slowest pitch of all time.

Ravmani looked back and forth between the patient and me. He said nothing, which let me know that, at least for the moment, I wasn't doing anything wrong. When the patient bore down, the head moved farther.

A long green turd snaked out of the patient's ass. It coiled up on the edge of the bed. The smell was awful. Just a few short centimeters above, the baby's head was emerging.

"Okay, grab the head and start pulling," Ravmani said.

I wrapped my hands around the tiny skull, trying to grip it. My fingers slipped. I grabbed it again. I didn't want to lose my grip. Should I squeeze tighter? Would I crush its skull? What the hell was I supposed to do?

I gripped slightly harder, and I pulled backward. Nothing happened. The patient was gasping for air. She sucked in a deep breath and pushed again. The nurses counted to ten. As she pushed, I pulled. The head moved more quickly. The baby was coming out!

The head was about halfway out now, and the patient stopped. Ravmani screamed at her. In a mix of languages, he told her to keep pushing. She took another deep breath and pushed again, and the baby's head slid out of her vagina.

The baby was the color of ash. It furrowed its brow and wrinkled its face. I never knew a baby could wake up while it was being delivered.

Ravmani slapped my hands. "*Not there! Hold it here! Jesus!*"

He shoved my hands below the baby's jaw and told me to keep pulling. My strength slackened. I didn't feel comfortable doing it this way.

"*Pull goddammit!*" he screamed. I pulled again but nothing happened. The patient pushed harder and grunted loudly.

"What the fuck are you doing? Do you want a live baby or a dead baby? Just deliver it!" Ravmani snarled.

I pulled again, this time with downward traction. The baby's shoulder popped out. But I hadn't moved quickly enough. Ravmani body-checked me out of the way. His hands were around the baby, and he delivered it in a flash.

I was barely able to stand up. I swayed side to side. My heart slammed in my chest. I wanted to escape, but I couldn't. I had to stay with Ravmani because I was a medical student. I was destined to stand here and take it, because if I didn't, I would fail the rotation and be totally screwed.

Ravmani forgot I was in the room. He delivered the placenta, and stitched a small tear in the vagina endured during the delivery. When he finished, he regained his effeminate voice. "Okay, the baby's here," he said lyrically.

He waltzed out of the room.

Fate spared me, and none of the other patients delivered during my shift. I sat and read at the Nurses Station. I managed to avoid Ravmani's wrath.

At night, I tossed and turned in bed. I stirred with dread. I couldn't work another day with that lunatic. I got out of bed and went to the kitchen. I had a six pack of beer in the back of the fridge. My hands shook as I drained the first and then the second.

After a while, my nerves calmed. I found sleep came easier after that.

~~~

The month was a manic-depressive roller coaster. Brookstone and Ravmani alternated days. On days with Brookstone, the ward was relaxed. Unfortunately, I was relegated to delivering placentas. At first this was a relief, but it became a waste of time. Every day moved in slow motion. The alternate days, the ones with Ravmani, were a whirlwind of high energy. Every event on the monitor, no matter how minuscule, was a catastrophe. Ravmani pimped me mercilessly. If I didn't know the answer, he went ballistic. He expected me to have every chart memorized while he checked them over and over again.

To my surprise, he let me do everything. I put in catheters, I assisted with cesarean sections, and I delivered babies. My technical skills improved dramatically. The first delivery I did on my own was slow and shaky. By the end of the month I had done so many I looked like a pro.

Ravmani never let up. There was always a reason to scream. I always did something wrong. No matter how hard I tried, it wasn't good enough. But the better I got, the more he let me do. This didn't endear him to me. I hated the sight of his face, and cringed at the sound of his voice. I boiled inside, and suppressed it, each time he blew up.

I had two on-call nights during the month, one with each of the Attendings. Those nights were just like the days. Brookstone didn't need me, and let me sleep in the call room. Ravmani cracked the whip, and had me deliver babies, bleary-eyed and sleep-deprived.

As the month went on, I found that I needed a few more beers each night to calm me enough for sleep. Sleep was still restful, but when I awoke in the mornings, I was plagued with dry mouth and headaches.

~ ~ ~

"Okay, get her prepped for surgery!" Ravmani shouted.

A nurse flew out of the room. Another gathered the various cords and lines attached to the patient. She was going to be moved quickly.

The situation was grim. Oxygen saturation had dropped and the fetus' pulse had plummeted. The fetus may have had the umbilical cord wrapped around its neck. At this point, there was no way it could survive a vaginal delivery. It would need to come via c-section.

In the center of the oval ward was a pair of surgical suites. Usually, they were dark, but every so often, they housed a flurry of activity.

Ravmani kicked his way into the Prep Room. He vigorously scrubbed his hands and forearms over a stainless steel basin. "Get your ass in gear!"

I stood beside him and mirrored his movements. I meticulously cleaned every millimeter of my skin from fingertips to elbows. Ravmani was much faster than me. He rinsed off and raced into the Operating Room.

By the time I was completely soaped-up, the nurses were wheeling the patient into the OR. I had to move faster or Ravmani would have my head. I pressed a lever down with my foot. Water rushed out of the faucet. I ran my hands under it, careful to keep them upright.

I entered the OR. The patient was already on the operating table. The anesthesiologist had just arrived and was setting up her equipment. Ravmani was in full surgical attire. He was draping a sterile blue sheet over the young girl.

"Let's go, let's go!" he shouted.

The nearest nurse dropped what she was doing and helped me don my gown and gloves. Once I was ready, I helped Ravmani set up everything else.

"How're we doing?" Ravmani asked the anesthesiologist.

"Good to go," she replied.

"Listen up," Ravmani said. He glared at me from the other side of the patient. I stiffened. "You do exactly what I say and when I say it. Do *not* do anything without my say-so. Understand?"

"Yes, Dr. Ravmani."

With the other c-sections, there had always been two surgeons. Each knew what to do and when to do it. This was a demanding surgery with two lives in the balance. Now, there was only one doctor. However, if I followed his orders exactly, his experience should be enough to carry us through.

Ravmani sterilized the abdomen with Betadine, and made his incision. He sliced through layers of skin, fat, and muscle. As he cut, blood seeped everywhere.

"Irrigation."

That was my cue to flood the cavity with a device that sprayed sterile water.

"Suction."

I drained the excess liquid with a long plastic wand like a vacuum cleaner.

"Bovie."

I handed him a small pen-like apparatus that cauterized bleeding tissues.

I kept everything in close reach. The things I couldn't get were handed to me by the Scrub Nurse. I obeyed each order with speed. I hadn't made any mistakes. I felt a growing sense of excitement.

Ravmani had cut all the way down to the uterus. "Traction."

I grabbed the metal retractor. I hooked it over the abdomen and pulled back. The surgical opening widened.

"You hold that. Don't let go. Not unless I say."

Ravmani sliced carefully into the uterus. It started to open, but he hadn't cut deeply enough. He sliced again. A tidal wave of warm, yellow liquid erupted onto my chest and arms. Ravmani's mask was hit. A small plastic screen attached to the mask protected his eyes.

Ravmani reached into the uterus and extracted the fetus. The umbilical cord was wrapped twice around its neck. Carefully, he uncoiled it, freeing the baby. He placed the baby on a very wet section of the surgical field and severed the umbilical cord.

The nurses had the infant now. They hurried it to a small table and began routine procedures. It cried loudly. Ravmani had done it. He saved the baby, but he didn't look happy yet. "Hold the traction," he said.

He traded out his scissors for suturing equipment. He sutured the uterus, and then moved upward methodically, closing the muscles and skin. He gave me fewer instructions now, but I did them well.

Ravmani tied the final suture, and breathed a sigh of relief. "Great job, everyone," he said to the nurses. His effeminate voice returned once more.

I finally understood why obstetricians were surgeons.

~~~

One of the monitor-alarms chimed. "I need help with Flores!" a nurse shouted down the hall.

Brookstone was nowhere to be found. This kind of thing always happened when the Attendings were gone. I looked around the station and saw everyone was missing. The nurse was yelling at me.

I raced to the patient's room. She was a girl of about eighteen, delivering her second child. An older woman, perhaps her grandmother, was standing by her side.

The nurse shot over to the cabinets and rattled through them. She tossed out everything we would need for the delivery. "Do you know how to get everything set up?" she asked.

"Yeah," I said. I had been doing this for a few weeks now. I could handle it.

The girl groaned something in Spanish. The grandmother squeezed her hand, and replied in a soothing voice.

I hurried to the foot of the bed. The baby's head was already crowning. We weren't going to have time to set anything up. The nurse smashed a button on the wall, paging anyone for help.

I hurtled across the room and grabbed sterile gloves. By the time they were on, the baby's head was halfway out. "Here it comes!" I said.

I grabbed the head and pulled. It was sliding out quickly. The girl pushed again, but there was no movement. I readjusted my grip. She pushed again. The head moved toward me. I rotated it. She pushed again, groaning in pain.

The grandmother said something in Spanish. The nurse counted to ten. I rotated again and pulled, and then the head was out. The girl stopped, trying to catch her breath. "Keep going! It's almost there!" I said.

The nurse and grandmother encouraged her. She pushed again. I pulled down hard. A shoulder popped out. I pulled up and the second shoulder emerged. An instant later, the rest of the body slid out. The nurse and grandmother cheered. The girl withered from exhaustion.

I did it!

I turned the infant around. Amniotic fluid ran off it. It started to cry. With a rubber bulb, I sucked mucous from the baby's nostrils.

The sound of clattering footsteps filled the room. Two nurses and Brookstone appeared. He surveyed the scene. He slapped me on the back and said, "Don't drop it." He took charge and completed the rest of the delivery.

Once the baby was out of my hands, I headed for the locker room. I was drenched in fluid. While I changed clothes, I smiled. It was the biggest smile I ever had.

~~~

At the month's end, I needed to have my evaluation completed. I could give it to Brookstone or Ravmani. There was no question in my mind who to give it to. Brookstone, the consummate professional, would no doubt give me a decent grade. I did everything he asked, and never once did he accuse me of being a lazy, good for nothing idiot.

"Dr. Brookstone, would you fill out my evaluation?"

"Sure," he said with a smile.

Using the wall as a flat surface, he filled out the form in seconds. He circled a score of three for every category. He put no thought into it at all. He scribbled his signature at the bottom. "You did a great job," he said.

"Oh, uh, thanks," I said, feeling deflated.

My final day was spent with Ravmani. The screaming was worse than usual, but when I blinked, the day was over. When Ravmani and I returned to the Nurses Station, we stared awkwardly at each other. I wondered if he knew how much I hated him.

Trying to remain professional, I offered my hand. "Thanks for everything, Dr. Ravmani."

"Where's your eval?" he asked, not interested in a handshake.

"What?" I asked, dropping my hand.

"Your eval. I want to fill it out."

"I already gave it to Dr. Brookstone."

"Give me a copy. I get CME credits for it."

Ravmani would simultaneously crucify me with a bad grade, and get points toward his mandatory continuing medical education requirement. He was a great guy.

I dragged myself to one of the computers and printed off a blank copy of the evaluation. Filling it out, he took considerably longer than Brookstone had. He was carefully plotting my demise.

When he handed it back to me, he said nothing. One of the monitor-alarms dinged and flashed. He walked down the hall to investigate.

I looked at the paper. He had given me a perfect score. At the bottom was a section for comments. He had written, "Great job. Hard worker. Will be an excellent doctor."

I was dumbfounded. He had pushed me hard, expected a lot, and had taken notice of my effort. Ravmani, while an asshole, now seemed far less malignant. I decided to wait for him to return so I could thank him again. After several minutes, I heard him yelling at someone in the distance. I decided not to press my luck.

DECEMBER ANESTHESIOLOGY

It was Saturday evening. The sun had started to set. Long shadows stretched across the ground. There was a chill in the air. Even though this desert climate precluded snow, it did get cold at night this time of year.

Christmas decorations popped up across the city. Lines of sparkling white lights snaked their ways up the trunks of palm trees. Santa hats appeared on top of cacti. Inflatable reindeer and Nativity scenes stood proudly in the rock-landscaped neighborhoods. It looked like the Twilight Zone version of Christmas.

To my surprise, Brad had called me and asked if I wanted to get together for a drink. My first impulse was to decline, but I decided to go. Perhaps making a friend would be a good thing.

The inside of the local brewery was lit with a soft orange glow. People filled the room, wall to wall, elbows pressed together. I elected for the patio where it was less crowded. It was chillier outside, so portable heaters had been set up. I found an out of the way table and claimed it. Almost as soon as I sat down, Brad appeared.

"What have you been on?" he asked, after we exchanged the usual pleasantries.

"OBGYN."

"Did you like it?"

"Not really."

"Oh, too bad."

"You?"

"Surgery."

"How'd that go?"

"Shitty. They were bustin' my balls morning to night."

"No kidding?"

"Yeah, man. Remember that day Weismer got pissed at Abbas? It was like that every day, except ten times worse."

"Damn," I said, cringing.

Our conversation was typical. Any time medical students got together, the conversation invariably turned to school. It didn't matter if the venue was a hospital or a bar, rotations were always at the top of the conversation.

A waitress took our orders. She returned with two pints of beer, and I thirstily gulped mine down. Brad watched me, as he sipped his, with a look of surprise. "Damn, dude. Rough week?" he asked.

I set the glass down hard. The remaining beer sloshed at the bottom. "Rough month," I answered. There was an elongated pause. Brad and I didn't know each other that well. He must have been afraid to ask what was on my mind. I finished my beer. After that, I broke the silence.

"There was this girl. Things were going great, and then they weren't."

Brad took another sip. "What happened?"

"She works at the hospital."

"What's she do?"

"She's a tech or something. I'm not sure. Anyway, I met her when we were on Medicine."

"No shit?"

"Yeah. We flirted a lot. We had great chemistry and everything. But we couldn't hang out on account of me being so busy on the rotation. At the end of the month, we went out. After that I never heard from her again."

The waitress reappeared. "Would you like another?" she asked.

"Sure," I said.

"And you?" she asked Brad. Only half his beer was gone. He declined, and the waitress walked away.

"You two hook up?" Brad asked.

"Yeah."

"No kidding?" he asked rhetorically.

"It was good, too. I thought so, anyway."

The waitress returned with my drink, and then scampered to another table. I began to down the next beer as quickly as the first.

"You call her?" Brad asked.

"Coupl'a times. She never answered or called back."

"That's the problem with cell phones."

"Whaddaya mean?"

"Back in high school nobody had one. So, no automatic Caller ID. You called a girl, she answered 'cause she didn't know who was calling."

I drained the second pint and slammed the glass down. I was lucky I didn't break it. With two pints of beer and no food in me, I was starting to feel loopy.

The waitress returned again. I got my third beer, and Brad his second.

"How 'bout you? Any ladies in yer life?" I asked.

"Yeah, my wife."

"You're married?"

"You didn't notice my wedding ring?"

"I don't pay attention to that kind of stuff on men."

Brad chuckled. He nodded at our waitress who was at another table. "How 'bout her? She's cute."

"Nah. Not my type."

"Not your type? You see her ass? How could she not be your type?"

We both laughed. My belly was full. The pace of my drinking slowed. Brad continued to sip his beer.

"Where's yer wife? Why dinn't you bring 'er?"

"She's back in L.A. She's got a full-time job. We're doing the long distance thing until I can go back to California for Residency."

"Yer wife got a sister?"

Brad finished his second beer. The waitress came and went again, bringing new drinks.

"I wish she did, man. I'd totally set you up. She does have a brother if you're interested."

"Fuck you," I said with a laugh.

We drank more, laughed more, groaned about the miseries of school, and made fun of Attendings. The camaraderie wasn't something I experienced very often. A part of me didn't want the night to end. Unfortunately, it did.

Brad offered to drive me home. He seemed to think I couldn't hold my liquor. I told him I was fine. I staggered to my car and drove home drunk. The next thing I remembered was waking up on the floor of my apartment the following afternoon. My head was hammering.

The front door of my apartment stood open. The TV, stereo, and DVD player were all in their proper places. My wallet was in my back pocket. I was lucky I wasn't robbed. Or killed. Or raped. Or all of the above.

Shaking my head in disbelief, I closed and locked the door. As I did, I saw my cell phone lying on the floor. I picked it up and flipped it open. The display read, "1 missed call. 2:42 AM. Anne."

I decided not to call her right away. It was better to not seem overeager.

~~~

It was Tuesday. I was two days into my new rotation, and I was already bored out of my mind.

I dragged myself into the ice-cold operating room, sat down on a backless rolling stool, and watched. There was little for me to do, and staying awake wasn't easy. I observed with eyes half-open as the anesthesiologist injected chemicals into the patient's IV.

She told them to count backwards from ten. Nobody ever made it past seven, and most only got to nine. Once they were asleep, she intubated the patient's airway and hooked that tube up to a ventilator. The apparatus pumped up and down, pushing air into the patient's lungs.

Afterward, the surgeons sauntered in like rock stars, practically high-fiving each other. They erected a sterile blue drape at the patient's neck, blocking my view of them.

During the surgery, Flenderson, the anesthesiologist, did a crossword puzzle. She occasionally looked up to check vital signs and make small adjustments to her equipment.

I couldn't touch anything. Even if I was allowed to, I wouldn't have known what to do. Too much gas would lead to death. Too little and the patient would wake up. Knowing my luck, I'd wake the patient up and kill them at the same time.

Flenderson struck up a conversation with me now and then. It helped fill the excruciating silences in the OR. We chatted in fits and starts. It was superficial stuff. She didn't see the point in going deeper. A month from now I'd move on and never see her again.

The first day I arrived wearing my short white coat and business-casual attire. I was shown to a locker room where I changed into a pair of short-sleeved green scrubs. I nearly froze to death. The surgeons had control of the thermostat, and they preferred the OR to be at subzero temperatures. Today I wore a long-sleeved t-shirt underneath my scrubs and felt a little warmer.

When the day's cases were completed, Flenderson sent me home just after noon. Apparently anesthesiologists valued their golf game, too.

Even though it was December, it was still warmer outside than it was in the OR. I let my skin warm under the winter sunlight. The sun was a pale white circle holding fast in the sky. The ground below me was dirty and hard.

I grabbed my cell phone and dialed Anne's number. It rang several times and went to her voicemail. I was well-acquainted with the message. I snapped the phone closed. Letting out a sigh of frustration, I trudged to my car. As my fingertips touched the door handle, my phone rang.

I quickly dug it out of my pocket. Anne's name lit up the digital screen. I pried it open, nearly dropped it in the process, but managed to catch it. "Oh, hey, Anne!" I said excitedly.

"Long time no see," she said.

"What's up?"

"You called me."

"I was just . . . returning your call . . . from the other night."

A pause left me wondering if she even remembered calling. Maybe she had done it in a drunken haze?

"Oh that," she laughed. It sounded forced. "I was wondering if you were busy, that's all."

"I'm not busy now."

Another pause. I felt nervous, but I had to give it one more try. "Maybe we should get together sometime?" I asked.

"Sure, that'd be fun," she said warmly. "I get off work at seven. Why don't you pick me up around nine? Do you remember where I live?"

"Yeah, I'll be there."

If anyone walked by they would have seen a look of shock on my face. After all that time, she finally wanted to see me again. Shock transformed into glee. I drove home sporting a goofy smile.

~~~

I debated whether I should arrive promptly at nine or show up casually late. I showed up early. I restrained myself from jumping at the front door. I stood on the stoop, hands in my jacket pockets, and turned back toward the street.

Palm trees ran along both sides. It was dark now and the lights in the trees twinkled brightly. The lights were pleasant in their festive, yet non-specific form of holiday cheer. Cars inched by in either direction. The traffic was horrendous despite the late hour.

I checked the time. It was two minutes until nine, but I couldn't wait any longer. I knocked. I waited. I knocked again. I waited again.

What the hell? Was she actually pulling this on me again? Not answering the door instead of not answering the phone? That bitch. She had some nerve to pull a stunt like that. The next time I saw her I would–

The brown door creaked open. Anne, looking more radiant than I remembered, stood on the other side.

My face involuntarily broke into a smile. "Hi!" I said.

Damn. I was being too enthusiastic. She probably noticed that.

"Sorry," she said. "I was upstairs when you knocked."

"No problem."

"Wait here one sec. I'm just gonna grab my purse."

She disappeared into her apartment.

I bounced nervously on my toes. I must have looked like an idiot to anyone walking by. I was standing in front of an open door, staring inside like a reluctant burglar. Anne was only gone for thirty seconds, but it felt like thirty minutes. When she finally returned, I moved her along as quickly as possible.

As we walked, I stole glimpses of her, too shy to stare but wanting to fully take in her beauty. She wore slim blue jeans and an orange sweater. Her hair was in a ponytail. She exuded casual sexiness. My heart raced. I was glad to be seen in public with such a beautiful woman.

We walked downtown. We went to one of those American-style bar and grill franchises. Anne could have suggested a date at the garbage dump, and I would have gladly accompanied her.

We ordered drinks: a beer for me, a margarita for her. As she lifted her drink with her left hand, that damned diamond ring flashed at me, scattering the light from above. Did she wear that thing for show? I'd ask her if we managed to get beyond one date this time.

"How've you been?" I asked.

"Not bad, I guess."

"Working a lot?"

"The normal amount."

"So . . . let me ask . . . what took you so long to call me back?"

Her eyes shifted as she sipped her drink. "Was it that long?"

"Kind of."

"I guess I had a lot going on," she said, disinterested.

Figuring this could only lead someplace bad, I changed the subject.

"How long have you lived downtown?" I asked.

"So, what's it like being a med student?"

"Uh, good," I said, not feeling eager to talk about myself. "Sometimes it's really hard. Some of the Attendings like to yell. And pimp."

"Pimp?"

"It's what they call it when they drill you with questions."

"That's a weird thing to call it."

"I didn't come up with it."

"You know, I was thinking about going to med school."

As she spoke I looked into her brown eyes. I nodded and said "yes" and "okay" and "uh-huh" in all the right places. I leaned forward slightly. My body language told her I was hanging on her every word. The reality was I could hardly pay attention. As she blathered, the only thought in my mind was: are we having sex tonight?

"–don't you think?"

"Uh, err, sure, I think so."

"That's great!"

My bowels acted up. What had I just agreed to? There was no time to ask, because our meals arrived. I stuffed my face while Anne talked. It was easier to let her go on endlessly.

The rest of the night moved swiftly, and before I knew it, we were back on her front stoop. She took a step up toward her door. Quickly, I grabbed her by the wrist and spun her around.

I kissed her. This time, I was far less drunk. Anne kissed me back. We speeded up to her bedroom. In my eagerness, I only pulled our pants down, not bothering with the rest of our clothes. She moaned with pleasure this time. After I climaxed, she gave me a final, passionate kiss. My entire body felt lighter.

Needing to arrive at the OR by early morning, I opted to return home instead of spending the night with her. As I walked out, Anne cast a lingering look upon me. Last time I stayed and she wanted me to go. This time, it was reversed. Somehow, this made me feel great.

~~~

My butt hit the hard vinyl cover of the swivel chair. The icy cold of the seat seeped through my scrub pants. The OR was set to arctic temperatures. I froze throughout the morning.

Flenderson thumbed through a newspaper. The surgeons talked about their swimming pools and how it was too cold to go swimming, but their kids still used them despite it being December. I thought it strange that two men who worked in a freezer would complain about it being too cold to go swimming.

Case after case rolled in and out of the OR. I had to do something to stave off boredom. I brought an Anesthesiology book with me. By the time I reached the halfway point of the rotation, I had read the book twice. I started bringing other books with me, but concentrating on them became harder.

Anne hadn't called. I called her twice a day and never got an answer. How could she do this to me again? Was I something disposable to her? Eventually, I found a way to warm up and get my mind off Anne at the same time.

I started to bring coffee into the OR, only my coffee had whiskey in it. Time passed more quickly. I became more conversant. Flenderson became more engaged in our conversations. I endeared myself to her. When I ran out of coffee at home, I brought in cups filled entirely with whiskey.

~~~

It was Thursday. Flenderson had her face buried in a financial magazine. She was worried about losing money in the stock market. I took a long sip of whiskey. It burned down my throat.

The patient was in an artificial coma. To my right stood the giant apparatus where all the gases resided. The respirator pumped rhythmically. What would happen if I reached out and turned one of those dials? Dropping the patient into cardiac arrest might liven things up a bit.

My right hand, feeling lighter than usual, moved toward the machine. My fingertips touched the cold controls. I expected Flenderson to jump out of her chair. She would scream at me, and I would fail the rotation. I would be expelled from school. I would face criminal charges.

I turned my head and saw she was still reading the magazine. The patient was still comatose. The surgeons still jabbered on. If I wasn't here, nobody would even notice.

My arm dropped. I slouched. The surgery continued uninterrupted.

Time passed uneventfully. All this time spent quietly sitting, drinking, and thinking allowed me to realize something. Anne wasn't going to call me. She didn't give a shit about me. I had called Brad a few days ago to lament my situation. He commiserated with me and told me to forget about her. Whiskey helped ease my mind.

I noticed patterns in the OR. They were so consistent I devised a game. Any time a surgeon talked about his house, his car, or his wife's plastic surgery – take a drink. Any time the patient became combative while waking up from the anesthetic – take a drink. Any time Flenderson fell asleep – take a drink – two drinks if she snored. It got to the point where I had to bring two cups of whiskey every day.

Nobody noticed.

The rest of the month lumbered along like a half-dead animal in anticipation of the end. As always, I found myself on the last day of the rotation. When the final case wrapped up, Flenderson stood and yawned. Stretching, she made her way toward the exit. She hesitated, as if she had forgotten something, and then turned back. "Good job today. See you next week."

She walked away. I started to tell her I wouldn't be back, but stopped. It wouldn't matter. She'd have a new nondescript student sitting next to her soon. I'd be forgotten in no time.

Everyone had left the OR. All that remained was the anesthesiology equipment and a mess of blue towels on the floor. They had been dropped to hastily mop up a wash of bodily fluids. I closed my eyes and listened to silence. The OR sounded like a tomb.

~~~

My school was gracious enough to bless us with a full week of vacation for the Christmas holiday. I decided I would take the train home instead of flying. It would take two days to travel home and two days to travel back. That left only three days to spend at home with my family. It was perfect.

The train ride was mercilessly boring. I sat beside the window and watched the world pass by. The brown desert terrain gave way to vast open fields which were dusted with snow. Those fields gave way to rolling hills covered in deeper layers of snow. The window fogged.

Every few stops the passenger next to me would change. Sometimes they wanted to quietly read, other times they were eager to talk. I wasn't interested. A few of them were not dissuaded by this and continued to talk to me, not caring if I didn't answer.

I sipped the whiskey in my coffee cup. It didn't make the journey faster, but it did make my discomfort manageable.

My parents waited for me at the train station. They were excited to tell me about all of my sister's adventures. I got sick of that, so I feigned falling asleep as we drove home.

I awoke the next day feeling like my head would explode. Groggy, I stood in a scalding shower for the next thirty minutes. After I got out, I dressed sloppily and made my way down to the kitchen where there was a ruckus. As I neared, the noise grew louder and my head pounded harder. The smell of cookies wafted toward me. My stomach lurched.

It was Christmas Eve. Traditionally, my mom, my sister, and I made cookies and watched some holiday crap on TV. My dad would visit the party at the VFW and come home later.

When I entered the kitchen, Mom was cradling a fat bundle of yellow cloth and making weird cooing noises. My sister stood beside her, rolling out cookie dough.

"Mornin', sleepy head," my sister, Eve, said.

"Morning," I groaned.

Mom took no notice of me. She continued to rock that fat bundle and make those ridiculous sounds.

"Where's Rick?" I asked.

"Dad took him down to the VFW. Wanted to show off the father of his new granddaughter," Eve said.

"Why didn't he just take the baby instead?"

"Stop being such a grouch."

"Whatever."

I maneuvered around Mom and the baby, and made my way to the refrigerator. I poured a glass of orange juice and returned to the kitchen table. I slid as far down in my seat as possible.

"How've you been?" Eve asked.

"Fine. Just tired."

"You look hung over."

My sister, always the observant one. My eyes darted to Mom. She was on Planet Baby. I looked back to my sister. "Only way to pass time on the train."

Eve was three years older than me. She had a Master's Degree in business. She had a job as Vice President of Fancy Shit at a famous computer company that marketed to yuppies. She was always one step ahead of me. When I got on the honor roll at school, she made Valedictorian. When I got accepted to medical school, she got engaged. I started clinical rotations, she had a baby. Every time I had some exciting news to offer, she upped the ante, and my achievement was soon forgotten. If I ever married someone rich or talented, Eve would probably become President of the United States.

When I told my parents I was coming out for the holiday, Mom kept on saying how great it was that Eve would be home with the new baby.

The TV blared commercials for last-minute holiday sales. I turned the volume down, and my headache eased a bit.

"How's school?" Eve asked.

"Fine."

"Know what kind of doctor you're gonna be?"

"Nope."

"What's the kind of doctor that specializes in taking care of assholes?"

"A proctologist."

"You'd be great at that."

"Go to hell."

"Don't swear in front of the baby!" Mom said.

"Eve just did."

Mom didn't notice. "Evelyn, could you hold her for a minute? I need to use the bathroom," she said.

Mom handed the yellow bundle over and bustled down the hallway. Eve gave me a sly grin. I knew something was coming. Growing up with her, that smile always heralded something bad.

"Rick got a raise," she said.

"Good for him."

"We're going to Hawaii in February. Mom and Dad are going to babysit while we're gone."

I took a long sip of my orange juice. The glass was almost empty.

"We got a new Mercedes on order. You still driving that old shitbox of yours?"

"Give it a rest, Evie."

"Please don't call me that."

"Whatever you say, Evie."

"We have to be civil for the next couple of days. Why don't you try being nice for a change?"

I turned my attention back to the TV. "What position did you guys use to conceive the baby? Doggy?"

"Fuck you."

I finished my drink and went back to my room.

That evening we had our annual Christmas Eve get-together. Family from throughout the state converged upon my aunt and uncle's house for a night of mediocre food and forced fun activities.

Mom, Dad, Eve, Rick, the baby, and I crammed into one vehicle. I was squished against a door with Eve next to me, holding the baby. I looked down at its face. A bubble of snot had formed on one of its nostrils. I looked at my sister, my mouth turned down in disgust. Was she going to clean that thing or what? She didn't meet my gaze. She was pretending she didn't see my judgmental look.

When we got to the party I distanced myself from my immediate family. I walked into the kitchen and found my uncle with his head in the refrigerator. "Hey, Uncle Bill," I said.

"Oh, hi there. Can I getcha somethin' to drink?"

"A beer if you got one."

Bill rummaged around. He pulled out a bottle of light beer and handed it to me.

The mere act of taking that first sip set my nerves at ease. If I could keep one of these handy at all times, I would make it through this party alive.

A moment later, Aunt Patty, a wiry woman with a huge gray afro, wandered into the kitchen. She squealed my name with delight. We hugged, and I gave an embarrassed smile.

"How are you?" she asked with way more energy than any normal person.

"Fine, fine. And you?"

"Bill and I are doing just great. Aren't we, Bill?"

Bill's head was still stuck in the refrigerator. "Yep, doin' great."

Patty put her hands on her hips and said, "Tell me what it's like now that you're a big-shot doctor."

"I'm not a doctor yet, Aunt Patty."

"You're seeing patients now, aren't you? That's what your mother said."

"Yeah, but I can't write prescriptions or anything like that."

"Well, it sounds fa-sci-na-ting."

"It's all right," I said, taking another swig of beer.

"What was your favorite specialty so far?"

"I don't know."

"Did you see anything really crazy like on TV?"

"Not really. You know, I should probably go say hi to everyone. I'll catch you later."

"Okay. Have fun!" she said with unadulterated delight.

I escaped from the kitchen and moved to the living room. A crowd had gathered around Eve and the baby. The house was getting loud.

I went to the dining room. My younger cousin was sitting at the table, playing a game on his cell phone. I sat across from him. His gaze was locked on his phone.

Jack was a walking stereotype. He wore one of those multi-colored Rastafarian hats. A thick cord of hemp encircled his neck. He wore bracelets and a ratty Army jacket. His family had plenty of money. He didn't have to get his clothes from a second-hand store. He was one of those guys that worked hard on his image, but pretended he didn't care about it. Also, he reeked of pot.

"What are you playing?" I asked.

"Some game."

"Yeah, no shit. What game?"

Jack ignored me.

"How've you been?"

Jack shrugged.

"How's school?"

Jack gave no response.

What was this kid's problem? I steeled my resolve. I knew I could get him to give me more than a one or two word answer.

"How are the ladies treating you?"

Jack shrugged.

"Got a girlfriend?"

"Nah."

"Boyfriend?"

"Nah."

"You wanna get high?"

His fingers paused for a second. "I don't do that," he lied.

At this point I didn't care anymore. He wasn't interested in talking. I decided to try and find someone that wouldn't piss me off.

I was unsuccessful.

I managed to be a ghost for most of the party. Family members would see me sitting in a corner, and come over and ask me questions about medical school. But they weren't really interested. They talked to me because they were obligated. They would listen for a minute and then tell me how great they were doing. I didn't want any part of it.

Six beers later, I found myself wedged in the family car, heading home.

Back in the house, I stumbled around. Even though it was late, my parents asked me to sit down and watch a Christmas movie with them. Growing up, we always watched a Christmas movie on Christmas Eve.

"Come on," Mom said. "I feel like I haven't seen you since you got home."

"I don't know, Mom, I'm pretty tired."

"I know, but you're only here for a few days."

"I should really go to bed."

"Okay. Did you at least enjoy the party?"

"Sure, it was all ri–"

"Mom! Can you hold the baby? I really have to pee!" Eve said, half-drunk herself.

Mom was suddenly back on Planet Baby. She wrapped the baby in her arms and resumed the cooing noises. Dad started the movie while he and Rick talked about basketball. I went back to my room and crashed.

Christmas Day I awoke with another headache. I stalked down to the kitchen to drink some water. I felt like I didn't belong in my own body, like I was an alien.

As I passed the living room I saw that the presents had all been opened. Rick was struggling to put together an age-inappropriate toy for the baby. Dad was engrossed in the TV. Mom was playing with an electronic book reader. Eve was simultaneously instructing Mom how to set up the device and Rick how to put the toy together.

"You guys started without me?" I asked.

Nobody heard me.

I repeated it, louder this time.

"Sorry, sweetheart. We thought you'd feel better if you got to sleep in," Mom said.

"Yeah, thanks."

After I had a glass of water, I showered and dressed. I opened my presents without any fanfare. My grandparents visited and fawned over the baby. They asked me how school was going, but I was an afterthought. For the rest of the day I drank soda spiked with vodka.

That evening my family watched another Christmas movie. I sat in the living room with them, drinking and staring at the TV, but not really watching it. When I went to bed that night, I had a dreamless sleep.

The next morning marked the final day with my family. My train left in the early afternoon. It was a lucky thing, too. Eve and Rick were planning to head back later that day, too. The last thing I wanted was to be alone with my parents. Not much happened that morning. I talked a little bit with Mom and Dad, but only because I had to.

I talked to Rick, but it was a stilted conversation. Eventually, Eve came into the living room carrying the baby wrapped in different yellow blanket. They had a yellow blanket for every day of the week. She handed the baby to Rick who immediately disappeared.

Eve plopped down on the chair Rick had vacated. "Still warm," she said.

"Huh?"

"The chair."

"Oh."

"So, you're headed back in a couple hours?"

"Yeah."

"Meet any girls down there?"

I adjusted my position in my chair. "Eh, I don't know. Sort of."

"Sort of? Ooo, what's her name?" Eve asked with a sly grin.

I readjusted. "Don't worry about it."

"Come on. You were never a ladies' man. Now you've finally met one and you aren't going to tell me about her?"

I shifted around in my chair. No matter how I sat, I couldn't get comfortable. "I don't even know if it's a thing or not. There's no point talking about it."

"You get in her panties yet?"

"Evie, knock it off."

"Is my little brother a man now?"

"Fuck off."

Eve could barely contain herself. She always pulled this crap. She would pretend to be interested, and then make me into a joke. Living with her had been awful. I had counted down the days until she left for college.

"Sorry. If you ever need anything, you know you can give me a call, right?" she said.

"Call *you*?" I asked incredulously.

"You know what I mean. For shit you can't tell Mom and Dad."

"Sure."

"Good luck at school."

"Thanks."

She left the room, and I didn't talk to her again. As I got in Mom and Dad's car, Eve and Rick waved to me from the open door of the house. I gave a half-hearted wave back. When we got to the station, the train was already boarding. I jumped on as fast as my feet would carry me.

The train pulled away from the station. I was free. I felt different again. As the train pushed southwest, I saw the same countryside as when I came up, only in reverse. Rolling hills gave way to snowy plains which gave way to arid desert. My short stint in surreality was over. Now, I was back to my life as an almost-doctor.

JANUARY PEDIATRICS

The alarm clock was an air raid siren. The shrill beeping stabbed my eardrums. I reached behind me, groping blindly. My fingers clumsily found the plastic box. It clattered to the floor. Sweet silence enveloped me. I drifted back to sleep.

~~~

There it was again. That horrible beeping. I sat up in bed, heart racing, my underarms slick with sweat. The pale morning light glowed gray in my bedroom. I squeezed my stinging eyes shut. What day was it?

Memories of yesterday slowly returned. After knocking the clock to the floor, I slept until 2:00 PM. I decided not to bother with my rotation. I didn't need another blundering first day, and another introduction to an Attending who wouldn't give a shit about me.

The old me would have been panic-stricken to skip out, but now I didn't care. I spent the rest of the day on the couch, watching TV and drinking beer. When evening came, I went back to bed and returned the clock to the nightstand.

And now the next day had come. If I went in, I would be starting all over again. Another month of learning the ropes, getting to know the staff and procedures, and then moving on just as I was getting the hang of it. Every month was exactly the same.

Looking at that baleful clock, I knew I had to make a choice. I stayed in bed another five minutes. I slapped the clock and went to take a shower.

~~~

I stood in the the back office. The layout was odd. There was a central hub with several desks and computers. On either side were two hallways, each with four exam rooms. The central hub was open to give an unobstructed view of each hallway.

One of the front office staff had escorted me back here and told me to wait for Dr. Edwards to arrive. I showed up fifteen minutes late. The Attending hadn't shown up yet either. And so, I waited.

I perused the schedule. The day was fully booked. The first patient was already waiting in an exam room. Should I see them or wait for Edwards to arrive? What would he say about me skipping yesterday? No doubt he would be furious. Why had I not gotten my ass out of bed? I was a fool.

There was a clacking behind me. I turned and saw a short, pudgy man with canes that snapped around his wrists. He gave me a nod. "You the new med student?" he asked in a gruff voice.

"Yes," I said, introducing myself.

He clacked around to one of the desks and dropped into a high-backed leather swivel chair. "Where ya from?"

I was taken aback. No Attending had asked me anything like that before. "The Midwest. I only moved out here for med school," I said.

"Right on. Whatcha wanna go into?"

"I'm, uh, not really sure yet. I think I need to do all the rotations before I decide."

"You like workin' with kids?"

"I don't know. I haven't worked with kids before."

"Well, go see what's in Room One, and come present to me when yer done."

"Oh, okay . . ."

My exposure to children until now was limited to getting annoyed when parents brought their screaming infants to the movies. I had no idea what I was supposed to do. I slowly moved toward the exam room. I had hoped Edwards would show me what to do, at least for the first one.

Halfway there, Edwards called, "Hey!"

"Yeah?" My heart lifted. I hoped Edwards had changed his mind.

"Take off the white coat. You'll freak out the kids."

My heart dropped again. I slipped off the jacket and tossed it onto the nearest chair. I walked to the exam room and pulled the chart off the wall.

The patient was a four year old male here for "vomiting." Their vital signs were normal with the exception of a slightly elevated temperature. It wasn't high enough to qualify as a fever.

I held my breath and looked back. Edwards was absorbed in his computer. He scratched his goatee and typed something. My stomach burned. I let my breath out and felt my body loosen. I entered the room.

I had expected a tornado of destruction, but the room was serene. The child was lying quietly on the exam table. His mother sat beside him and lovingly stroked his hair.

"Hello," I said. "I'm Dr. Edwards' medical student. Would you mind if I see you first?"

"That's fine," the mother said with a weak smile.

I approached the table and sunk to my knees. I wanted to be at the same height as the patient, not tower over him. "How are you doing?" I asked in a ridiculously soft voice.

The kid groaned.

"He started getting sick yesterday," the mother said. "His day care said he threw up. So, I took him home. He's been running a fever all night, and he threw up a couple of times."

"How high was the fever?"

"One hundred and three."

"That's high. Did you give him any medications?"

"Just some Tylenol."

That would explain why his temperature was recorded as normal in the chart. Tylenol will lower a fever without treating the cause. "Did you give him anything else?" I asked.

"No."

"Is he keeping food down?"

"He won't eat. That's why I brought him in."

I asked a few more questions. After that, it was time for the physical exam. Since he was already supine, I would examine his abdomen first. There were no bruises or masses, and nothing obviously wrong. I uncoiled my stethoscope and heard all the usual noises, although they were moving faster than normal. I pushed deeply into each part of his belly with my hands. He groaned, but I felt nothing abnormal.

The mother looked at me hopefully. I was afraid I had no answer for her. I moved on with the exam. "Come on, buddy, can you sit up for me?" I asked in the weird voice.

His mother sat him upright, but he slouched lethargically. I pulled his shirt up higher to expose his chest. I placed my stethoscope on his chest. I closed my eyes so I could focus on his heart's rhythm. He heaved suddenly. I opened my eyes and stood up, about to ask what was wrong, when his mouth opened and vomit exploded onto my chest.

My shirt and tie were soaked. Green chunks dripped to the floor. It seeped through my shirt. I could feel it penetrating my skin. My face was a thousand degrees.

The mother gasped. "I'm so sorry! Are you all right?"

"Fine."

Fortunately, there was a sink in the corner of the room. I handed a few paper towels to the mother. She cleaned off the patient's chin. The rest of him had been spared from his projectile puke. She left the rest of his vomit on the floor for someone else to clean up.

I cleaned myself as best I could. I looked ridiculous with a wet green shirt and tie. I returned and sat beside the patient to finish the exam.

At length, I said, "Let me get Dr. Edwards. We'll be back in a few minutes."

"Thank you," she said as I evacuated the room.

I took short, slow steps down the hallway. My eyes were locked on the floor. When Edwards noticed me, he pushed away from his desk. "How'd it go?" he asked with a wry grin.

"The patient's here for 'vomiting' and, well . . ."

"He's still doin' it, huh?"

I snorted and my face twisted into a smile that matched Edwards'.

"I can't tell you how many really nice ties I had ruined by some kid puking or peeing on them. So, I don't wear ties anymore," he said.

"Good thing you had me take off my white coat."

Edwards nodded. He didn't dress like a conventional doctor. He wore blue jeans, gray sneakers, and a Hawaiian shirt. I tried to imagine him much younger, as a medical student in dress attire and a white coat. My mind strained, but the image wouldn't come.

"Dr. Edwards, what should I do about . . . this?"

I held my arms out. The vomit had splashed itself into the pattern of an ink-blot test.

"Tell ya what. Present the case to me, we'll go see him together, and then I'll let ya go home and change. Sound good?"

"Great. Thank you."

"Okay, so let's hear it."

I fumbled with the chart. My mind flooded with thoughts of past presentations. Every doctor had a different style and order.

Which order would Edwards want? I realized I hadn't asked about the patient's past medical history. If Steinway was here, he would kill me. I was completely screwed.

"Well?" Edwards asked.

"Oh, um, the patient is a four year old male who presented with a Chief Complaint of vomiting–"

"Obviously," he chuckled.

"–and he, uh, started vomiting yesterday while at day care, and his mother brought him in. He ran a fever of one-oh-three, she gave the patient Tylenol, and now he's afebrile. He vomited several times in the night and once today. No blood in the vomit. No appetite. He looks kind of lethargic–"

Oh shit! That wasn't part of the Subjective. I was already giving objective findings, and half-assed ones at that. Even so, Edwards watched and listened.

"–but he has no known sick contacts. No other symptoms. His past medical, um, past medical . . ."

I fumbled again with the chart. I rifled through the previous notes to find something, anything.

"That's fine. How was your exam?" Edwards asked. I began to run through a list of every normal exam finding. Looking bored, Edwards said, "Just give me the pertinent positives."

"I didn't really find anything."

"Just a positive vomit sign."

"Yeah, I guess so."

"Whaddaya think it is?"

"My first thought was gastroenteritis. But with that fever, I'm not sure."

"No fever now, though."

"But he took Tylenol."

"How long ago?"

"I don't know. I didn't ask."

"That's okay, I'll find out. Let's say you're right. Whaddaya wanna to do?"

We had reached the Assessment and Plan. This was the part that my other preceptors never had time for. It was nice that Edwards took an interest in actually teaching me something.

"Keep the patient hydrated. Avoid antibiotics because if it's viral they won't do anything. Use more Tylenol if the fever comes back. And come back in a week for follow up," I said.

"Okay, let's see this kiddo."

We walked toward the exam room. Edwards clacked away with his canes, and I followed close behind him. I felt relieved.

~~~

I opened the sliding glass door and stepped onto the patio. A small patch of scorched brown grass stretched before me. The backyard was surrounded by a tall maroon block fence. All the backyards here were like this. It was easier to not have to get to know your neighbors if you couldn't see them.

The sky was overcast, a sickly gray color. The sun burned anemically behind a mass of clouds. A propeller airplane droned somewhere in the distance. I sat down in a dusty chair, part of an unkempt set of patio furniture.

Behind me, from within the house, I could hear the faint crackling of bacon. Breakfast was almost ready, but I had to step out for some fresh air. I needed a moment alone.

It was strange being here again. Today marked another morning waking up with Anne. She offered to cook me breakfast. Since Edwards' office didn't open until nine, I accepted.

Anne called me yesterday afternoon. I was so busy seeing patients I didn't notice my phone ring. I got her voicemail later that evening. She invited me out for drinks. We met and repeated the events of our previous encounters. It was an unhealthy routine, but not one I would decline.

"It's ready!" she called.

In the kitchen, Anne held a sizzling frying pan. She tilted it, and scraped eggs onto a plate. The plate beside it was already heaping with food.

"Help yourself," she said. "There's orange juice in the fridge if you want."

"Water's fine."

A glass had been set out for me. I filled it with tap water and sat down to eat. I wasn't particularly hungry, and the food wasn't particularly good. But she went to all this trouble, so I didn't want to disappoint her.

We ate in silence. Words only flowed naturally between us when lubricated by alcohol. Why she had wanted me to stick around for breakfast was perplexing.

I watched her, stuffing food into her mouth, her left hand wielding the fork more like a shovel than a utensil. It was then I noticed her left hand was bare. Where was the diamond ring?

She caught me gazing at her and looked up. "Are you going to work today?" she asked with a mouthful of eggs.

"Yeah. But not until nine."

"That's cool."

"I had to get up really early last month, so sleeping 'til seven feels like sleeping in."

She nodded and looked back at her food. She chewed noisily, smacking her lips and slurping her drink. I pushed the unseasoned eggs around my plate with my fork.

"What do you want to do tonight?" she asked. She said it like a date was a forgone conclusion.

"Um . . . do you want to get together?"

"Yeah. Maybe I can cook you dinner?"

I set the fork down. My appetite was gone. I tried to think of an excuse. Nothing came to mind. And now she was staring at me, waiting for a response. The longer I waited, the worse the silence became. "Sounds nice."

"Great!" she exclaimed before she resumed chomping her eggs. There was a pile on her plate large enough to feed three grown men.

I pushed back from the table. "I have to go."

"Okay. Byyye."

She puckered her lips, ready for the kind of kiss you see between lovers who have been together for decades. I timidly pressed my lips against hers. An instant later, I backed off and left the house.

I arrived at Edwards' office twenty minutes late, but he hadn't arrived either. I looked over the schedule and saw we were fully booked. Several patients were already stuffed into exam rooms.

A familiar clacking heralded Edwards' entrance. He sauntered in, and his persona filled the room with charismatic energy. The office manager, a petite brunette woman named Sharon, walked at his side, wringing her hands, her face pensive.

"Dr. Edwards! Some of the parents have told me they're going to leave!"

"Oh, come on, Sharon," he said jovially. "The parents'll be fiiine."

"But Dr. Edwards!"

"Sharon, ya know I just got married."

"Yeah."

"Well, ya gotta realize that sometimes my wife's gonna be feelin' frisky. And this mornin' was one of those times."

"Gross," she said with a grimace.

Edwards guffawed. His laughter boomed up and down the hall. He turned to me and said, "Got married 'bout four months ago. She's twenty."

Edwards was in his mid-forties, old enough to be his wife's father. That sort of thing didn't bother me, so I simply congratulated him.

"Didn't even faze ya, huh? I like that. Most people are shocked when I tell 'em. How 'bout this, I'll take Room One, you take Room Two, and we'll move on from there." Edwards turned to Sharon and said, "Can you run down the street and get me the usual?"

A deep crease formed on Sharon's forehead. "Only if you start working."

"Deal," he said with a wink.

The patient in the second exam room, a little girl, was running around in a circle, coughing, with a line of snot trailing from her nose halfway down her shirt. The patient's mother or grandmother, I couldn't tell which, sat on a chair with her legs crossed, reading a magazine.

"Hello," I said.

The girl continued running in circles. I introduced myself to the grand/mother, but she couldn't have been less interested in me. I collected the history. "Let's have a look at you," I said to the girl.

The little girl was still hacking and running laps. The grand/mother had returned to her magazine. Normally when I said this, the parent would help gather the child for the physical exam. I had only been doing this a day, but it seemed like an unwritten agreement between parent and doctor.

"Okay, I'll just pick her up," I said.

I crouched and waited for the girl to make another pass. When she circled around again, I grabbed her. Her shirt felt like a wrung-out washcloth. I tried not to think about how her snot-soaked shirt was in direct contact with my bare hands.

I hoisted her onto the exam table and asked her to hold still. I went to the sink and washed my hands. When I turned around, she was back on the floor doing laps again. The grand/mother's nose was buried in the magazine.

I caught the patient again, put her back on the exam table, and began the examination. I didn't expect to find much. The history implied she had otitis media, a middle-ear infection. I moved quickly through the abdominal, cardiovascular, and respiratory exams, all of which were normal. Finally, it was time to examine her ears.

Edward's office did not have an otoscope in every room. Instead, he had two portables that he carried from room to room. One of them was tucked in my back pants pocket. I slipped it out. "I'm going to look in your ears. Hold really still, okay?"

I had examined dozens of adult ears before today. It wasn't too difficult. How much different could it be on a kid?

I turned the otoscope's light on. I pulled up gently on the patient's ear with my left hand. I slowly pushed the device into her ear. She unleashed a piercing scream. She jerked away from me. Her grand/mother looked up with a scowl, no doubt wondering what kind of torture I was inflicting on her grand/daughter.

"I'm sorry! It's okay, it's okay," I said in the most soothing voice I could muster. "I just need to look in your ear."

The grand/mother finally came to my aid. She gently stroked the patient's head and held her tightly. On my reattempt, the little girl shuddered in a desperate attempt to push me away. If she only realized remaining still would cause her less pain, it wouldn't have been so excruciating.

The grand/mother held her tighter. I readjusted and finally visualized the tympanic membrane. It was a bulging, angry red, just as I had expected. I pulled away, and the patient relaxed. It was short-lived, though, because I still had to examine her other ear.

When I exited the exam room, I saw Edwards standing at his desk, scribbling in a chart. "What were ya doin' to that kid?" he asked.

"Trying to examine her ears."

"Sounded like ya were murderin' her."

"I wanted to, just so she'd sit still.

Edwards laughed. "Whatcha got for me?"

"Right sided otitis media."

"Okay. Whaddaya wanna do?"

"Amoxicillin."

"Right on. Dose?"

"Oh, uh, I'm not sure."

"Don't worry. I'll show ya."

Upon my reentry to the exam room, the patient immediately hunkered down and cried. Edwards clacked in and chatted with the grand/mother like they were old pals. He then turned to the patient and quickly examined her. He deftly moved his otoscope in and out of her ears. She winced, but didn't scream. He was skilled.

"What side did ya say?" Edwards asked.

"Right."

"Yep," he said with a nod.

I was elated. Affirmation was something I rarely got. Working with Edwards was so different than anything I had done before. I was learning, and he was teaching and giving me independence. I was actually having fun.

Edwards showed me how to calculate the antibiotic dose, and then we moved on. We were behind schedule the rest of the day, working at an exhausting pace. By the time we finished, I was spent. But I was looking forward to tomorrow.

The next day, we had a lull in the afternoon. We had caught up on work. Eyeing the clock, I counted ninety minutes until I could go home.

Edwards was clattering away at his computer. A strange light flickered in his eyes. "Guess what, guys?" he said.

"What?" Sharon asked from the back corner of the hub.

"The big football game is here next month!"

"And?" she asked, still looking at her paperwork.

"There's gonna be tons of escorts coming from out of town. Really hot ones, too, I bet. Let's check 'em out."

Within moments, Edwards had navigated to a website featuring escorts. Most were locally based. A few were listed as visiting the city for the week of the game. Edwards had been right. "Let's see the talent," he said mischievously.

He clicked a link. A tall, thin woman filled the screen. She had dyed blonde hair, unnaturally large breasts, and a thick covering of intricate tattoos. She was naked and contorted in various positions.

"Hey, stand over there," Edwards said to me with a shake of his head.

I stood on the opposite side of his desk, in the hallway, looking into the hub. I took a wide step to the right. Edwards considered my position. "A little more to the right."

He had positioned me so I would block the computer screen in case any patients walked down the hallway. I couldn't believe his boldness. He was crazy.

"Whaddaya think about her?" he asked.

I leaned over the desk to get a better look at the screen.

"Aren't you married?" I asked.

"It doesn't hurt to look. Sharon, what do you think of this chick?"

Sharon looked up from her paperwork. "Ugh, she's gross. All those tattoos."

"Yeah, but the *body.*"

Sharon shook her head and resumed working. Clearly, Edwards' behavior didn't bother her. It must have been nothing new.

"Well?" he asked me again.

"She's okay," I said.

"What the hell's wrong with the two of you? She's hot."

"She's gross," Sharon repeated.

"I wouldn't kick her out of bed," Edwards said.

"You wouldn't kick anyone out of bed, Dr. Edwards," Sharon said.

The three of us laughed.

~~~

I stepped into the house. It was hot. "Dinner's almost ready," Anne said.

I followed her into the kitchen. The entire house was permeated with the smell of beef. Anne tended to a large boiling pot. "You look nice," she said.

I had come straight from Edwards' office. It was on the far side of the city, so I didn't have time to go home and change into something casual.

Anne sprinkled spices from an anonymous plastic bag into the pot. She could have been poisoning me for all I knew. She had cooked me dinner yesterday, and thought it was so successful, she decided to do it again tonight.

We ate her bland chili dinner. Whatever seasoning she had used, she should have added more. She asked me how it was, and I told her it was delicious. Afterward, we got drunk and had sex. By the time we went to bed, my buzz was wearing off.

"Oh my God, it was so cold out today," Anne said absent-mindedly.

"I suppose."

"You don't think it's cold?"

"It's *cool*. But where I'm from, I don't think it's cold unless it's below freezing."

"Well, I think it's cold."

"Is that why you have the heat cranked up?"

Anne laughed.

"So," she started, "do you have a girlfriend back home?"

"No, of course not."

"It's okay if you do. I'm just curious."

I thought about asking her the same question, especially with that ring of hers, but I held my tongue.

Anne snuggled closer to me. Her breasts pressed against my ribs. She draped her arm across my chest. "What would you say about me?" she asked.

"What do you mean?"

"I mean if we were out together. Would you introduce me as your girlfriend?"

My body became rigid. I was attracted to Anne, and I liked having sex with her, but we hadn't spent much time together. I wasn't sure how to answer. The question felt like a trap. Saying no would almost certainly put an end to our encounters.

"I suppose so," I replied passively.

"I've thought about getting married since I was a little girl," Anne said dreamily. "I'd be standing in the park in a beautiful dress. My Prince Charming would ride up on a horse and pull me onto the saddle with him. Then we'd ride off somewhere majestic. The sun would be setting. That's when he'd ask me to marry him."

Her voice trailed off and her eyes closed. She slept peacefully. I wasn't sure what to make of the fantasy. It was one of the cheesiest things I'd ever heard.

I turned my gaze to the ceiling. It would be better not to worry about her fantasy. The bigger worry was that Anne was apparently my girlfriend. I had no idea what to do with her now.

~ ~ ~

Edwards' office ran as usual. He was always late. He was always jovial. He made lewd jokes to Sharon and me. No matter how far behind schedule we got, the parents never seemed to mind. They loved him.

Half the time we ended up behind schedule because he was too engrossed in something on his computer. He was constantly checking Internet auction sites, bidding on useless junk like cards, bottle caps, old toys, and Hawaiian shirts. Eventually, these items would be shipped to his office. Mail time was like Christmas. Edwards, Sharon, and I tore into the packages, completely forgetting about the people waiting in the exam rooms.

As time went on, I became more skilled. I grew proficient with the pediatric ear exam. I gained confidence in my diagnoses and treatment plans. I wasn't always right, but the collegial environment helped me feel at ease.

As with all my rotations, by the time I got a handle on things, it was almost time to move on. And so, I began my last day with Edwards.

I strolled into the office thirty minutes late with Edwards nowhere in sight. I set a gigantic cup of coffee down on his desk. It was an extra-large caramel macchiato with nine shots of espresso. His usual. I had brought in coffee every day since the second week.

One day Edwards had shown up looking ragged. All the exam rooms were full. Sharon was hounding him to get going. "Sharon, I need my coffee first," Edwards grumbled. Sharon said something snarky back to him and he replied, "I can't see the patients if I haven't had any coffee." I burst out laughing.

Subsequently, we came to an arrangement. I'd pick up his extravagant coffee every day along with something for myself, and he would pay for both. By the end of the month, I had tried everything on the menu.

I took a sip of my coffee and looked at the schedule. There were only ten patients. It was going to be a nice, light final day.

My first confrontation was against a family of four. All four children were here for a routine physical exam, and all four would be seen simultaneously. The chart rack bulged, barely keeping the charts from spilling onto the floor.

I grabbed the charts and dragged myself into the exam room. A plethora of unidentified people were crowded into the room. Everyone was talking, one kid was crying, and two others were shouting.

"Excuse me!" I shouted over the din. "I'm Dr. Edwards' medical student. Could I ask who Mom and Dad are?"

Mom and Dad identified themselves.

"Thanks. You know, it's a little crowded in here. Why doesn't everyone else step into the waiting room?"

Reluctantly, the mystery relatives left. One of them gave me an irked look as she exited. Didn't these people have better things to do? Didn't they have jobs?

With the others out of the room, the noise level dropped considerably. Everyone was silent now except for the one screaming kid. One screaming kid I could handle.

This was not my first time dealing with a multiple-patient visit. Edwards scheduled these things all the time. I told the two older kids to sit side-by-side on the exam table. I picked up the two younger kids and put them beside their older siblings. With all four sitting in a row, shoulder to shoulder, I examined each one in turn.

First, I examined their hearts, one after another. Then their lungs, then their throats, and so on until each had a thorough examination. Everything was normal, except the screaming kid had impetigo, a superficial oral bacterial infection. When I finished, I reported my findings to Edwards.

The day went smoothly except for the "emergencies." As Edwards had plenty of open space in his schedule, he was able to squeeze in a lot of unscheduled patients. Every time I thought we were caught up, another "emergency" walked in and we got off track again. Almost every "emergency" was a cold or upset stomach, certainly not things that couldn't wait.

The final patient was a nine year old boy who presented with stomach pain. In the world of Pediatrics, nine is the perfect age. The patients are old enough to tell you what's wrong with them, but they aren't aloof like teenagers. I was tired, and this seemed like a good way to end the day.

The patient was on his back, sprawled across the exam table. He looked like he was dead. His concerned mother sat on the corner of the table, stroking his head.

I did my usual introduction and history gathering. Nothing was out of the ordinary other than vomiting. He had a high fever, but his mother kept it at bay with Ibuprofen. There were no other symptoms. It was probably another case of gastroenteritis.

Since he was already supine, I started with the abdominal examination. I pulled his red t-shirt up. His abdomen looked normal. I lightly placed the diaphragm of my stethoscope against his skin.

He roared. His limbs flailed. He kneed me in the ribs and smacked me in the face. I tried to hold him down, but he screamed and thrashed violently.

The stethoscope amplified each terrible cry, and my eardrums felt like they were going to burst. And then, as suddenly as he had started, he stopped. I waited a beat. Then another. I looked at his mother who was doused with fear.

Cautiously, I leaned forward. I placed the stethoscope on him again, and he reanimated. His body was electrified. He bucked on the table. His arms and legs jerked in an unsynchronized fashion. His eyes squeezed shut, and his head turned side to side.

Oh, shit! This *was* an emergency!

I blurted out something about getting Edwards, and I bolted from the room. I found him at his desk, perusing a chart.

"Dr. Edwards!" I shouted breathlessly.

"Hey, what's wro–"

"Quick! The patient's having a seizure!"

Edwards dropped the chart, and clacked as fast as he could to the exam room. I imagined a call to the paramedics and an ambulance rushing to the hospital. What if he died? What if they blamed me?

When we entered, Edwards' tense body relaxed. The patient was no longer seizing. He was sitting upright with his mother's arm around his shoulders. They were gently rocking back and forth.

Edwards asked how he was doing. The patient smiled and said he felt fine. Edwards examined his mouth and saw he hadn't bitten his tongue. His pants were dry, so he hadn't become incontinent. Edwards reassured the mother that her son was fine. He diagnosed him with gastroenteritis and sent them on their way.

With the final patient gone, the office was quiet. It felt emptier than usual. Edwards and I both dropped into chairs in the hub. He told me to give him the details of the seizure.

After I did, Edwards stroked his goatee and said, "Yeah, I think that kid's fine. Sounds like a pseudo-seizure."

"What's that?"

"It's like a seizure, but it's not."

"It sure looked like one to me."

"These are different. Usually brought on by stress. But they don't have the same changes in electrical activity in the brain like a true seizure."

"It's from stress?"

"Some people get sick to their stomach, other people have pseudo-seizures."

"So, he's fine then?"

"Well, people with pseudo-seizures can still hurt themselves if they fall or bang their head. You should take them seriously. But yeah, that kiddo should be fine."

"That's a relief."

"You did a good job with him. Pretty exciting for your last day, huh?"

We had a hearty handshake. Edwards gave me a perfect score on my evaluation. I couldn't remember ever feeling so good. He encouraged me to go into Pediatrics because he thought I'd be good at it. No matter what the specialty is, the doctors always tell you to go into that one. But I think Edwards was sincere.

As I walked away, I felt sad. I wasn't ready to leave.

"Hey, one last thing," Edwards said.

I came back to the hub. Edwards was on his computer with the escort website pulled up. A busty redhead was on the screen. "What about her?" Edwards asked.

"Aren't you married?"

"It doesn't hurt to look."

"I guess not."

"Well, whaddaya think?"

I smiled. "I wouldn't kick her out of bed."

FEBRUARY
NEUROLOGY

Something rattled deep in my chest. I buried my mouth in the crook of my arm and let loose a torrent of coughs. Something wanted to come up, but was stuck inside my lungs. I must have caught something from one of those little bastards on my last rotation.

My coughing fit finally ended, and I took a sip of water. I was sitting at the Nurses Station on the sixth floor of the hospital. I was back in the hospital where I had my OB/GYN rotation. It was nice to drive to a part of town where I wouldn't have to worry about my car being stolen every day.

My preceptor hadn't showed, and I was starting to wonder if I was in the right place. I caught several disapproving glances from the nurses as they worked around me. To them I was a hacking monstrosity who was in the way.

My head swam. The whole world was skewed off-axis. Every muscle in my body ached. I coughed again, and quickly stifled it with another drink of water. I stretched my neck and hoped the muscles would feel better. They didn't. Whenever the neurologist showed up, I'd probably ask him if I could go home.

As if the universe had heard me, a tall man in khaki pants and a blue-striped shirt walked in. He wore no tie or white coat. A stethoscope hung around his neck, and a reflex hammer poked out of his pants pocket. He was talking on his cell phone. His name was Fisher, and he was in charge of Neurology consults.

Not wanting to be rude, I thought it best to wait for him to finish his conversation. He sat down a few feet away from me and logged into a computer. I tried not to listen to the details of his conversation, but with how loudly he was talking, it was impossible.

"Yeah, yeah, Marty, I know, but cut me a break here." Fisher paused and listened to the person on the other end of the phone. He eventually went on. "But Marty, how long have I been coming to see you, huh? (pause) And in all that time, haven't I always paid what I owed? (pause) So why won't you cut me a break this time, huh? (pause) The car's beautiful that's for sure, but you're ripping me off. (pause) I love you, Marty, but I'm going to have to get an estimate from someone else, okay? (pause) Sure, Marty, thanks. I'll be back tomorrow to pick it up. Bye."

He ended the call and dropped the phone on the table. "Bastard wants to charge me an arm and a leg for some body work," he said to no one in particular.

This was my chance. "Dr. Fisher?" I groaned.

"Yes?" he said, looking up from his computer.

"Hi, I'm–"

Another torrent of coughs exploded from my mouth. I turned away while my lungs spasmed with fire. I nearly doubled over. When the attack ended, I went back for my water and took a long drink. Then I tried again. "Hi, Dr. Fisher. I'm the third year rotating with you this month."

"Don't take this the wrong way, but you look like crap."

"I feel like crap."

"What's wrong?"

"I had Peds last month, so I must have caught something."

"Never fails. Everyone gets sick on Peds."

"Yeah."

"You're in no shape to see anyone today. You shouldn't have even bothered coming in. Why don't you take off? Get some rest."

"Thank you, Dr. Fisher. I was hoping you'd say that."

"No problem. Feel better."

"Okay. What time do you want me here tomorrow?"

"Nine o'clock if you're feeling better. Otherwise, just stay home."

I finished my water, and then staggered out of the hospital. As I passed the ER on the way out, I half-entertained the idea of admitting myself. But Fisher had told me to get some rest. And being in the hospital was no way to feel rested.

~~~

The next Monday, Fisher and I met at the Nurses Station. "How're you feeling?" he asked.

"A lot better, thanks."

"Good. Let's go. We have quite a census today."

Fisher flattened his list of patients on the table. Ten names were printed on it. I followed him to the first patient's room. We stopped just outside the door. "This one got admitted yesterday for seizures. Let's go say hi," Fisher said.

"Sounds good," I said, like it mattered what I thought.

The patient was a middle-aged woman with brown hair, which had once been done up in curls, but was now messy from lying in a hospital bed. Fisher gave her a friendly pat on the lower leg, and chatted with her about nothing in particular for about five minutes. He told her he was going to change her anti-epileptic medication dose. She nodded in agreement, but it seemed like she didn't understand what he said. When he was done, he told her to have a good day, and he quickly exited the room. I followed him out, a bit confused about what had just happened.

"The new dose should give her better control. It was decreased a few months ago, but it looks like that was a mistake. She'll be fine now," Fisher explained while jotting down a few notes.

He drew a line through her name on the census and said, "You know, with this many patients, I'm going to have to fly through these cases, and I'm not going to be able to do much teaching today."

"Oh, that's okay," I said. The prospect of shadowing him was dull but all right.

"I have an idea. There's a bunch of supplies I need to pick up for my office, but I never have time. Why don't you get that stuff for me? After that you can go home and take it easy."

My head twitched with surprise. I had already missed an entire week, and now he was going to let me go home after seeing one patient? Why had I even bothered to come?

"That sounds good," I said, trying not to reveal my excitement.

"Great. You're really helping me," he said. He took a business card from his wallet and handed it to me. A list of five items was written on the back. "There's an office supply store down the street. Tell them to charge it to my account."

I ran his errand. When I told the person at the register I was Fisher's medical student, they immediately knew what to do. Apparently, he had been sending medical students to this store for some time. Afterward, I delivered his things and headed home. I watched TV the entire afternoon. The longer I sat there, the farther into the couch I slid. I could almost feel my brain congealing inside my skull.

~~~

I closed the apartment door as Anne shuffled past me holding two heavy grocery bags. She eased them onto the counter and pulled out food. She had bought things I had never heard of before. She put them away with the comfort of someone who lived here.

When I was sick last week, Anne took it upon herself to nurse me back to health. She came over four evenings, made me soup, tidied the house, and kept me well stocked with tissues.

"How are you feeling?" she asked, crumpling the shopping bags.

"One hundred percent."

"That's good."

I stood beside her. She gave me a quick kiss on the cheek, and then started to make dinner. "I can't believe you had to work being as sick as you were," she said.

I hadn't bothered to tell her that Fisher had given me as much time off as I needed. That way I'd be free, and not have to bother seeing her in the middle of the day.

"Dr. Fisher's a good guy. He let me leave early today."

"That's nice. What time did you get home?"

I had returned at eleven. "About three o'clock."

She was chopping an onion. The knife clacked on the cutting board with each stroke.

"How about you? How was your day?" I asked. Not that I really cared, but this is what people did in a relationship. They asked how their partner's day went.

"It was kinda boring. Oh, but you know that one nurse, Gabby? Well, you won't believe what she said to me. I was pretty much working my ass off all day, and in the one minute I sat down to rest, she . . ."

I tuned out. This is what she always did. She jabbered on about this girl or that guy or a stupid coworker or an annoying patient. She would talk forever. None of her stories interesting, and they all ended the same way: the person she interacted with was either an idiot or an unreasonable bitch. She'd have me believe she was a saint with the IQ of Einstein. It was only bad luck that had her working a low-level hospital job.

". . . ever that way, right?" she asked.

My attention snapped back. "Yeah, you're absolutely right."

She finished the onion. She moved on to chopping carrots. "I knew it. She's such a bitch." She went on for a few more minutes. I interjected a bland sentiment of agreement every so often, and she never knew I wasn't listening.

"You know what I realized when I was driving over here?" Anne asked.

"What's that?"

"How long we've been together."

"Oh, yeah, uh, it's been . . ."

"Three months! Can you believe it?"

I wasn't sure how she came to that number with all the false starts we had. I rubbed my hand tenderly across the back of her shoulders. "It doesn't feel like that at all," I said.

"I know! The time has just flown by!"

She scraped the vegetables off the cutting board and into a large bowl. She unwrapped a package of chicken breasts and began to cut them into small pieces. "So, I was thinking," her voice had once again taken an odd lyrical quality, "if things keep going well, we should start looking for a place to live together."

I squeezed her ass and whispered in her ear. "You know what we should do? We should do it, right here in the kitchen."

I pressed my lips against the nape of her neck, and she giggled. "Stop. I'm trying to make dinner."

"I can't stop."

She craned her neck around, I leaned over her shoulder, and we kissed. Within moments, she turned and we were kissing hard and groping each other. And then she was on the counter, and we were having sex clumsily. Her head banged against an upper cabinet, and my hand sent a few items clattering to the floor. After we finished, Anne stroked my cheek and smiled. Lights danced in her eyes.

We put our clothes on, and Anne resumed cooking. She gossiped about one of her best friends and the guy she's dating that's totally wrong for her. The subject of cohabitation was forgotten.

~~~

I woke up earlier than usual. Last night I had been restless, and had strange dreams in aqua-marine colors. I woke with a start and found myself staring at the ceiling. Anne snored lightly beside me. Her blonde hair was splayed across the white pillow like a fan. I liked her best this way. Things got confusing when she was awake.

I got up carefully, so I wouldn't wake her, and crept into the kitchen. I opened the coffee maker and dumped in some coffee grounds. This cheap appliance was half the reason I made it through the first two years of school. Staying up until four or five in the morning to cram for a test, and doing it two or three times per week was a feat made possible only with the aid of caffeine.

As the coffee maker gurgled, I stalked into the living room and drew open the curtains. The world was cast in a pale blue light, the sun not quite ready to show its face. A few people walked by, hunkered down in winter coats. It was cold enough to see wisps of hot breath meeting the cool morning air.

The coffee maker spurted out a last puff of steam and fell quiet. I poured myself a cup, using a little sugar and cream. It tasted nice but it needed something else. I removed a half-empty bottle of whiskey from the cabinet above the refrigerator. I gave it a healthy pour. Now the coffee was perfect.

I sat on the couch in silence. I took long sips of my drink. I watched the hands of the clock slowly crawl across the dial. For some reason, Brad came to mind. I hadn't heard from him since Anne and I started seeing each other regularly.

Rotations did that. They made it a struggle to maintain relationships. It took a great deal of effort to keep from being alone. And it seemed I only had the energy to maintain one relationship at a time.

I passed the remainder of my early morning on the couch in silence, taking long sips of Irish Coffee.

~~~

A few hours later, I found myself back in the hospital with Fisher. He printed out his daily census and frowned at it. "Hmm, lots of people today. Going to be really busy."

"How many do we have?" I asked.

"Four new consults plus the follow ups from yesterday."

Since he sent me off on an errand yesterday, I had no idea how many patients that equaled.

"Intractable headaches in Two A. Should be straight-forward. Come on."

As Fisher and I entered the elevator, he got a call on his cell phone. He immediately became engrossed in a conversation about concert tickets. The details of his life were open to anyone within earshot. He continued his conversation all the way to the patient's bedside.

The patient looked annoyed. I mouthed "sorry" to her and gave an apologetic shrug. After an eternity, Fisher ended his call.

Fisher slid his phone into his pocket. He gave the patient a big, stupid grin. "Hi, I'm Dr. Fisher with Neurology. How are you doing today?"

"Shitty," the patient replied.

"I hear you're having some nasty headaches."

"You could say that."

"When did these start?"

"It's not 'these.' It's just one big-ass headache," she said, irritated.

"Oh, I'm sorry," Fisher said without a trace of sincerity. "When did it start?"

"Two days ago. Just hit me out of the blue."

As the questions went on, I felt myself becoming smaller. Fisher and the patient continued their back and forth. He asked a question and she gave a snarky answer.

"What do you normally take for headaches?" Fisher asked, scratching the back of his head.

"Whatever I got."

"Which is?"

The patient gave a bitter sigh. "I dunno. Percocet, I guess."

"Ah," Fisher said like a detective finding a clue. "And how much do you usually take?"

"A couple."

"How many times a day?"

"Three or four."

"So, you take up to eight a day?"

The patient shrugged. She and Fisher continued their repartee, and I felt as if I had shrunk to microscopic size.

"What kind of pain was the Percocet prescribed to you for?"

"Chronic."

It was now Fisher's turn to act irritated. "I mean, what is the origin of your pain?"

"Fibromyalgia."

"Of course."

The patient scowled. "You almost done? I'm getting tired of answering all these damn questions."

"Yes, almost. Did you recently run out of Percocet?"

"Yeah, a couple days ago."

"I see. Well, I believe you are having a rebound headache."

She looked at him quizzically. He explained. "Percocet contains a narcotic, and your body has become reliant on it to treat the headaches. When you ran out, the headache returned. But it rebounded and it's worse than ever. This is something I see quite often."

"What do I do about it?"

"What other medications have you tried?"

"My doctor said I can't use Ibuprofen because I have a stomach ulcer. And I tried Tylenol, but that don't work."

"You know, Percocet is mostly Tylenol."

The patient shot him a deadly glare. "I'm done talking to you. Why don't you get out?"

"Just to let you know, your CT scan was normal. So, I'm going to give you a trial of a completely different type of medication to see if it will help."

"Fine," she said flatly.

"And in the future, don't use narcotics to treat your headaches."

She glowered at him. He told her to have a nice day and we left. Fisher went to the Nurses Station and found the patient's chart. He wrote some orders. "She's fine," he said. "Her symptoms will go away with treatment. I'll give her a beta-blocker."

"Sounds good," I said, even though I had no idea what I was agreeing with.

Fisher wrote a progress note, and then crossed her name off his list. "It's going to be another one of those crazy days. Not much time for teaching."

I knew where this was heading.

"I'm not going to have much time to go over stuff with you."

Of course not.

"So, if you don't mind running another errand for me, you can go home early."

"Sure, Dr. Fisher."

"Great. My wife's car is in the body shop. She's got to pick it up, but as you can see, I'm swamped. If you could drive her there, I'd really appreciate it."

He wrote his home address on the back of a business card. As I left the hospital, I tried to sort out my conflicting emotions. On the one hand, I liked not having to kill myself admitting patients and delivering babies, but on the other hand, this rotation was a complete waste of time.

~ ~ ~

The doorbell rang for the second time. I felt conspicuous standing in front of Fisher's house in the middle of the day. I decided to wait another minute and then, if no one answered, I would leave.

Just when time was up, I heard a rustling behind the door. It slowly opened. A cute, short woman with closely cropped black hair peeked out from the other side.

"Hi," I said with a wave.

She blinked dumbly at me.

I told her my name. It took a moment to register. "Oh yeah, Bob called me about you. Do you mind waiting another minute? I'm almost ready."

"Sure."

The door closed again. The minute she asked me to wait turned into ten. When the front door finally reopened, she emerged holding a baby carrier. She set it gingerly on the ground as she locked the door.

An infant, bundled warmly, slept inside the carrier. Its left fist was against its mouth. It was dressed in green, and I couldn't tell if it was a boy or a girl. I hadn't expected this, but after a month with Edwards I was prepared for anything this baby could do.

The woman hefted the carrier and gave me a wan smile.

"Right this way," I said, directing her to my car.

As we walked I got a better look at Fisher's wife. If I hadn't known better, I would have guessed she was his daughter. She couldn't have been older than twenty. She was cute, though, and that short hair really worked for her. It's too bad she was married.

"Can I put her in the back?" she asked.

"Okay."

I opened the car door, and she left the baby carrier on the seat, unsecured. Weren't these things supposed to be hooked to a seat belt? She was the mother so she must have known what she was doing, right?

I closed the door. We moved to the front, and I hit the gas. As we drove, the silence was palpable. I tried to break the ice. "It's been great working with your husband."

"That's nice," she said, disinterested.

"How long have you been married?"

"About six months."

That explained a few things. Fisher was bound by an antiquated sense of duty.

"I'm sorry," I said, "I didn't catch your name."

"It's Cat."

"And what's your little one's name?"

"Jocelyn."

"Beautiful."

Actually, it sounded too old-fashioned. The only people named Jocelyn were women in medieval tales.

The car ride couldn't end fast enough. At least the baby was calm. Still, the desire to avoid the awkward silence kept me talking. Cat must have thought I was a madman.

"How did you meet Dr. Fisher?"

"Bob and I met at the club where I used to work."

"A night club?"

"A gentleman's club," she said. She meant a strip club. "I worked there for a couple years. I was one of the dancers." She meant she used to be a stripper. My pulse increased and my hands became sweaty.

Amazingly, she kept going. "He came in one night with some buddies. He was the best man for his friend's bachelor party."

The car went over a huge bump in the road. The baby carrier bounced. I glanced back. It was still upright, and the baby was still asleep. Cat hadn't noticed.

"I was working the floor. I gave him and his friends a couple of dances. I ended up taking him back to the Champagne Room. He asked me if he could pick me up after my shift ended. He was cute, so I said yeah. He took me back to his place and, well, now we have Jocelyn."

I hadn't expected her to give me a blow-by-blow of the events leading to her unplanned pregnancy. Either Cat was the most forthcoming person on the planet, or she had been waiting a long time to tell that story. And who better than a stranger she would never see again?

I groped for something to say. "Where did you work?"

I felt like a moron. Cat didn't care. She answered in the same detached manner she had told the story. "Panthers. That place by the VA hospital."

We fell back into silence for the remainder of the drive. When we reached our destination, Cat asked, "You mind watching Jocelyn for a minute?"

"Okay."

She slammed the door and ambled toward the building. As soon as she was inside, the baby started to wail. Oh, no. What was wrong with it?

I tried to reach back, but the seat belt restricted me. The little girl's face was bright red. Her toothless maw opened wider than I thought possible. I grabbed for her again, but she was just out of reach.

I unbuckled and went to the rear of the vehicle. My hands hovered over her. I didn't know what to do. I looked up to see if Cat was heading back. No luck.

I picked the baby up. Her screams became louder and more pained, so I put her back. I sniffed her butt. It didn't smell like she had pooped. I touched her belly, and found her shirt was damp. Why was every baby I touched always wet?

I grabbed one of two small stuffed toys that were inside the baby carrier. "Look!" I exclaimed. "Look! It's your horsey!" I made it gallop across the air. The baby quieted, her eyes opened as she examined the toy. She decided the toy wasn't good enough and resumed shrieking.

I tried the other toy with less success. I stepped away from the car for a minute. I looked around. A couple of passers-by gawked at me. They probably thought I was kidnapping the baby.

I ducked back into the car and tried again.

"It's okay, honey. It's okay. Shhh. Your mom's going to be here soon."

That didn't work either. Maybe she wanted to scream for the hell of it? And where was Cat? She was taking an eternity in the office. Was she giving the guys in the building a private dance?

This went on until I felt like crying. I hung my head and pleaded, "Please stop crying. Please."

The baby quieted. Thank God. I offered her the slightest smile. And then, just to torture me, she wailed even louder.

The other rear door opened and Cat scooped up the baby. She bounced it, and whispered something in its ear. After a few seconds of that, the baby lost her motivation to cry.

"Thanks," I said. "I tried everything I could think of."

"It's okay. Sometimes I can't get her to shut up."

I pulled the baby carrier out. A blue convertible was parked next to my rust bucket. Cat nodded toward it. "Can you put that in my car?"

I complied without saying a word. She could have asked me to do anything at this point. I was glad to get that thing out of my car. Cat secured her baby in the carrier, and then got into the front seat of the car. She revved the engine. "Thanks for the lift."

~~~

The next day, we saw an interesting case, but Fisher tried his damnedest to be blasé about it. The patient was a forty year old male out of emergency surgery yesterday. He was tied to his bed with fat Velcro restraints over his arms. A police officer sat nearby reading a newspaper.

"What's this guy's story?" Fisher asked.

The cop looked up. "Shot in the head."

"No shit?"

"Yeah. He was robbing a liquor store. Only he didn't see the black-and-white across the street. He started shooting, and we–" The cop made his finger into a gun, and made a hollow "pop" with his mouth.

The entire left side of the patient's face was caved in. It was wrapped in layers of bandages. Surgical hardware had been implanted to rebuild his skull, but he still looked deformed. His head bobbed back and forth, and he smacked his lips purposelessly. His eyes were dead. Whatever spark of intelligence he once had, had been carved out of his brain by the trail of a bullet.

"I wonder how much tax money got wasted on him," Fisher said.

"Too much if you ask me," the cop said.

Fisher examined the patient more quickly than the others. Reflexes, light in the eyes, and a few other tests. They were all abnormal. Fisher never mentioned what any of these findings indicated, only that they were abnormal.

Fisher slid his reflex hammer back into his pocket. "I hope this bastard learned his lesson," he said.

"Think he'll recover?" the cop asked.

"Not a chance."

"Good," the cop snorted before returning to his newspaper.

"Come on," Fisher said, heading out of the room. "I can't believe they wasted my time with this crap."

On the way out, I cast one final look at the patient. I wondered what fate awaited him. Unlike Fisher and the cop, I did not hold him in contempt. I pitied him.

The days continued with the same routine, short visits with patients followed by favors. Sometimes it was something as simple as getting a cup of coffee. Other times I had to drive around and pick stuff up. Once, Fisher had me call his cable provider so he could add premium movie channels to his account. I waited on hold over an hour for that favor.

In the afternoons I studied, at least for a while. When that got boring I went to matinees at the movie theater. That gave way to long naps. Eventually, I became tired of all these and fell back into a pattern of mindless drinking.

~~~

Somehow, I found myself at Cat's former place of employment. Being early afternoon, the club was deserted. One girl did a half-hearted pole grind on the main stage. A couple of other women were giving lap dances to a few patrons who dotted the room. The music was turned down. This place was sad.

I ordered and rum and cola from a waitress, fully clothed, who was a lot prettier than any of the nude girls in the room. The drink tasted like water with a hint of rum flavoring. And at eight bucks, it was quite a deal.

When the current song ended, another began and the girl on stage rotated out with a different girl. The new one danced just as half-heartedly as the first. They probably saved their energy for the evening.

I scrutinized the girls. I hoped to see Cat, like she was bored at home and decided to pick up an extra shift. The idea was ludicrous, but I was hopeful nonetheless.

"Like a dance?" someone asked.

I craned my neck. A stripper with long blonde hair, a tiny pink thong, a slight rippled scar on her stomach from liposuction, and large waxy breasts stood beside me. I set my drink down and stammered, "Uh, n-no thanks.

She shrugged and walked away.

I finished my drink, and the cute waitress returned. I ordered another. Eventually, another stripper came along and asked if I wanted a dance. She looked like the first stripper only as a brunette. This time I said yes.

Afterward, I tracked down my waitress and asked if she wanted to go out sometime. She firmly told me that she did not date customers. I left the club with my head hanging. She probably thought I was a pervert.

~~~

Thursday night, Anne wanted to have a get-together with her girlfriends. She sprung it on me at the last minute, and I didn't have time to think of an excuse to get out of it.

I found myself waiting in the kitchen. I wore black pants and a yellow collared shirt. Anne was in a knee-length skirt that bore a colorful abstract pattern.

Freshly purchased bottles of liquor stood proudly on the counter. A stack of red plastic cups sat next to them. A variety of mixers were in the refrigerator at the ready.

Anne was in the living room selecting music. A steady bass line began to thump. "I can't believe you haven't met any of my friends yet!" Anne shouted.

"Me neither!"

"Usually, when I start seeing a guy I introduce him right away!"

"Is that right?"

"Yep! I don't know why I didn't do it this time!"

I picked up the bottle of rum and inspected the contours of the glass. Briefly, I entertained the notion of drinking nothing. But I'd be meeting new people tonight. It would be better to have a few drinks to ease the tension.

The doorbell rang. After a few moments, I walked into the living room.

Anne and a friend squealed and hugged. Her friend was tall and dark-skinned. She was incredibly sexy. My eyes drifted down to her left hand. No ring.

She brought her friend over and said, "Sabrina, this is my boyfriend."

Sabrina and I shook hands and exchanged the usual greetings. The doorbell rang again, and Anne answered it.

"So, where do you know Anne from?" I asked.

"High school," Sabrina said.

"You've known each other that long, huh?"

"Yeah. We were really close the whole way through."

"I haven't stayed in touch with anyone from high school."

"That's too bad. I bet you're too busy being a doctor and all."

I didn't bother correcting her. I wasn't interested in staying in touch with any of the people I knew from high school. Most of them were hillbillies. It would have been a complete waste of time.

Sabrina's attention was suddenly elsewhere. Several new girls had appeared. It was obvious Sabrina was eager to ditch me. "Well, it's really great to finally meet you," she said.

"You, too."

"Excuse me."

She raced over to her friends. We didn't speak again the rest of the evening. She was gorgeous, so it wasn't due to a lack of interest on my part.

Anne introduced me to each of her closest friends, five in all. They were all very pretty, which confirmed my suspicion that beautiful people flocked together. I didn't belong.

I had a few mixed drinks and tried to chat with Anne's friends. They each put on a good show of interest, but nobody was entirely convincing. They weren't impressed. They must have wondered why Anne was dating me.

As the night wore on, the music grew louder, the squeals shriller, and the girls drunker. The girls danced with each other, but I hung back.

"Hey!" someone called from the couch.

It was Becky, Anne's friend who was not as attractive as Sabrina, but still quite attractive.

"Hey," I called back.

"Whachoo gonna do wit Anne?"

"Huh?"

"Annie! Whachoo gonna do wit her?"

"What do you mean?"

"When you gonna git married?"

"Married?"

"You looove her, don'choo?"

"Becky!" Anne shouted, pausing momentarily from grinding on another girl.

"What? I jus' wanna know!"

Anne held out both hands, inviting Becky to dance with her. Becky hauled herself off the couch. She grabbed each of Anne's hands, and they danced uncoordinatedly.

I dropped onto the couch. The six girls carried on until midnight when one of them suggested they go to a dance club. Anne stumbled over to me. She leaned forward. Her shirt drooped, exposing her cleavage. "You wanna go with us, baby?" she asked. Her breath was hot and reeked of alcohol.

"Sorry, I can't. I have my rotation tomorrow."

"Skip it."

"It's the last day. I have to go."

"Who gives a shit? Come out with us."

"I can't."

"Fine," she said sternly. What was her problem? I couldn't be absent on the final day. I needed to get my evaluation filled out, otherwise I wouldn't pass.

Anne and her friends gathered their belongings and made their way out. I turned off the stereo, and the apartment fell quiet. The pulse of the bass still thumped in my ears.

The kitchen counter was sticky with dry booze. Red plastic cups were tipped over and drooled soda and liquor. I picked up the bottle of rum again. This time it was only half-full.

I caught my reflection in the glass. I was a featureless figure. I closed my eyes and replayed Becky's question in my mind. I hadn't considered that until she shouted it drunkenly. When I looked at my reflection again, it grew darker.

I took a swig from the bottle. Then another. Then another.

~~~

The next morning I rose from Anne's bed, my head aching. I dressed quickly, putting on the same rumpled clothes from last night. Anne was snoring. Careful not to wake her, I crept out of the room. She groaned and turned over.

When I reached the hospital, showered and in fresh clothes, Fisher was already waiting for me. That had been a first.

"Good morning," I said.

"What's good about it?"

"Um, I don't know." I hadn't expected that. I was merely exchanging the routine morning banter. People were supposed to say they were fine and leave it at that. "Anything I can do to help?" I asked.

"No, not really," he answered glumly. "Not unless you could tell my wife to stop being such a whore."

"I-I'm sorry."

"I went home early yesterday and caught that bitch fucking some other guy."

Several nurses were trying to look busy, but were obviously eavesdropping. Fisher leaned back in his chair, drumming his fingers on the desk. "Yeah, it's over. I'm gonna make sure I get full custody of Jocelyn. My wife is getting kicked to the curb."

One thing was certain, both Fisher and Cat had no qualms speaking their minds. Fisher dropped his chair forward. He looked me up and down. Was he going to ask if I had sex with her? Not that I wouldn't have enjoyed it.

"Today's your last day, right?" he asked.

"Yes."

"When's your test?"

"Tomorrow morning."

"Why don't you take off and study?"

"That would be great. Thanks."

"You bring your eval?"

I pulled a folded piece of paper from the pocket of my white coat. Fisher clicked his pen nine times, and then he wrote hard.

He tore a hole through the page in one place. He gave me a score of three in every category. He scratched something in the comments section and messily signed his name. He folded the paper and handed it back without looking at me.

He stood up and stomped away. When he was out of sight, I realized I had been holding my breath. My diaphragm shook as I exhaled. I held the paper up and read the comments. "Professional. Friendly. Weak medical knowledge. Didn't show much interest in Neuro."

That son of a bitch pushed me away every day. He didn't want me around. How the hell would he know if I wasn't interested in Neurology? He wasn't interested in teaching. He never even pimped me once, so how could he say I had weak medical knowledge?

I jammed the paper in my pocket. I stormed out of the ward, glad that his marriage was over.

After my test the next day, I came home and watched TV. I called Anne four or five times and left four or five voicemails. She never returned my calls. By now I was getting used to this kind of thing. On Sunday afternoon she called.

"Hey, I missed you yesterday," I said cheerfully.

"Did you?" she said flatly.

"Of course."

"Oh."

"How come you didn't call?"

"I was tired."

Silence. My cheerfulness quickly drained. She was upset with me, but I didn't have a clue why. I waited and heard only her soft breath.

"Can I come over?" I asked.

"You know how to get here."

"Do you want me to come?"

". . . sure."

She had given me a key last month, so I let myself in. I found her draped across the living room couch. The TV was on, the volume blasting. Her eyes were glassy.

"Hi," I said.

Anne didn't reply.

"How are you?" I asked, forcing myself to sound extra happy.

Still nothing. If she hadn't wanted to talk, why had she called me in the first place?

I sat on the far end of the couch. There was barely enough room for me to fit on the cushion. I touched her leg, but she pulled it back. "What's wrong?" I asked.

"Nothing."

"Are you sure?"

"Yeah."

"Really?"

"I told you, I'm *fine!*" she snapped.

She didn't sound fine. She sounded pissed off. I thought about saying that, but a sarcastic comment would only make things worse.

"Okay, but if something's bothering you, I'd be glad to talk about it."

She curled into a ball. "Don't act like you don't know."

My face flushed, my heart thumped, and that old familiar anxiety fluttered in my stomach. "I'm sorry, honey. What did I do?"

"Stop playing dumb, you asshole."

Now my heart pumped in overdrive.

"A-Anne. I-I don't know what I did. Please tell me. I'm so sorry," I said. I was a sniveling idiot. I didn't even know what I was apologizing for.

"You wouldn't go out with me and my friends," she said.

"Huh? You mean on Thursday?"

"Yeah."

"I partied with you 'til you left."

She sat up. Her eyes were ablaze. "That's not what I'm talking about!"

I edged as far back on the couch as I could go. "What do you mean?"

"You acted all high and mighty. Not wanting to go out on a weeknight. Only alcoholics do that. You too good to drink on a weeknight?"

"No, I was drinking–"

"Well, you must not be interested in me. Don't think I can't tell. It's because you're gonna be a goddamn doctor, you think you're better than me, don't you?"

"No, not at all."

"What then? You don't really love me?"

"That isn't true."

"You can go to hell!"

"Anne, I'm sorry."

"Get outta my house!"

I pleaded more, like a baby, but she threw me out.

I returned home. Sliding the key into the deadbolt, I tried to remember the last thing she had said to me. I opened the door and walked into the dark apartment. Was it over? Had we broken up? I'd probably never see her again. And God only knew when I'd find another girl willing to have sex with me.

MARCH
PSYCHIATRY

I found myself back at the county hospital. During the drive in, my body filled with dread. I could taste it in the back of my throat. Anne worked here. I was afraid what a chance encounter with her would lead to.

As I made my way into the building, the rooster crowed. I went to the fourth floor, where the inpatient psychiatric unit was located. I walked down a long, brightly lit hallway toward a pair of gray metal doors. Each door had a narrow rectangular window. They glowed from within like a pair of eyes.

An intercom was on the wall. Above that, where the wall and ceiling met, was a video camera angled at me. They didn't want anyone getting in or out of this place.

I pushed the button. A few seconds later I heard the voice of a woman who sounded as ancient as the hospital. "Can I help you?"

"I'm a medical student starting today."

"Hold on."

I heard a heavy click as the metal doors unlatched remotely. I pulled one open and stepped inside. It closed behind me, and the lock snapped shut.

Before me were multiple hallways going forward, right, and left. Patient rooms lined the far hallway. To the right of the first hallway was the Nurses Station. Unlike any I had seen before, it was closed. It had full walls, large windows, and a door. To my left was a room marked "Laundry." To my right was a conference room. A small note was affixed to the door, reading, "Medical Students." I tried the handle, but it was locked.

The door opened. "Can I help you?" an extraordinarily fat woman asked. Before I could reply, she figured out who I was. The short white coat was a giveaway.

She brought me into the room, and I found three other faces staring at me. They each had a flimsy spiral-bound notebook in front of them. The fat woman ushered me to one side of the table. "Please, sit. Here's a book for you. We're only on page two."

I sat next to the other two medical students, one male and one female. The fat woman sat on the other side, next to a remarkably skinny woman. "Now that we're all here, let's do some introductions, shall we?" she said with a clap of her hands.

I told them my name without any fanfare.

"I'm Rachel, a fourth year," the girl next to me said. "I rotated here last year. I'm back because I really want to go into Psych."

"That's wonderful," the fat woman said with another clap. "Did you apply to our program?"

She meant the hospital's Residency program. This was one of many places where doctors could do their post-graduate specialty training. Rachel nodded. "This is my top choice."

"Well, good luck!"

Now it was the other student's turn. "Hi, I'm No-Name. I'm a third year. I'm going into Pediatric Cardiothoracic Surgery," he said.

To be honest, I couldn't remember his name. Or his face. He wasn't all that interesting.

The skinny woman spoke next. "I'm Sally, Nursing Coordinator."

"And I'm Sandy," the fat woman said, finishing off the group. "I'm the Nursing Supervisor. It's really a pleasure to have you all with us for the next month."

Rachel and No-Name returned the platitude. I simply nodded. Sandy gave another clap. "Let's get to it. We're going to spend the day learning about CPST. That stands for Crisis Prevention and Safety Training."

We'd be spending the entire day in here? Were we really going to prevent any crises? Maybe Rachel would, but I certainly wouldn't. No-Name looked doubtful, too.

The training was excruciating. It focused on how to handle situations in which patients became agitated or violent. Every situation in the book had five stages, each given a philosophical name. Each stage was accompanied by a drawing that represented it. The people in the drawings had no faces, their heads were blank ovals. I suppose the reality of Medicine is that all patients are just bodies with blank faces.

After an exhausting three hours, Sandy clapped her hands. "Good job, everyone," she said. "Why don't we take a break for lunch? Let's meet back here in an hour for part two."

"Y'all wanna get some lunch?" No-Name asked.

"I brought my own, but I'll come with you," Rachel said.

They turned their eyes to me. My skin crawled. There wasn't going to be any way out of this. "No thanks, I'm good," I said.

"Just come along," No-Name said. It sounded more like an order than a friendly request.

"Okay."

Rachel was well-tanned with auburn hair and dark brown eyes. Her figure was the inverse of an hourglass. No-Name was incredibly hairy. Thick black tufts of hair peeked out from the neckline of his shirt. His hands were dark and coarse. His face was a blank oval.

I bought some disgusting slop from the cafeteria. It was labeled as Mexican food, but it looked more like meat paste slapped on a tortilla. No-Name got something that looked like a sandwich and smelled vaguely of tuna. Rachel brought a square Tupperware container filled with salad that oozed dressing.

The dining area was crowded, but we found an empty table. We ate in silence for a bit, interrupted by the occasional ice-breaker. I felt the need to keep checking over my shoulder to look for Anne. Eventually, No-Name struck up a real conversation.

"What do y'all think about this trainin' nonsense?" he asked.

"It's not so bad. I had to do it last year," Rachel said.

"Seems pointless to me."

"It might come in handy. Better to know it and never have to use it."

"Only thing I got to know is how to use these," No-Name said as he flexed his bicep. His shirt sleeve bulged. He was probably right. That was likely the only thing he knew. "If those wackos gimme any trouble, they'd better watch out."

I looked down at my food. The tortilla was wet and flimsy, sopped with grease. I stabbed it with a plastic fork.

"How about you? What do you want to go into?" Rachel asked me.

She forked a small bite of salad into her mouth and looked at me with wide eyes. No-Name chomped half of his tuna sandwich in a single bite.

"I'm not sure," I said.

"Dude!" No-Name said, his mouth full. "It's already March! What's wrong with you?"

"There's still lots of time to decide. What rotations have you liked?" Rachel asked.

My mind turned blank. Which rotation had I liked best? Which tedious specialty did I want to get stuck in and grind away at until I died? Was that a trick question?

I took a bite of meat paste to buy a few extra seconds to come up with an answer. "I liked my Peds rotation the best," I said.

"Peds, oh that's great," Rachel said.

"Peds. Pff," No-Name said.

"I thought you were going into Peds Surgery," Rachel said, sounding annoyed. I got the feeling she thought as little of him as I did.

He raised his index finger correctively. "Pediatric Cardiothoracic *Surgery.* Emphasis on the surgery. A chance to cut is a chance to cure."

"You still have to learn Peds before you get to slice them open."

"The medical part's nothin'. Just memorization. Which drugs kill which bugs. A monkey could do that. The real trick is cuttin' open a live person."

"You don't think you have to memorize anatomy to do that?"

"Obviously. But we did that already in first year. Unless you guys didn't dissect cadavers wherever you go to school."

Dissecting cadavers was a first-year tradition in every medical school. In Gross Anatomy, groups of four students spend the entire year cutting a corpse apart, piece by piece. While it was a great learning tool, I'd be an idiot to think I still remembered every tiny nerve and vessel two years later.

"Sounds like you're going to be in Residency for a long time," Rachel said.

"Ain't no thing," No-Name replied. "I'm gonna be making so much bank, it'll be totally worth it."

"Where did you do your Surgery rotation?"

"I got it here in two months."

I shook my head and took another bite of meat paste. After swallowing, I pushed my tray away. Two bites were enough. I didn't want to get sick.

We reappeared upstairs a few minutes later. Sandy welcomed us back. "Now it's time for part two of CPST. This is the really fun part!" she said, punctuating her statement with her trademark clap. "Let's clear a space in the middle of the room."

After we cleared the room, Sandy continued. "We are going to show you the CPST maneuvers for self-defense and escape. There are several you will need to know before going into the milieu. They might just save your life."

How dangerous was it in there? Was this a lockdown for the criminally insane? Should I hire a bodyguard for the month? No, I'd just stick close to No-Name. His overconfidence would buy me enough time to run away from any situation.

Sandy and Sally began to demonstrate the various maneuvers. Each time they finished one, they had us practice. Rachel attacked No-Name, No-Name attacked me, and I attacked Rachel. During each maneuver we shouted, "No!" as a means of startling the aggressor. Rachel said it enthusiastically, No-Name said it while trying not to laugh, and I said it with indifference. If a patient attacked me, I wouldn't remember any of this.

We finished at 3:30 PM, and Sandy gave a final clap. "Congratulations! You've completed CPST. Hopefully, you won't have to use it, but if you do you'll be ready."

The line was obviously rehearsed and refined over years, one month at a time, to each group of new students starting their Psychiatry rotation.

We were dismissed and buzzed off the unit. I had no interest in taking a leisurely stroll to chat with Rachel and No-Name. As I hurried away, I looked down every hallway, paranoid that I'd see Anne. I didn't. When I got home, I made myself dinner. She didn't call me, and I didn't call her. I didn't want to risk it.

~~~

The next day I was back on the unit. A man and a woman, casually dressed, power-walked by me. Who were they? This seemed like a strange place to exercise.

As I approached the Nurses Station, I saw a multitude of people bustling inside. Rachel was already there, talking to an older guy with a beard, probably an Attending. I didn't see No-Name.

I entered, surprised at the weight of the door. The room was cramped. People were huddle by computers, clacking away at keyboards. A large TV screen displayed live feeds from eight security cameras. Cubby holes held patient charts which were labeled with first names only. At the back of the room was a dry-erase board that listed each patient along with their corresponding treatment teams. There were thirty entries, and the unit appeared to be full. This room looked more like a military command center than a Nurses Station.

"Hey," someone said, startling me. A man in a green and white striped shirt stood behind me. "I'm Matt Danforth. You're working with me."

"Are you one of the Residents?" I asked.

"Yeah. Second year. You're M.S. . . ."

"Three."

"Okay. Is this your first time on a psych unit?"

"Yeah."

"First thing you should do is lose the white coat. There's no rule against it, but people find it easier to talk if it doesn't look like you're about to perform a science experiment on them."

"Got it," I said, hanging my coat over the back of a nearby chair. "You want me to get started seeing people?"

Matt inspected his list of patients. "Why don't you just shadow me today? Tomorrow I'll give you two patients to follow."

This was for the best. I had never seen a psychiatric patient before. I wasn't even sure what kind of questions to ask.

We exited the Nurses Station and headed down the far hallway. The pair of power-walkers blew past us. "Good morning, Dr. D!" the man said. He was one of Matt's patients? I hadn't expected the patients here to be dressed in normal clothes. If everyone looked normal, how could they tell who were the patients?

Farther down the hallway was a bank of interview rooms. They were all identical, housing a table, computer, telephone, and chairs. The door to each room had a large window. This was so staff could monitor patients' behavior while in the room with the doctors.

We entered the only vacant room. "Wait here. Don't let anybody steal our room. I'll go get the first patient," Matt said.

I waited, feeling useless, until Matt returned with a woman in her mid-fifties. She was dressed in a pair of black jeans and a baggy purple sweatshirt.

"And this is our medical student," Matt said.

"Hello," she said. "Are you going to be a psychiatrist, too?"

"I'm not sure. Maybe," I said as pleasantly as possible.

We sat around the table. Matt asked this seemingly normal woman a series of questions. She answered them easily and coherently. Why was she here anyway? She didn't seem crazy at all. I thought this was supposed to be the loony bin.

"How's your mood today?" Matt asked.

"Still depressed," the patient answered.

"Compared to usual?"

"Better."

"Any suicidal thoughts today?"

I couldn't believe he would come right out and ask that. He was so blunt about it. Was that how it was supposed to be done? Perhaps, because the patient was completely unfazed.

"No, not so far."

"And last night?"

"Yes, one or two."

"Any plans?"

"No, nothing like that. Just thinking it would be nice if I died in my sleep."

"I see." Matt said. He changed subjects. "How'd you sleep?"

"Good!" she said, brightening. "I didn't wake up one time."

Matt nodded with approval. "Any thoughts of hurting others?"

"No, never."

"Hearing any voices today?"

"No."

"Seeing weird stuff?"

"No."

"Paranoia?"

"Only that I'll be locked in here forever," she said with a laugh. Matt joined her, but his laughed seemed forced.

"Great. Well, I think you are doing a lot better. But you still have a bit to go."

"When will I get to go home?"

"I'm not sure yet. We still need to check a Lithium level, and the soonest we can do that is tomorrow. Plus, I'd like you to have a day without any suicidal thoughts."

"Oh, I see."

"You know, it's better you stay in here a couple days longer and never have to come back, instead of leaving early and winding up here again in a few days."

"You're right. Thank you, doctor."

"Have a good day," Matt said as he ushered her out of the room.

The heavy door closed, all the doors here were heavy, and Matt sat down at the table. He quickly wrote a progress note.

"Why is she here?" I asked.

"She overdosed on Xanax. She told her FP she was depressed, so he put her on Xanax and Prozac."

"I take it that didn't help."

"Nope. She's Bipolar. When you give Bipolar people antidepressants, especially one like Prozac, they can get worse. In her case, she decided to kill herself."

"All that from the wrong meds?"

"Well, not all. She's been non-compliant with all her medical stuff for decades. And she lost a lot of her family's money gambling in a manic episode. It was right after that she got depressed."

It was hard to believe such a normal looking lady could have gone through all that.

"All right, we're done with her. Stay here while I get the next one."

The next patient was a homeless guy who was admitted for suicidal ideation without an attempt. He seemed just as normal as the lady. The one after that was a guy with depression and auditory hallucinations. He described it as "noise" like the sound of a crowd at a sports stadium. He and Matt were very matter-of-fact about it. Each patient we saw seemed as normal as the next. I had expected something different.

We cleared out of the interview room once Matt had finished writing all his progress notes. We returned to the Nurses Station and found it less chaotic than earlier. Matt pulled out charts and began writing orders for his patients. Random Attendings popped in and out and staffed cases with Matt. They usually agreed with his plans, but always added a bit more: order an Internal Medicine consult for Patient X, or gather collateral information for Patient Y. I was amazed by the volume of his work.

I stood at Matt's side while he wrote orders, called families and pharmacies, and dictated discharge summaries. Around noon he sent me off to get lunch. I ate mindlessly, opting for salad instead of meat paste. When I returned half an hour later, Matt was wrapping up his morning's work. I wondered what we would do next.

The answer became clear quickly: admissions. With thirty beds and a multitude of discharges, all of the Residents were kept busy filling the empty spots. People from all over the city with suicidal ideation, suicide attempts, mania, and psychosis were funneled to us.

Between 12:30 and 4:30 PM, Matt admitted two patients, bringing his census back to six. The first had been a crotchety guy who was crashing off meth and wasn't in the mood to talk. Matt got the bare essentials from him and then let him sleep. The second patient, however, was far more interesting.

We all sat down in the interview room. Matt and I sat near the door. The patient was on the other side of the table, near the back of the room. Matt told me this was safer, so we could escape in case things escalated.

The patient wore an ill-fitting hospital gown. He looked around the room quizzically, paying no attention to us. Matt introduced himself, but the patient said nothing. He said the patient's name, but got no response.

"Zeus," Matt said at last.

"Yes?" the patient said, looking at Matt.

According to the information we received prior to his arrival, the patient thought he was the king of the Greek gods.

"How are you doing?" Matt asked.

"The cake," Zeus replied casually.

"I'm sorry?"

"I ate all the cake."

"I see. Is that why you're here today?"

"Mom told me I couldn't have any. She wanted it all. But I wanted some, too. So I ate the whole thing."

"How'd you get to the hospital, Zeus?"

"Mom brought me."

"And why did she do that?"

"I told you, because of the *cake*," he said, irritated.

"Okay. How are you feeling today?"

"I feel like eating more cake."

"Hearing strange voices?"

"Yes."

"What do they tell you?"

"To eat cake. And Mom's a bitch."

"Anything else?"

"I hear the wind."

"Really? What does it say?"

Zeus replied with a string of gibberish. I bit the inside of my cheek and looked at the floor to prevent myself from laughing. Matt continued as professionally as ever.

"Did you try to hurt your mom?"

Zeus turned his palms up. Matt tapped a piece of paper and said, "It says here you stabbed your mom with a kitchen knife. Is that right?"

"I just cut her arm, no big deal."

"And you did that because of the voices?"

"Well, yeah."

"What if you had killed her?"

"I would have resurrected her. I *am* Zeus," he said nonchalantly.

Zeus was crazy, but there was consistency in what he told us. The interview continued with Matt asking questions and Zeus answering them like we were a pair of stooges. He denied having any other psychiatric symptoms. He denied homicidal ideation, but qualified it by stating he would kill anyone who prevented him from eating cake.

"Have you ever tried to kill yourself?" Matt asked.

"Yes."

"How many times?"

"Eleventy. Or twelvety."

"And how do you usually try?"

"I smoke clove cigarettes."

"Do you think that will work?"

"Eventually."

I stifled another laugh, but Zeus was completely serious.

"How many times have you been in the psychiatric hospital?"

"One million five hundred sixty two thousand and four."

"That's a lot."

"If Mom had her way, she'd always have me in here. But she can't. I know I'm legally allowed to have cake."

"What about psych meds? Which ones have you tried?"

"I'm not taking any of those. I've already tried them all. All they do is make me feel worse."

"What happens?"

"Would you make Marilyn Monroe take meds? Or the President of Mars? No, you can't. You fucking fascists can't make me do anything I don't want to!" Zeus suddenly cracked at the seams. We had been talking for about twenty minutes, which must have been his limit.

Matt forged ahead, moving quicker now as Zeus was about to lose it. "Do you have a psychiatrist?"

"I don't see no fucking scientist."

"Use any drugs?"

"Just clove cigarettes and cake."

"How about marijuana or meth or heroin?"

"I already *told* you!"

Matt flipped through the pages of the H and P. Even though he moved fast, he still had a lot of ground to cover. With each new question, Zeus fidgeted more in his chair. Matt attempted to perform a brief cognitive exam, but Zeus refused to participate.

"Fuck you, you fucking fascist! You can't keep a god locked up in here with the mortals and no cake and the jukebox from hell and the fucking Creature from the Black Lagoon eating all the mashed potatoes!"

Zeus was fuming. I felt an urgency to escape the room. I didn't want Zeus to think I was preventing him from eating cake.

"Okay," Matt said, tucking his pen into his shirt pocket. "Why don't you go out to the Day Room and relax?"

Matt and I got up and exited the room. Zeus stormed off. We went to the Nurses Station. Matt told the nurse to increase Zeus' safety precaution level. He completed the admission note, and then staffed the case with an Attending over the phone. There were a lot of "yes's" and "uh-huh's" from Matt's end.

"Well, that's it," he said. "Zeus should be all tucked in for the night."

"What meds are you giving him?" I asked.

"Haldol for now."

"That's one of the antipsychotics?"

"Right. Why don't you read up on it tonight and tell me about it tomorrow?"

Great, a homework assignment.

A nurse approached Matt and solicited him for help with one of the other patients. As they walked off, Matt excused me. The Unit Secretary buzzed me out. I drove home feeling more exhausted than I had in quite some time. During the drive, my cell phone rang. Anne's name flashed on the outer screen.

I reached for the phone, which was sticking upright in the cup holder, but then I stopped. Maybe I shouldn't answer? Maybe I was better off without her? I turned the thought over in my mind. When I finally decided, I flipped the phone open and pressed it to my ear. It had fallen silent.

~~~

The next day was a blur. I correctly recited the risks and benefits of Haldol to Matt before we rounded on his patients. The meth guy was still detoxing. He cursed at us several times and refused to get out of bed. Zeus didn't look much better. He regaled us with a story of how one of the other patients sent him telepathic messages overnight. Matt increased his dose of Haldol. In the afternoon we admitted another new patient, a man who had stabbed himself in the abdomen in a suicide attempt.

Once I was outside the unit, the day's work was no longer there to distract me. The looming task that sat before me was inescapable. I had to call Anne. I would have to confront her about her behavior. I'd give her an ultimatum: treat me with respect or it's over.

When she picked up, her voice was indignant. "Why didn't you return my call?"

"This is me calling you back."

"What took you so long?"

I supposed she didn't see the irony in her question. "Sorry, I was busy," I replied.

"Too busy for me. Typical. You don't care about me, do you? Not really."

"Of course I care about you, Anne."

"What kind of a man are you, anyway?"

"What do you mean?"

"Why am I wasting my time with you? You keep stringing me along. I don't have time for this shit."

"Anne, slow down. Listen–"

"No, you listen. I don't think this is working. I need someone capable of feelings. I don't need to be with another narcissistic asshole."

"Anne! Wait! I'm sorry!"

"Sorry about what?"

"About the way I treated you. I was being a total jerk, you're right. But you have to believe me when I tell you it wasn't on purpose. I didn't even know I was doing that."

". . . oh."

"Please don't break up with me, Anne. I love you."

". . . why don't you come over? We'll sort things out."

"Okay. Great. Thank you so much," I blubbered. I was always blubbering when it came to dealing with Anne.

I raced to her place. We sat on the couch and talked things over for a good half an hour. "I'm done dating casually, you know?" she said. "I need someone I can settle down with. So, if you think you're ready for that, we can move forward."

"I will. I mean, I am."

"I love you," she said with a smile.

"I love you, too."

My heart felt lighter than ever before.

We adjourned to the bedroom. Afterward, she asked me to go downstairs and fetch her a glass of water. I opened the refrigerator and found several bottles of beer left over from the other night. I pulled one out and chugged it.

The next evening, I met her at a restaurant for happy hour. I hadn't bothered to change out of my attire from the day. She hadn't either. I found her at the table, wearing scrubs.

"Hi, honey," she said.

I hefted myself into the chair. The table was elevated, with tall chairs around it. My feet dangled in mid-air.

"How was your day?" she asked, sipping a pink cocktail.

"Fine. The same as yesterday."

A waiter appeared, and I ordered the largest beer on the menu.

"You wanna get some food?" she asked.

"Yeah, I could eat."

"Good, 'cause I don't have the energy to cook after the day I had."

"Oh," I replied, looking around the restaurant.

The sun was setting and shades had been pulled over the windows to keep the patrons from being blinded. Business was picking up. There were only two open tables in the bar area. Several large TV screens hung from the ceiling, each displaying a different college basketball game.

"Don't you wanna know what happened?" she asked.

"Oh, uh, yeah. Sorry. What happened?"

"There's this new girl I work with, Janie. She's been a CNA for, like, twenty years. Why anyone would want to do that for a career is beyond me. At least I'm smart enough to know to get out in a couple years . . ."

My beer arrived. I immediately started to drink it.

". . . and of course Janie thinks she knows everything. She only got hired a couple days ago, so she doesn't know how we do things. So, today, I had the fullest case load. They always dump everything on me because I'm the most efficient. Well, some old guy shit his bed, and my other call lights were on. I asked Janie for help . . ."

To my right a pair of cute college-aged girls hopped up to one of the empty tables. They were both wearing very short cotton shorts adorned with their college's logo. One was a brunette, the other a redhead. I'd never been with a redhead before. It had always been a fantasy of mine.

". . . and I'm yelling at Janie to get her ass down to the room and help me out. And she's yelling down the hall back at me that it'll be a minute. But it had already been, like, *ten minutes,* and this old guy was covered in shit . . ."

I imagined the redhead wrapping her smooth, pale thighs around my waist. She gripped my shoulders tight and arched her back, moaning in ecstasy.

". . . and the bed's still filled with shit when Janie finally comes waltzing in . . ."

I'm in and out, a slow but powerful rhythm. Her face is clear, youthful, blemish-free. Her nose is small and cute. Her eyes are a bright, shimmering green. Her fiery hair is tussled. She grips me tighter as I increase the tempo, and–

"Hey, are you listening?"

My attention snapped back to Anne. She looked annoyed. Her dirty blonde hair dripped over her shoulders, flat at the sides, frizzy on top. Her nose was wide and her eyes a dull brown. Looking at her now, I was surprised that I had never noticed her many imperfections.

"Yeah, of course."

"Then what did I just say?"

Quickly, I gulped down as much beer as I could. I racked my brain. If I didn't get this right, we'd have the world record for shortest reconciliation. She glared at me with a deep crease in her brow. I set the beer down. Only a third of it remained.

"You were just telling me how you don't like Janie because she's a know-it-all, and she kept stalling so she wouldn't have to help you clean up the old guy," I guessed.

"Okay, yeah," she said. "So, Janie finally walks in and helps me, but she's groaning the entire time. And it's not like I haven't helped her before, she's just a bitch."

As Anne carried on, I finished my beer. I looked at the two girls again. My thoughts drifted back to their young, supple bodies gliding and intertwining around me. The fantasy shattered when two college-aged guys showed up and joined them. It figured those hot girls would have boyfriends. I never had any luck in that department.

When I looked back at Anne, she put her hand over mine and said, "Looks like you've got something on your mind."

"It's school. The last couple of months have been tough. And I still don't have any idea what specialty I want to go into."

"When do you have to decide?"

"There's not a deadline or anything. In the fall I have to interview for Residency, but I can't do that until I pick a specialty. So, I'll have to figure it out in the next few months."

"That's the point of these rotations, right? To help you decide what to do?" she asked, giving me a comforting smile.

"Yeah."

"You still have a few left. Maybe you'll love one you haven't done yet."

"Maybe. I just feel like I'm the only one who hasn't decided."

"I'm sure that's not true."

I was starting to feel antsy with her examining me in such detail. I pulled my hand back. "Where's that damn waiter? I'm starving."

Anne surveyed the room and saw him talking to the bartender. She waved him over. Only a woman could accomplish that. If I had waved at him, he never would have come. We ordered dinner, and I got two more beers for myself. I didn't want to wait between drinks.

~~~

"How are you feeling today, Zeus?" I asked.

"Fine."

"How did you sleep last night?"

"Fine."

Zeus wasn't in the mood to talk. It was Monday morning. I had three weeks left in the rotation, and Matt wanted me to get as much experience working independently as possible. For now I was assigned to Zeus and the meth guy.

I saw the meth guy first. Over the weekend he had finished his withdrawals. Today, he was out of bed, alert, showered, and pleasant. He denied all psychiatric symptoms. The only thing he was interested in was discharging. I deferred to Matt, stating that as a medical student I was not allowed to make those kinds of decisions.

After that I found Zeus in the Day Room watching a game show. He grudgingly agreed to let me interview him. Since I didn't have a key to the interview rooms, we found an empty corner of the hallway to talk. He barely tolerated it.

"Hearing any voices today?" I asked.

"Yes."

"What are they saying?"

"I don't wanna talk to no scientist."

"Don't worry, I'm not a scientist."

"You're a lying fuck."

"Oh, okay then."

The hairs on the back of my neck stood up. The pit of my stomach swirled. I smiled falsely and said, "I guess that's all. Thanks for your time."

Zeus walked back to the Day Room muttering.

I returned to the Nurses Station. Matt was there with a thousand loose pieces of paper in front of him. He signed them with his left hand and clutched his head with his right.

"You okay?" I asked.

"Yeah, fine. Just a killer headache, that's all."

"Can I get you anything?"

"No, I'm good. You see those two?"

"Yes. The meth guy seems better. No SI or HI. He wants to go home."

"What do you think?"

"I think it would be fine."

Matt shook his head. "Not until he gets an appointment with a chemical dependency clinic. Otherwise, he's gonna use again and wind up back in here. Once he does that, he can go. What about Zeus?"

"He's definitely more irritable today. I didn't get to ask him much."

"Don't worry. I'll take care of it. Damn, I can't believe he's not any better. He's already up to eight milligrams of Haldol. It hasn't even touched him."

"So . . ."

"We're gonna have to add another agent."

Matt fell silent. He dropped his pen, and clutched his head with both hands. His eyes passed back and forth over his mountain of paperwork.

"Can I give you a hand?" I asked.

Stress had carved deep lines on his face. "I've got four discharges. That means four admits. One of them is already waiting in the ER. Maybe you could do the H and P? If you did that, I'd have more time to get this other stuff done."

There was an unspoken rule about being a medical student. Whenever you were asked to do something, you accepted. It didn't matter how dirty, disgusting, or tedious the task. Saying no could result in a poor evaluation and raised eyebrows in a Residency interview. No program wanted to hire someone who refused to pull their own weight. It was forced volunteerism.

I liked Matt, and I felt bad for him. He was overworked, and if I could do this one thing to help him, I didn't mind. I grabbed an admission form and headed downstairs.

All I knew about this patient was a preliminary diagnosis of Bipolar Disorder. When I got to the ER and asked a nurse where to find him, she smiled wryly. "Oh, you're from Psych, aren't you?"

"Yes, I'm a med student."

"He's in Room Three. Have fun, dear," she said, her voice laced with sarcasm.

While most of the patient rooms in the ER were stalls divided by curtains, there were half a dozen actual rooms for special patients. This guy was in one of those rooms.

The door was made of sliding glass. It was closed, but I could see inside. A scruffy man paced back and forth. I knocked on the glass and entered.

"Who'reyou?" he asked.

"I'm with Psychiatry. Is it okay if I talk with you?"

"Yeahyeahsurewhateveryouwant."

"You can have a seat if you like," I said, motioning toward the empty bed.

The guy sat down on the bed. I sat on a small rolling stool. I took out my pen and wrote his name at the top of the admission form. When I looked up, he was pacing again.

"What brings you in today?" I asked.

"WhatbringsmeinAbusbringsmeinWhatkindofstupidquestionis thattoaskaperson?"

He was flying. The only person who spoke this fast was Az the radiologist, and this guy had him beat. He spoke so fast he was tripping over his own words.

"Why did you come to the hospital?"

"MydoctortoldmeIhadtocomeandmywifetoobutmostlymydoct orIdon'tknowwhy'causeeverything'sjustfine."

"Why did your doctor tell you to come in?"

"HesaidIwasmanicbutI'mnotmanicIhaveADHDmywifejustpai dhimofftosaythatIcame'causethedoctor'sagoodChristianhallelujahp raiseJesusButalsomywife'smadbecauseofmyaffair."

"Are you, um, having any feelings of depression?"

"NolikeItoldyouIjustgotADHD–"

"Any suicidal thoughts?"

He was pacing faster now, and making full circles around the room. His face darkened to the shade of a beet. "Idonetoldyoualready I'mfineit'smywifewantstogetbackatmeforthea ffair."

"You cheated on her?"

"DamnsonyouwouldtooifyousawthesefinebabesAllthreeofemf ineassVegasshowgirlsrealhotstufffivehundreddollarsapopbuttotally worthittogetmydickwetyouknowpraiseJesusamen."

"You spent fifteen hundred dollars on prostitutes?"

"NofivehundredapopbutIhadeachthreeorfourtimesandonceall atthesametime."

"So you spent, um, six thousand dollars on prostitutes?"

He stopped pacing for a moment and put his hands on his hips. He flashed the proudest smile I'd ever seen. "YougotthatrightsonitsliketheysayinJohn3:16theLordis—"

"Did you do anything else impulsive?"

"IdunnoMywifesaysIspentfifteenontravelingandhotelsandcom putersandliquorbutIthinkshe'sexaggeratingShe'sliketheharlotinJoh n3:16Youknowtheonewho'stryingtosuckJesus'dickandall?"

"Fifteen . . . hundred dollars?"

"Thousandson."

"Fifteen thousand dollars?"

The patient resumed pacing. He was trying to get some kind of unnatural energy out. He looked like he couldn't stop even if he wanted to.

"How did you end up back here?"

"MywifefoundmeupinTexasIhadtogotherebecauseIseentheligh tAllthegamblingandfornicatingistheDevil'sworkandIseenthelightO ursaviorJesusChristtheonetrueGodnotthatevilatrocityLasVegasAsit saysinJohn3:16AndJesuswillsmitetheevildoersandnonbelieversandt hewhoresandtheprostitutesshallperishfromtheearthOnlyChristbrin gssalvationtothetruebelievers—"

"How long ago did this happen? Going to Vegas and Texas and back?"

If I hadn't interrupted, he never would have gotten off that ludicrous tangent. And while I was no biblical scholar, I was fairly certain his reading of John 3:16 was less than accurate.

"TwoweeksagoIguessyeahsonVegaswasafuntimethoseladieskn owhowtopartyTheladieslovemeIgotthemagicfingersyouknowwhatI meanGladIgottoseethelightbecauseIcanusethemagicfingersforgood

andholyworksnowIgotsavedandwon'tburninhellYougotyourselfsav
edson?"

"How'd you sleep the last two weeks?" I asked, dodging the question.

"SleepPffIdon'tgottimeforthat."

"Any sleep?"

"Maybeanhour."

"For two weeks straight?"

"LikeItoldyousonnowwhen'sitgonnabemyturntoasksomequest
ions?"

"I'm sorry, sir, but I need to ask you a lot of things so I can get you admitted."

"Allrightsongoaheadandthenwe'lltalkaboutsavingyourimmortal
soulafter."

Our conversation went on like that for quite some time. It took me two hours to complete the H and P. When it was over, I felt like I had run a marathon. At least I had saved Matt from that nonsense. I hoped he had gotten some real work done.

When I presented the case, Matt nodded and occasionally chuckled. "Clearly this guy's got hyper-religiosity. We see it sometimes when people are manic."

"He was quoting John 3:16 a lot, though most of it seemed made up."

"John 3:16, that's a good name for this guy."

"This guy's Bipolar, right? So, what do we do with him?"

Matt took my admission form and rifled through the pages. When he got to the Assessment and Plan section, he wrote something down, and then flipped the packet closed. "What medication do you want to give him?" he asked.

"A mood stabilizer," I said.

"Okay. Which one?"

"I'm not sure. Lithium?"

"Are you asking me or telling me?"

"Telling you. Lithium."

"How's his kidney function?"

"I don't know."

"Well, we'd want to order some labs then."

"Right," I replied, feeling stupid for having missed such an important step.

"Which labs do you want?"

"Um, CBC, CMP, TSH, and um . . ."

"Not bad. Throw in an EKG and a urine drug test, too."

"Okay."

"If his labs show he has renal failure, is there a problem with giving Lithium?"

"Um . . ."

"Lithium is metabolized in the kidneys, so it would make it worse. But let's say his labs are normal. What then?"

"Give him Lithium."

"What if he's a rapid cycler?"

"I don't even know what that is," I said with a laugh.

Matt smiled and leaned back in his chair. "Read up on it tonight," he said.

I was stunned. Here I was thinking this specialty didn't involve "real medicine," but I had been completely wrong. Psychiatrists had to pay as much attention to labs, medical conditions, and drug interactions as any other doctor.

When we wrapped up, it was about 3:00 PM. Matt was feeling generous and let me go early, thanking me for my help. At home I read up on my assignment, and was eager to tell Matt about it the following morning.

~~~

The majority of the patients on the unit were regular people. They got better and eventually went home. They weren't locked up for years like in the movies. Unfortunately, Zeus and John 3:16 were having a string of bad luck. No matter what we did for them, they never improved.

One morning, John 3:16 caught me in the hallway and said, "HeydoclistenIstillcan'tsleepatnightnothing'sworking."

Fatigue was catching up with him. He was already on the maximum dose of Lithium and a decent dose of Depakote, and he was still going a mile a minute. "How many hours did you get last night?" I asked.

"Onlytwoandtheyweren'tnogoodDocyougottagetmeonsometh ingelsemaybesomeSeroquelsoIcansleepThat'stheonlythingthatwork sforme."

"I'll let the team know."

"OkaydocthanksalotpraiseJesusandLordhavemercyonyoursoul IfyouwantI'llpraywithyouYouknowJohn3:16don'tyouOhyeaitisthe Lordwhogivethandtaketh–"

"Thanks, but I have to run. Have a good day."

I stepped around him and headed down the hallway. Before I reached the end, I was accosted by Zeus.

"Let me ask you something," he said.

"What's that, Zeus?"

"How much longer am I gonna be in here?"

"I'm not sure. It's not up to me."

"Forever?"

"No. I promise you won't be here forever."

"Almost forever?"

"No."

"Middle from forever?"

I held my breath and clenched my fists to keep from laughing. I simply shook my head. Zeus stared at me, looking earnest. When the urge to laugh faded, I gently exhaled. "How are you feeling today, Zeus?"

"Sad."

"Why sad?"

"Because I realized I'm not the sun."

Zeus' eyes became teary. He was truly upset that he was not the giant yellow ball of gas in the sky. I asked him the other daily questions. He seemed just as crazy as ever, but more on the depressed side today. When we finished, he walked back to the Day Room, wiping tears away with the backs of his hands.

I walked to the Nurses Station, looking for Matt. The room was at its usual level of disarray. Near the back, an Attending, Resident, and No-Name were discussing a patient. No-Name's eyes were glazed over.

Suddenly, there was a crash. Everyone turned their heads toward the sound. Through the Nurses Station window, I saw staff members race into the Day Room. My curiosity getting the better of me, I followed.

The Day Room was in a frenzy. There was an overturned table with a shattered wooden leg. Several chairs had been kicked over. Papers and books were scattered about. The patients had been collected on the far side of the room by a nurse. In the middle of the room, John 3:16 was pacing the floor in a tight circle. Close by, two techs and two nurses were struggling to keep a patient pinned to the floor. It was Zeus.

He tried to break free. He screamed profanities. He looked like a fat animal taken down by hunters. Matt knelt by Zeus' head, trying to talk to him, but Zeus ignored him.

The unit doors slammed open. Four hospital security guards rushed past me. They joined the techs and nurses. Their combined weight kept Zeus firmly on the floor.

"What's next, doc?" one of the guards asked.

"Take him to the Quiet Room," Matt said.

Matt strode past me. He unlocked a thick wooden door halfway down the hall. The nurses and techs backed off, and the four security guards hefted Zeus. They dragged him away, following the path Matt had taken. I pressed my back against the wall to make room for them. As they brought him into the Quiet Room, Zeus cursed louder than before.

The other patients stared, dumbfounded. A few curious ones began to walk toward the Quiet Room, but various staff members stopped them.

The Quiet Room was actually two rooms. The first was empty except for a single chair. The chair faced the second, connecting room. It was just big enough to fit a mattress, which lay unceremoniously on the floor without a bed frame or box spring.

Zeus was on his back on the mattress. His arms and legs were spread akimbo. The guards busied themselves securing his extremities in padded restraints. Zeus continued to struggle, but he made less progress as each restraint closed tight. He continued to fight, never losing steam.

Matt stood nearby. "Zeus, Zeus, listen to me."

"You goddamn fucking cake eating scientists! My nanobots have the nuclear launch codes! It's blasphemy to do this to a god! You'll all go to hell you bastards!" he screamed.

"Zeus," Matt said calmly, "we're going to give you some medications to help you calm down, okay?"

"Stupid asshole motherfuckers! Get your goddamn hands off me!"

"Zeus, you can cooperate and take pills, but if you can't, we'll give you shots."

"Fuck you, scientist! Shove your fucking shots and your fucking pills up your fucking ass! You can't make me do anything!"

"It'll be the shots then," Matt said. He turned to Zeus' nurse who was nearby. "Get the HAB for him. I'll work on the restraint orders."

Zeus was now firmly secured. The security guards backed away and filtered into the larger part of the Quiet Room. Nobody seemed alarmed at what was happening. This was another day at work.

Zeus fought the restraints until his face was red, but he didn't budge. He hurled crazed insults at everyone. Zeus' nurse returned with three syringes. She gave Zeus three shots in his left shoulder. A few minutes later he struggled less fiercely and stopped cursing. His eyelids became droopy. Another few minutes elapsed and he was asleep.

Everyone exited the Quiet Room. A single tech stayed behind to keep an eye on Zeus while he slumbered. Matt thanked the security guards, and then they departed.

I followed Matt into the Day Room. John 3:16 was still there, pacing in his tight circle. A tech was next to him, trying to get him to sit down and relax. He may as well have been talking to the sky. The other patients had returned to their books, board games, or the TV.

"Let's go talk," Matt said.

Matt immediately headed toward one of the interview rooms without waiting for John 3:16's reply. Whether it was Matt's tone of voice or mere presence, the patient obeyed.

"Tell me what happened," Matt asked while he sat down.

"ItwasthatcrazyZeusguyHe'stotallycrazyyouknowhedoesn'tlistentoanybody."

"Please, what happened?"

"OkayrightsorrydocIwasinthedayroomIjustsatdowntowatchTVandZeuscameinandstartedbarkingatmetogivehimtheremotebutIwouldn'tdoitHecalledmeafascistandIain'tnoNaziIlovetheLordpraiseJesusSoIcalledhimacocksuckerandhethrewthetableatme."

"You argued over who had control of the TV," Matt said, clarifying that verbal mess.

"Yeahthat'srightdoc."

"I can't have you antagonizing other patients."

"Ididn'tdonothin'he'stheonewhostartedit."

"Even so, if someone gets in your face, if you push back, things can escalate. There are some very sick people here, and they aren't able to make good decisions right now."

"OhIsee," John 3:16 said, like a light bulb turned on inside his head.

"If this kind of thing happens again, I want you to just walk away."

"SurethingdocjustwalkawaynoproblemanyonegetsinmyfaceIjustturntheothercheekjustlikeJesusourLordandsaviorwhosaidharktheheraldangelssing–"

"Okay then, have a good day."

We returned to the Nurses Station, and Matt slumped into a chair, his body oozing into liquid. He let out an exhausted sigh.

"You all right?" I asked.

"I'm fine. It's just I haven't gotten started on my discharges yet, and now I have more paperwork from putting Zeus in restraints. Plus, I'm on-call tomorrow night."

"I think I'm supposed to take call with you."

"The more the merrier," he said with a farcical smile.

~ ~ ~

Matt's pager beeped. He clicked a button, silencing it. "Got one already," he said. "A psychotic guy. He just hit the floor."

It was 4:31 PM. All of the other Residents had signed out to us for the night. Now we were alone and in charge of the entire psychiatric unit. It hadn't taken long for the first admission to arrive. It looked like we might be in for a long night.

The patient, a guy named Tom, was sitting in the Day Room, off to one corner, with one of the techs in a chair beside him. Matt approached. "Hi, Tom? I'm Dr. Danforth. Can I talk to you for a few minutes?"

Tom looked at the tech and grumbled something incomprehensible. The tech encouraged him to go. Tom grumbled again. The tech told him he would go, too. As Tom rose, I appreciated his size. He was six-and-a-half feet tall, barrel-chested, burly-armed, and had a rough, uneven face. I hoped he didn't get physical, because no amount of CPST could stop this guy.

Matt led us to the interview room. Tom and the tech held hands. Apparently, this set him at ease. We all sat down around the table. Tom stared at Matt, unblinking, with a sort of vacant intensity behind his eyes.

"How are you doing today, Tom?" Matt asked.

Incomprehensible grumbling.

"Can you tell me why you're here?"

Incomprehensible grumbling.

"Are you hearing voices?"

Tom turned to the tech and said, intelligibly but gruffly, "Not this shit again."

The tech encouraged Tom to try and answer Matt's questions.

"Any strange voices today?" Matt asked again.

Grumble.

"Seeing strange things? Visions?"

Grumble.

"How about paranoia?"

"I'm gettin' tired'a this bullshit."

"Okay. How about suicidal thoughts?"

Grumble.

"Do you think you can stay safe on the unit?"

"Fuck yourself."

Tom stood up, once again revealing his mammoth body. I felt like bolting from the room. If Matt was panicked, he didn't show it. He collected his clipboard and pen. "Thanks, Tom, we're all set," he said casually.

Incomprehensible grumble.

Matt and I exited the interview room, and Tom and the tech returned to the Day Room. Once we were inside the safety of the Nurses Station, I said, "That was intense."

"Yeah, no shit," Matt said, looking relieved.

"What's his story, anyway?"

"All we have to go on is the ER report. Police picked him up running down the highway half-naked. He was mumbling gibberish. Left him in a jail cell for three days thinking he was coming off something. When they realized he was crazy, they brought him here."

Matt completed his H and P, staffed the case with an Attending over the phone, and ordered an antipsychotic for Tom. After that, we moved on to the next admission.

The next patient was an elderly man who was severely depressed and addicted to alcohol. He had a bevy of medical problems. His name was also Tom. To keep our new patients straight, we decided to call him Old Tom and the first admission Bad Tom.

About the time we finished, one of the nurses stepped into the station and asked Matt for help. We followed her to the Day Room where Bad Tom shuffled back and forth with his pants around his ankles.

Bad Tom went to the bookshelf where a multitude of well-worn paperbacks were displayed. He pulled one out, grimaced at the cover, and threw it behind him. It sailed across the room and smacked against the wall. The tech asked him to stop, but he didn't listen. He grabbed another book and threw it without looking. Then another and another.

"Tom!" Matt shouted.

He didn't respond. He kept throwing books.

"Hey, Tom!"

He stopped.

"I need you to pull your pants up, okay, buddy?" Matt said.

Bad Tom grumbled and glared at Matt. The tech whispered something to him. After a very long pause, Bad Tom pulled his pants up.

Back at the Nurses Station, Matt asked Bad Tom's nurse to give him the first dose of his antipsychotic now instead of waiting until bedtime.

The third admission was ready. The busy night did not appear as if it would slow down.

Her name was Dawn. She came onto the unit holding a teddy bear and wearing a unicorn-print t-shirt. She told us a rambling story with tears in her eyes.

Two months ago her best friend died, and the next day Dawn attempted suicide by overdosing on five Benadryl tablets. She was hospitalized at a different psychiatric hospital. While there, she met "the love of my life," a man who was another patient. After discharge, he lived at her place because he was homeless. A couple of weeks later, things weren't working out because he was stealing from her and shooting up drugs in the apartment. They argued and he broke up with her. She promptly tried to kill herself.

We learned several things from her during the course of the interview. First, she wasn't great at making decisions. Second, she was addicted to benzodiazepines like Xanax and Valium. Third, she hates her psychiatrist and thinks her therapist is her best friend. And finally, she copes with stress by cutting herself.

At the end of the interview she agreed not to cut herself while here, and to let a staff member know if she couldn't stop herself from doing it.

We stood and Matt opened the door for her. She walked halfway out, then stopped and turned back. "You're such a nice doctor. Thank you for helping me," she said.

"Sure thing. Have a nice night," Matt said.

"Will you make sure I get my Klonopin tonight?"

Klonopin was another benzodiazepine.

"I have to call your pharmacy and verify your medication list first."

"Oh, I see. Will I get it tonight?"

"Hopefully."

"Okay. Please be sure I get my Klonopin. It's the only thing that works for me."

And it was working so well for her, too.

"All right, Dawn. Have a good night."

"Thank you," she said with a big phony smile.

I was amazed how she persisted on getting the medication, and how she called it hers like she invented it.

Matt closed the door. We sat back down and he finished his H and P. Afterward, he asked, "What do you think her main diagnosis is?"

"Bad decision making?"

Matt guffawed. "Well, it's part of that."

"I have no clue."

"She's Borderline."

"Borderline what?"

Matt laughed again. "Borderline Personality Disorder. She's got it bad. The two-minute mood swings, the weak suicide attempts, the cutting, the reliance on benzos, not to mention a few non-diagnostic criteria."

"What were those?"

"An adult with a stuffed animal or a shirt with an animated character on it."

"Really?" I asked with a laugh.

"You won't find that in any of the literature, but they're ninety-nine percent accurate. Find an adult who sleeps with a teddy bear and isn't Borderline, and I'll pay off your student loans."

Matt's pager cried out. He called the Nurses Station and was on the phone less than ten seconds. "Bad Tom's at it again," he said.

In the Day Room, the other patients had been cleared out. Bad Tom was sitting in a chair with his thick arms folded over his chest. He was muttering something under his breath. The tech was sitting close by. Matt entered the room, but I hung back.

"What happened?" Matt asked.

"Tom here got in John 3:16's face. Someone told Tom to chill, and Tom postured like he was going to punch him," the tech explained. It was funny how other people were calling him John 3:16 now.

Matt nodded. "Let's give him a little something extra to calm him down."

We went back to the Nurses Station and told Bad Tom's nurse to give him an injection of five milligrams of Haldol right away. Matt told the nurse it wouldn't knock him out, but combined with the other medication, it would slow him down. After that, we moved on to the next admission.

The next admission was a woman who had witnessed a homicide three months ago. She was having horrible nightmares and flashbacks. Her outpatient psychiatrist felt her PTSD symptoms were bad enough to warrant admission to the hospital. She agreed to go.

Seeing four back-to-back admissions, my attention span was fading. I watched and listened, but nothing registered. Matt was unfazed. Being this far in his training he was probably used it. When the admission was complete, it was 10:35 PM. Of course, another admission waited.

The next patient was a twenty-one year old female who had overdosed on ninety tablets of Ativan and ninety tablets of Oxycodone. She also took a bath and threw in a clock-radio for good measure. She spent a few days in the ICU before transferring to our unit.

We had only just begun the interview when Matt got an emergency page: "dr d – need you now – tom aggressive!"

"Excuse me," Matt said to the new patient. "There's an emergency. Please go to your room, and I'll find you later."

We booked it to the Day Room. Two security guards were there. One of them held a short leash on a big German Shepard. The dog had a muzzle on. The dog was more for intimidation than anything else.

Bad Tom paced. He growled and mumbled. He occasionally shouted a profanity. The tech who had befriended him stood in the far corner of the room. Bad Tom's nurse stood behind the security guards. Otherwise, the Day Room was deserted.

"What's happening?" Matt asked to anyone who might answer.

Bad Tom's nurse answered, "I gave him the IM, but after that he got even more agitated, throwing stuff and posturing again, so I called security to do a walk-through. As soon as security showed up he started swearing at them."

The guard without the dog, the head officer, turned to Matt. "What do you want us to do, doc?"

"We're going to give him some more IMs. We'll snow him this time. Stick around and help us make sure he cooperates."

"No problem."

Matt ordered different medications, a triple agent cocktail. "Hey, Tom," he said, "we're going to give you some more meds. I'd like you to agree to take them."

Bad Tom continued to pace but kept his gaze locked on Matt. "Fuck off," he grumbled.

"If you don't do it, we'll have to hold you down and make you."

"I don't want shit!"

"Let me call in a couple other guys to assist. Then we'll give him his meds," the head officer said. He pulled out his radio and called for backup. A few minutes later, four more security guards arrived. "We're ready," the head officer said.

"Okay, Tom, it's time," Matt said.

The posse of guards approached Bad Tom. He unleashed a furious roar. He lowered his shoulder and raced forward like a football player. His footsteps shook the floor with each pounding step. The dog growled and pulled at the leash.

Bad Tom dropped to his knees. His momentum slid him across the floor. He reached out. He grabbed the dog. His mouth snapped down on the back of its neck. It yowled in surprise and pain. The next instant, Bad Tom was tackled by the guards.

He was on the floor, fighting. The nurse hurried over. She rolled up Bad Tom's sleeve and gave him the injections. She quickly pulled away as Bad Tom struggled less.

As the medication circulated, he began to tire. He stopped struggling. His eyes closed. He let out a deep, rolling snore. The guards eased off, careful to see if this was a trick. He didn't move.

"You want him in the Quiet Room?" the head officer asked.

"No, drop him in his bedroom. If he tries this again when he wakes up, then he'll spend the night in the Quiet Room," Matt said. He turned to the guard with the dog. He was brushing back the fur on its neck, inspecting the area. "How's your dog?"

"Eh, he looks okay. I think it startled him more than anything else. That was a hell of a thing. Never seen anyone bite a dog before," he replied.

The guards and Matt exchanged a few more words. Then, they hefted Bad Tom and dragged him to his bedroom. Matt found the patient we had been seeing before the interruption and resumed the interview.

Matt looked exhausted, but he didn't slow down. It was now a quarter past midnight. I was bleary-eyed and yawning. Matt saw me drooping from fatigue.

"Why don't you go down to the call room and get some sleep?" he asked.

"No, it's okay, I'm fine."

"You can barely keep your eyes open."

"It's fine. I can help."

"No, really. Get some rest."

I rose from my chair, feeling three times heavier than usual. "Quite a night up here."

"Never a dull moment."

I was buzzed off the unit. It was serene now that Bad Tom was knocked out. I made my way to the call room, lurching along the way. When my face hit the pillow, I fell asleep instantly.

The next morning we did post-call rounds. Of all the patients he admitted, Matt only had room for one on his census. He elected to keep Dawn. Everyone else got distributed among the other Residents.

John 3:16 was now at the maximum doses of both Lithium and Depakote. He could still not sleep and was talking as fast as ever. Zeus was still totally insane, but far less irritable. The next three patients were average, depressed people who seemed to be recovering nicely.

When we got to Dawn, the first thing she said was, "What time am I getting my Klonopin?"

"I verified your med list with your pharmacy. Eight milligrams of Klonopin a day is way too much," Matt said, his voice a register lower than normal.

"So?" she asked, her body tightening. She was preparing for a fight.

"So, we're going to get you off it. You've developed a tolerance."

"What are you going to give me instead?" she asked, barely containing her rage.

"We're going to taper you off it, so you don't go into withdrawals."

"Then what am I going to get? Ativan? Xanax?"

"Probably an SSRI like Citalopram."

"*That's not gonna work!*" she exploded. "*I tried that before!*"

"It's worth trying again."

"No it's not!" she screamed. She was visibly foaming at the mouth. "It doesn't do anything for my anxiety or depression!"

"Actually, Dawn, SSRIs are the gold standard for depression and anxiety."

"You sound just like my other doctor! Except he has some goddamn compassion! At least he knows I *need* Klonopin to get better!"

"Okay, well, that's what we're doing," Matt said firmly.

He turned and walked away. I hoped Dawn wouldn't fix her ire on me next. In a way she was more frightening than Bad Tom. At least with him, you were probably safe as long as you weren't a dog.

We finished our work before lunch. "Thanks for the help last night," Matt said.

"I didn't do that much."

"You were great moral support."

"Anytime."

The ordeal was finally over. Twenty-eight hours is a long shift. Matt got far less rest than I did. As far as I could tell, he didn't get any sleep. He must have been fighting to stay awake. When I got home, I napped well into the afternoon.

~~~

The sky was bloody orange. The setting sun illuminated the smoggy haze that covered the city. I stared out the window mindlessly.

There was a knock at the door. I opened it and Anne bustled in, not waiting for an invitation. She kicked off her shoes and shrugged her jacket onto the floor. She fell into a chair and sighed. "You wouldn't believe the day I had."

"What happened?" I asked, pretending to be interested.

She launched into another rant about difficult patients and unhelpful co-workers. It was always the same story: Anne was a martyr who worked tirelessly for ungrateful patients, and her co-workers were all lazy slobs. I responded with a litany of canned phrases.

She exhausted herself from talking. I decided to get dinner ready. I put a pot of water on the stove, and started to cut lettuce for a salad. Anne, in full view via the pass-through, stretched her arms high above her head and groaned. "On my lunch break I found a few good listings for houses."

"Houses?"

"Yeah. I'm getting tired of driving back and forth from your place to mine. I'd like to spend every night in the same bed for a change."

There it was again, that shifting sensation in my bowels.

"What did you find?" I asked.

"A couple really cute one-stories up on the north side. And a bigger two story on the east side. They would definitely be in our price range."

Our price range? We had never discussed such a thing. She made crap money, and I was in massive debt. Our price range was nothing.

"How much are they going for?" I asked.

"The one-stories were around two sixty five, and the two story was two ninety."

We couldn't afford that. My forehead and underarms felt unnaturally hot. I moved on to slicing vegetables, but my hands shook. I had to slow down so I wouldn't slice a finger.

"You know, that seems kind of high," I said.

"It's not that bad. The market is shit right now. This is the time to buy."

"That's not what I meant. Sure, those prices are pretty good for a house, but I don't even have a job. And I have another year of school left. We'll never make the payments."

The water was at a rolling boil. I dropped uncooked noodles in. I unwrapped two pieces of bread and put them in the toaster oven.

"I thought you wanted to live with me," Anne said, pouting.

I hated when she pulled this self-centered shit. I stepped around the partition between the two rooms. I sat in the chair next to hers and held her hand.

"Of course I do," I said. "But I'm trying to be practical here. I can pay for my apartment with school loans, but not a house. How would I even get a home loan?"

Anne shrugged, looking upset, but refusing to express her feelings.

"It would be better if we waited until I was done with school and at least working a few months."

"It's not right," she said.

"What's not?"

"Living like this?"

"Like what?"

"Sleeping together, being in different houses. We should be married."

My heart worked its way into my throat. I wasn't sure how to respond. Evasion seemed best.

"Listen," I said, gripping her hand tighter, "we should hold off on any big decisions until after the Match. For all we know, I could end up in Miami, and then we'd be stuck with a house here and have to move across the country."

"If you match somewhere else, just turn it down," she said.

"I can't. It's like a contract. You have to go wherever you match."

"Well, I'm not leaving."

"What do you want me to do?"

"Just make sure you match here."

"I'll try my best, but it's somewhat up to chance. Besides, what if I want to go into a specialty that's not offered in this state?"

"Don't pick one of those."

"But I want to pick what I like."

I smelled something burning in the kitchen.

"You don't know what you want. So, just pick something they have here, and it won't be a problem."

"Anne, you don't understand."

"I do understand. I understand this is just another excuse to not commit to anything."

I leaned forward and kissed her. Her lips were rigid at first. After a few moments, her lips softened and she kissed me back. I ran my free hand across her legs and into her crotch. Anne pushed me away. "What the hell is wrong with you?!" she shouted. She stood up, knocking her chair over. Her hands were balled into fists. An aura of fire burned around her. "You always do that!"

"Do what?"

"Ugh, forget it. I'm done talking. Let's just eat."

She huffed loudly and stomped into the kitchen. A moment later, she yelled, "Goddammit!"

I raced into the kitchen.

Smoke escaped around the edges of the toaster oven door. The bread inside was black. The pot of water had boiled over, and some of the noodles had stuck to the side of the pot. They were crisp from the heat.

"You burned the spaghetti! And the bread!"

"Oh . . . I'm . . . sorry."

"You can't do anything right! You can't cook dinner, and you don't want to be with me! You're ruining my life!"

She stormed into the bedroom and slammed the door. My heart plummeted into my stomach. I steadied myself against the counter. I waited for Anne to return, but she didn't come out.

I ate in silence. I had to choke the food down. By the time I finished and cleaned everything, Anne still hadn't appeared.

I sat in my living room chair, watching the sun disappear below the horizon. The blood-orange sky gave way to the solemn blue of twilight. I didn't want to buy a house, and I didn't want to marry her. I had to break it off.

I had a beer, then two more. It had been over an hour since Anne exploded. It was time to talk to her. I entered the bedroom.

She looked at me with disdain. She didn't speak. I did all the talking. I apologized profusely. I went in circles, babbling about how much I loved her. Eventually, she accepted my apology. After that, she fell asleep, too tired for sex. I laid next to her and watched the ceiling for hours.

~ ~ ~

The rest of the month progressed smoothly. The normal patients came and went. Our three all-stars stayed with us for quite some time. Zeus was as psychotic as ever, but now he was pleasant and not causing trouble.

John 3:16 eventually got Seroquel. He remained manic until he was maxed out on it. Only then, he finally slowed down. He spoke normally, slept eight hours at night, and his religious preoccupation was gone.

Dawn was the biggest challenge. Each day was a crisis. She accused us of being the worst doctors ever one day, and the best doctors ever the next. Her erratic behavior and continued suicidal ideation prevented us from discharging her.

When the final day of the rotation came, I was excited. John 3:16 would be discharged, and Zeus would be transferred to a special long-term facility. I was glad to see the conclusion of their treatment on our unit.

I was in the Nurses Station, reading lab values on the computer. It was early, and I hadn't seen Matt yet. There was a hurried knocking on the door. One of the nurses opened it and asked, "Can I help you?"

Dawn was on the other side. "I need something for my depression, right now."

"I'll check your med list and see what I can get you."

"I'll take Xanax, Ativan, Valium, or Klonopin. Those are the only things that work for me."

"Okay, just a minute."

The nurse closed the door and checked Dawn's chart. I couldn't help but laugh, because none of those medications worked for depression. The nurse told Dawn she only had a non-benzodiazepine PRN available. Dawn screamed at the nurse. The nurse plainly told her it was the doctor's decision.

"Well, he a fucking Communist Nazi!"

I didn't interview her that morning. She hid in her bedroom. I never saw her again.

Zeus was in the hallway. He had taped a piece of paper to his forehead with the word "MEDS" written on it and an arrow pointing down toward his mouth. We went to an unoccupied part of the hallway.

"How are you feeling today?" I asked.

"Okay. I'm okay. Yeah, okay."

"How did you sleep last night?"

"Great. Excellent. Perfect. I dreamed the Cake Faerie visited me."

"Who's the Cake Faerie?"

"The faerie that brings cakes, duh."

"Can you see her?"

"Yeah, obviously."

"I can't see her. Maybe she's not real," I said, deciding to challenge him.

"You can't see her because she doesn't reveal herself to scientists. Only people who love cake. Or who can walk through walls."

"Oh," I said, amused, "can you walk through walls?"

"Duh, obviously. But not the walls here. They're too thick."

"Are you having any suicidal or homicidal thoughts?"

"Nah."

"Not even people who won't let you eat cake?"

"Hmm," he put a fist up to his chin like he was the Thinker. "I guess not. But I'd definitely call the cops."

Even though he was still crazy, he had improved. Hopefully, he would continue to get better and would eventually return to the outside world.

I ran into Matt a few minutes later. We saw John 3:16 together. When we found him, we were surprised. He was energized again. He could barely sit still. His speech was pressured, but not as fast as before.

"You look manic again," Matt said.

"Manic? No, I'm fine," John 3:16 said.

"How many hours of sleep did you get last night?"

"Seven, I think."

"How's your mood today?"

"Anxious. My clients are nervous because I've been gone so long."

"You take all your meds?"

"Yeah."

"I find it hard to believe you're fine. Something must have changed. People don't look this energized when they're nervous."

"Maybe it was the coffee."

"How much coffee did you drink?"

"The whole pot."

"Come on, man. You shouldn't do that. Now you're all revved up again."

"Oh, I didn't know. Sorry, doc."

"Maybe you need to stay here another day to show us you aren't manic."

"No, doc, don't do that! I'm fine! I really am better! I want to go home!"

"You have been doing better the last few days. We'll stick with the discharge plan."

"Thanks, doc," he said with a sigh of relief.

When we returned to the Nurses Station, Rachel was there, beaming. A couple of nurses offered her congratulations. One of the Attendings smiled and said something to her.

"Hey, Rachel, what's going on?" I asked.

"The Match results came out. I'm coming here!"

"That's great."

"I got my number one choice. Can you believe it?"

"I'm sure you'll do a good job."

"Thank you."

She turned back and talked to the Resident she had been assigned to for the rotation. I felt a twinge of jealousy. I would be in her position a year from now, but would I be as happy? I didn't even know what I was going to choose as my specialty. She had it all figured out while my life with a swirling clusterfuck.

The rest of the day was filled with the usual progress notes, staffings, and order writing. After that, we did one admission. By the time we finished, it was time to go. Matt and I walked outside the unit. "It's been fun," he said with a firm handshake.

"It's been a good month."

"I hope you learned a thing or two."

"I did. Thanks, Matt."

Matt looked anxious to move on. He still had several things to tidy up before he could leave. Clearly, he wanted our conversation to end so he could get on with it.

I pulled a double-folded piece of paper out of my pocket and handed it him. "I have a rotation evaluation," I said. "I was hoping you could fill it out."

"Sure," he said, shoving it into his pocket without looking at it. "I don't have time right now. Mind if I mail it in?"

"That's fine."

"Great. Good working with you. See you around."

I nodded and headed down the hallway. Halfway down the corridor, I turned back to see if Matt was still there. He had disappeared behind the metal doors. The hallway was stark.

Another rotation had ended. I was not looking forward to starting over again. That always happened, just when I was getting the hang of something.

APRIL
EMERGENCY MEDICINE

After spending an entire month not wearing my white coat, I nearly forgot it on my way out the door. It seemed like an eternity since I'd last worn it. I caught a glimpse of the white collar, permanently stained brown from rubbing against the back of my neck. It had been an eternity since I'd washed it, too.

As I pulled into the parking lot, I could see the hospital was smaller than the others I had been to. It was a low structure, only four-stories tall, with tan walls, a brown roof, brown columns, and a gray parking lot. The whole thing was rather drab. The hospital's ER was a Level II Trauma Center, which meant it wouldn't get the most extreme emergencies.

I had received my schedule a couple of days ago, and to my surprise I found I was not working every day. I was only scheduled to work three days a week, twelve hours at a time. The first two weeks I was on day shift, and the last two weeks I was on night shift.

Soon, I found myself in "ER Green." It was one of three sections that divided the department, and it was practically empty. A Nurses Station to my right had a chart rack with two charts in it.

The beds, separated by curtains, were all empty save two. The area was tidy, and the atmosphere was subdued.

I went to the Nurses Station and found a woman sitting there, stuffing a doughnut into her mouth. "Hello," I said.

She looked at me, embarrassed, and slowed her chewing. I told her who I was and, with a full mouth, she replied, "Dr. Chaturvedi's not here yet. She starts at seven. If you want, you can wait here 'til she arrives."

I sat in a swivel chair in a back corner of the station. I pushed myself left, right, left, right. As the clock crept toward seven, there was still no sign of Chaturvedi. I started to do full spins in the chair. Gradually, more patients were brought into the ER, and the chart rack began to fill. I didn't get started because I didn't know what the Attending would want me to do. So, I kept spinning.

At ten minutes after seven, another physician appeared. He was the night doctor, and he was visibly agitated. He paced back and forth, checking his watch every minute. He was waiting for Chaturvedi to relieve him.

Fifteen minutes later, a middle-aged woman blustered into the ER. Her hair was a frizzy mess, her glasses were crooked, and the pockets of her long white coat bulged with papers. She carried several textbooks in her arms. She dropped them on the Nurses Station desk and panted with exhaustion.

Instantly, the night doctor was upon her, thrusting a piece of paper at her.

"I'm sorry I'm late," she said.

"I need to get out of here. Here's my sign out. Everybody's comfortable. Got a few labs cooking. Those are marked in red. Any questions?"

Chaturvedi stuffed the paper into one of her coat's pockets, never to be seen again. "No, I'm fine. Thank you."

The night doctor left the ER at light speed. Chaturvedi pulled a chart out of the rack and grimaced as she read it. She put it back and inspected another. This one must have been more to her liking. She tucked it under her arm and ran off.

She hadn't noticed me sitting in plain sight. I hesitated to stand up. Introducing myself during an examination was probably a bad idea. I decided to wait for her to return. I resumed my spinning.

About ten minutes later, Chaturvedi returned. She scribbled in the chart and dropped it into a separate chart rack, this one designated for patients who needed further testing. She grabbed a new chart from the first rack and strode away.

"Dr. Chaturvedi," I said, standing up.

She stumbled as she looked back. I approached and introduced myself. I told her I'd be working with her for the next two weeks.

She nodded, but kept looking down at the chart. "Fine, fine. Why don't you follow me for the first one, then you can see people on your own," she said.

We entered the curtained stall to find a man sitting on the bed, talking on his cell phone. Despite seeing us enter, he continued talking. Chaturvedi interrupted him. "I'm Dr. Chaturvedi. This is my medical student. What brings you in today?"

The man stopped his conversation, annoyed. "I'll call you back," he grumbled into the phone before putting it away. Apparently, we were inconveniencing him. "I got this really bad stomach pain. I was hoping I could get something for it."

"Can you describe how it feels?" Chaturvedi asked.

"It hurts real bad," he answered vaguely.

"Is it a sharp pain or a dull pain?"

"I dunno. It just hurts."

"Have you ever had this before?"

"Yeah, once, a couple of years ago."

"And what happened then?"

"I got some pain killers. That fixed me right up."

"What were they?"

"Um, let's see . . ." he trailed off. He looked around the room, as if he might find the answer on the ceiling. "I think it was called Oxycodone."

"Okay. Lay on your back, please."

She helped him lay supine on the bed. He moaned in agony. Chaturvedi lifted his shirt. His abdomen looked normal. She unsnaked her stethoscope from behind her neck. She placed it on each of his abdomen's quadrants, lightly at first, and then pushed deeper. He laid comfortably. "Your abdomen sounds fine," she said.

"Oh, that's good," he said, sounding phony.

Next, Chaturvedi percussed his abdomen. With the first tap, he screamed and writhed on the bed. She continued without flinching. As she examined the rest of his abdomen with her hands, he screamed his head off. He bellowed like an actor on an audition.

Chaturvedi remained unaffected by his screams. When she finished she helped him sit up. "Well, doc?" he asked, panting.

"Your exam appears normal. But I'd like to get an X-ray just in case."

"Oh, okay, sure. But what about my pain?"

"I'll have the nurse bring you some Acetaminophen."

"Sorry, but that doesn't work for me."

"What works?"

"Well, that Oxycodone worked good. I think I had some Percocet once. That was pretty good, too. Either of those would be fine."

"No, I don't think so."

The man narrowed his eyes. "Why not?"

"I see no indication for it."

Like flipping a switch, the man became enraged. "What the fuck do you mean? I'm in the worst pain of my life! And you won't help me? I thought your job was to help people!"

"Sir, please, if you would calm–"

"If you don't get me my Oxycodone, I'm gonna sue your ass for malpractice!"

"I'm sorry, but all I can give you is Acetaminophen," she said coolly.

"Fuck you!"

He jumped off the table and left the ER in a huff. He moved pretty well for a guy in the worst pain of his life.

We walked back to the Nurses Station. Chaturvedi wrote a couple of things in the chart, and dropped it in the third rack marked "Completed."

She picked up another from the first rack and looked it over. She handed it to me. "This should be a good one for you," she said. "Go see it and present to me when you're done."

I took the chart and, in a blur, she was headed off to see someone else. I looked over the chart. It was nothing more than a single blank piece of paper in a folder. The only part that had been filled in was the Chief Complaint, "Abscess."

A young man waited in the curtained stall. He was laying on his right side. I let him know I was a medical student, and proceeded with the H and P. I had him turn onto his belly and pull down his pants. The abscess was just to the side of his rectum. Bulging and red, it was about three centimeters in diameter. With a gloved finger, I gently touched it. The patient's body gave a jolt.

"Sorry," I said.

"It's okay. Do what you gotta do," he said.

I told him to pull his pants back up and wait for me to return with Chaturvedi. I pitched the gloves, and walked back to the Nurses Station.

Chaturvedi was already there. She dropped a chart into the "Orders" rack and quickly grabbed another. She was oblivious to my presence. I waited for her to read the chart in her hands, and when she began to walk away, I said, "Dr. Chaturvedi."

She stumbled again. "What have you got?" she asked.

"A perirectal abscess."

"Okay, let's go take a look."

We barged into the stall. Chaturvedi gave the patient orders without introducing herself. He pulled his pants down again, looking more sheepish than the first time. "Yes, very good," she said. "Drain the abscess and I'll come back to check on you."

She started to exit, not cognizant of opening the curtain with the patient's butt exposed. "Dr. Chaturvedi!" I said nervously. "I've never done that before."

She continued out and let the curtain fall. "Ask the nurse to help you set up, and I'll show you what to do," she said from the other side.

Oh, great.

The nurse was chipper as she helped me gather the necessary equipment. We set up everything, and I had just put on a pair of latex gloves when Chaturvedi returned.

"Are you ready?" she asked.

I gave a nervous nod.

"Sterilize the area."

Using a sponge-tipped wand with built-in Betadine, I dabbed the top of the abscess, and then slowly spread out in concentric circles, careful not to go over any area twice. When I finished, Chaturvedi instructed me to put on a pair of sterile gloves.

"Inject the area with Lidocaine," she said.

She didn't wait for me to finish each step before she told me what to do next. Fortunately, this part was relatively easy. I tilted the tiny bottle of anesthetic, and drew out the fluid. I slowly exhaled and slid the needle into the patient's skin. He groaned. I pushed the syringe's plunger, releasing some of the Lidocaine. He groaned again. I was hurting this guy. I wanted to stop.

"Good," Chaturvedi said. "Next spot."

I did this three more times until the skin around the abscess had bubbled up with anesthetic. When I finished, I tapped the abscess with the needle. "Can you feel that?" I asked.

"No," he said.

I breathed a small sigh of relief. So far, so good. Chaturvedi continued, "Now, get the four-by-fours ready and make your incision." These were the vaguest instructions possible.

I picked up a handful of square pieces of gauze in my left hand and the scalpel in my right. I converged them over the abscess. "How far do I make the incision?" I asked.

"The length of the abscess."

My heart pounded harder and faster than ever.

In Medicine, there is an old saying, "See one, do one, teach one." It refers to the optimal learning process for procedures. Apparently, Chaturvedi subscribed to the philosophy of "Do one," but not the rest.

My hand shook. I breathed deeply and slightly loosened my grip. I pushed the blade against the abscess and drew it across.

The abscess burst like a giant zit. Yellow pus and red blood geysered. My head jerked back. The fluid didn't hit me. Once the initial pressure was released, the fluid oozed out.

I put the scalpel away and grabbed more gauze with my right hand. I soaked up the disgusting mix of fluids. Soon, the abscess stopped draining. "Push on it until you get everything out," Chaturvedi said.

Oh, great.

I pushed the Zit-from-Hell on all sides. A seemingly endless supply of pus and blood poured out. The patient moaned. I could only imagine how much worse this would be without anesthetic.

"Good, good," Chaturvedi said. "I think you got it all. Now, pack it and we'll be done."

As quickly as ever, she exited the area, leaving the rest of us behind. I looked at the nurse, my mouth hanging open. The nurse had seen a million of these and walked me through the final steps.

Using forceps, I slowly pulled a long strip of sterile gauze into the abscess. I did this until it was packed full. The idea was to let it soak and pull out whatever it had soaked up in a few days.

When that was finished, I dropped the gore-soaked materials into a red biohazard container. The room looked like something out of a horror film.

The nurse, still chipper, congratulated me on a job well done. I removed my gloves, washed my hands, and got the hell out of there. As I escaped, my legs felt weak. I thought I was going to collapse.

Chaturvedi stayed on the move. The ER remained steadily busy. Each time she deposited a chart in the "Completed" rack, another appeared in the "New" rack. Trying to get ahead was futile.

I saw three more patients, all with relatively straight-forward complaints. She also dragged me to two others she thought were interesting cases. When the clock hit 1:00 PM she sent me off to lunch. On my way out of the ER, I saw her scarf down a sandwich she had kept strategically hidden in one of her white coat's pockets.

Now that I was sitting in the cafeteria, eating something that resembled food, I felt like I was at a stand-still. My body was on the verge of withering. Nevertheless, I was in no hurry to go back to the ER.

Chaturvedi hadn't given me a time limit, so I stretched my lunch to an hour. I was going to be here for twelve hours, so what if I spent one of them eating? I doubted Chaturvedi even remembered I was gone.

The next few patients I saw were routine coughs and colds. People used the ER as their primary care provider. They weighed down the system.

I grabbed another chart and headed to the curtained stall. I found a young woman sitting on a small plastic chair next to the bed. Her head was in her hands. She looked up, and I saw she was wearing sunglasses.

I gathered the history and learned that she was a freshman in college, living in a dorm. Yesterday, she woke up with, "the worst headache of my life." Lights were bright and painful. Today, she developed a fever. I knew what was wrong.

I had her lay down on the bed. I gently placed her head in my hands. Raising her head forward elicited extreme neck pain. The rest of her exam was negative.

I asked her to wait while I presented my findings to Chaturvedi. A positive Brudzinki's Sign, photophobia, fever, and headache all pointed to meningitis. I described all of this to her as she wrote in another patient's chart. I couldn't tell if she was listening.

"Let's go," she said at last.

Chaturvedi examined the patient much faster than I had. "You're right," she said. "What tests do you want to order?"

"Um, definitely an LP. Also a CBC and CMP. And a blood culture."

"Good, but we need to do a CT Head before the LP to make sure she doesn't have a mass. Otherwise we could herniate her brain."

"Okay," I said, looking down at the patient. I imagined horrific thoughts running through her mind, hearing the doctor talk about her brain herniating.

"I'll order a stat CT. Go down with her and have the radiologist read the results ASAP. We don't want to waste a lot of time."

Someone from Patient Transport wheeled the bed to the Radiology suite. The tech and I stood on the other side of a wall, behind a plate of radiation-proof glass. The CT scanner hummed as it bombed the patient's head with radiation. The process only took about a minute.

While Patient Transport wheeled her back to the ER, I walked to the Reading Room. There was only one radiologist. "Excuse me, sir?" I asked, feeling uncomfortable.

"Can I help you?" the radiologist asked.

"I'm a med student in the ER. We just got a head CT of a patient who has meningitis. I was hoping you could look at the scan and let me know if there are any problems before we do an LP."

He grunted and faced his computer screen. He closed what he was working on and pulled up my patient's data. Images of her brain appeared in black and white. As he scrolled through the images, he would occasionally grunt, stop, and turn back. He spent about five minutes looking through the data.

"Looks okay. Go do your LP," he said.

I thanked him, and he grunted and returned to what he had been doing before.

Back in the ER, I found Chaturvedi talking to a nurse. I relayed the news to her. She fired back at the nurse to get ready for the procedure. In the meantime, she handed me a fresh chart so I could keep working.

The next stall housed a man who came in with a Chief Complaint of "allergies." Why someone would come to the ER for allergies was anyone's guess.

After I finished a focused physical exam, I was certain what was wrong. He was suffering from a viral upper respiratory infection. It was nothing serious. The only treatment is time.

"I believe you have a viral infection," I said.

"Can you give me something to feel better?" he asked.

"Typically, these take a week or two to get better on their own. You can keep taking Ibuprofen, and be sure to drink plenty of fluids."

"Can you give me an antibiotic?"

"Antibiotics don't work on viruses."

"I'd feel a lot better if I had an antibiotic."

"Like I said, that won't help."

"Okay, but if you don't give me one, I'll find someone who will."

I paused, trying to figure out if this was supposed to be a threat.

"Just wait here, sir," I said as I left him.

I went back to the Nurses Station and wrote my findings in the chart. The Unit Secretary told me Chaturvedi was back with the meningitis patient. I hustled over, not wanting to miss the procedure.

Chaturvedi sat on a stool, positioned behind the patient who lay on her right side. Chaturvedi waved me over with a gloved hand. "Have you ever done an LP?" she asked.

"No."

"Okay. Why don't you watch me do this one, and you can do the next?"

I was more than happy to watch. I wasn't confident enough in my skills to stick a needle into someone's vertebral canal. I moved behind Chaturvedi so I would have a good view.

"Pull your knees to your chest. All the way up. Farther. Good," Chaturvedi said.

The patient's body was curled into a ball. Chaturvedi worked quickly, and did not explain anything as she went.

She did the preliminary sterilization and anesthetization. Next, she got a large needle that would penetrate all the way into the vertebral canal. I watched in awe as the needle completely disappeared into the patient.

Nothing happened. She hadn't hit the intended area. She backed the needle out an inch, although most of it was still inside, angled it differently, and slid it forward again. Still nothing. The patient groaned. Chaturvedi did it again and again. On the fifth attempt she got it. There was an audible pop, and fluid began to rush out the other end of the needle.

Quickly, Chaturvedi attached a tall, slender glass tube to the needle. This measured the opening pressure of the cerebrospinal fluid. The fluid shot up to eighty millimeters of mercury. This was abnormally elevated.

Chaturvedi removed the glass tube. Fluid dripped more slowly out of the back of the needle. She positioned a test tube beneath the nozzle. It filled up with a cloudy yellow liquid. When it was full she handed it to the nurse who marked it, "1."

She did this three more times. Each time, the fluid in the subsequent test tube became clearer. The nurse arranged the tubes in sequential order, and prepared them for delivery to the Microbiology Department.

Finally, Chaturvedi drew the needle out of the patient. Chaturvedi taped a piece of gauze over the wound. With the needle gone, fluid would stop flowing out of the vertebral canal.

"That's it," Chaturvedi said.

True to style, she exited. After quickly writing in the chart, she resumed seeing the other patients. She didn't take a moment to relax.

The nurse took the test tubes to the lab. I stayed behind to clean up the mess. "Am I going to be all right?" the patient asked.

I had no idea.

"You'll be fine. They'll get you on some antibiotics, and you'll be better soon," I said.

She got IV antibiotics and was admitted to the hospital. I never saw her again. I hoped what I told her turned out to be true.

The rest of the day flew by. Before I knew it, the end of the shift had arrived. I felt like I was about to crumble. The "New" rack was still bursting with charts. The ER had been slammed. Only someone with superhuman endurance could keep up with this pace.

Chaturvedi walked out from behind a curtain. She dropped a chart into the "Orders" rack. She pulled two charts from the "New" rack. She handed one to me and walked away.

"Excuse me, Dr. Chaturvedi?"

She stumbled for the third time. "It's almost seven. I was hoping I could, um, take off soon?" I asked nervously.

She checked her watch. "No problem. Great job today. See you next time."

"Thank you," I said, putting the chart back. When I stepped away from the desk, Chaturvedi was already gone. Her replacement would be here in the next five minutes. Would she stop then, or would she keep working tirelessly?

I wasn't going to stick around to find out. When I got to my apartment I flopped onto the bed and fell asleep instantly. I slept for twelve hours. Every muscle in my body ached.

~~~

Instead of studying or spending time with Anne on my day off, I parked myself in front of the TV. I only ventured out to restock on alcohol. I drank everything, and then went out again to resupply. It was a good day.

Thursday morning I found myself back in the ER. Chaturvedi was late again, and the doctor she was meant to replace, the same as last time, was upset again. When she finally blew in, she apologized profusely.

She looked at the "New" rack and froze. It was empty. The gears in her brain stopped turning.

Chaturvedi blinked dumbly for a few moments. She eventually stepped around to the other side of the Nurses Station and sat down. I had never seen her sit down before. She rifled through her purse and pulled out a stack of mail.

I flipped my cell phone open. I had nothing to entertain me. I sent a text message to Brad. He never responded.

The hands of the clock rotated lethargically. I tried to see how many times I could spin around on my swivel chair with a single kick. My record was eight.

After that, I found a battered ER textbook on the back of a cluttered shelf. I flipped through it, studied abnormal EKGs, and read about meningitis and abscesses.

Chaturvedi paid her bills. A nurse read a trashy romance novel. A couple of techs tossed a foam football across the room. I yawned and put my head down on the table. I closed my eyes and found darkness.

Suddenly, there was a metallic slam. I swung my head up. My muscles tightened and sent a spasm of pain down my neck. I blinked and saw the clock come into focus. Three hours had passed.

Chaturvedi rose, salivating at the sight of the techs wheeling in a patient. The patient's right hand dripped with gore. He clutched his wrist, and cursed up a storm.

"What's going on?" Chaturvedi asked.

"Chopped up his hand pretty bad," a tech replied.

The other tech maneuvered the wheelchair into one of the curtained stalls. Chaturvedi hurried to the patient's side. I got up, still disoriented from my nap.

"What happened?" she asked.

"The lawnmower," the patient grunted.

"You put your hand in it?"

"Yeah. It's a riding mower. A stick got lodged in there, so I reached in to grab it, and this happened."

Chaturvedi rolled a small metal tray to the bedside. The patient put the back of his hand on it. He stretched his fingers as far as he could while she inspected the damage.

His hand looked like a bloody hamburger. She soaked up the blood with a pair of four-by-fours. The tips of his second, third, and fourth digits had flaps of skin peeled back. The center of his palm had a wide gash. The split skin revealed fatty tissue.

My head swam and my body felt weightless. I thought I might topple over. I held my breath and squeezed my eyes shut. I counted to ten. When I exhaled, I felt better.

"You're very lucky. You didn't cut anything important," Chaturvedi said.

"Thank God," he replied.

"We'll suture you up, okay?"

Chaturvedi turned and saw me. She looked surprised, like she had forgotten who I was. The bewildered look dissipated. "This is a good case for you," she said. "Let me know when you're done suturing." She walked off to finish her bills or something.

In my second year I learned how to suture on pig feet. I had experience on a dead animal. How hard could it be on a living person? The nurse helped me get the equipment set up.

After cleaning the wound, I snapped the needle into the jaws of the hemostat. The room fell eerily quiet. Both the nurse and patient were boring holes through my head with their stares. Time stood still. I held my breath and inserted the needle.

It easily slid through the subcutaneous tissue. I rotated my forearm and watched as the needle emerged from beneath the skin. Their staring intensified. My heart was sprinting in my chest. Every centimeter of my body was on fire.

I grabbed the needle with the forceps, released the hemostat, and pulled the needle through. I repeated this process on the opposite side of the wound. I pulled the needle again, until only an inch of suture remained. With an instrument in each hand, I wound the suture around and around, and pulled it into a tight knot. As I did, the two edges of the wound closed together. I snipped off the excess with a pair of scissors. The knot looked good.

Sweat dripped from my forehead onto the sterile field. Fortunately, nobody saw. The patient had looked away. The nurse strolled to the Nurses Station.

As I continued, my anxiety didn't diminish. I wished I could calm my nerves with a drink. I made a lot of errors as I worked: I inserted the needle too shallow or too deep, I pulled the suture out before tying the knot, I pulled the suture through while tying the knot.

In total, I did eight sutures. The patient looked at his hand and said, "Looks good. Thanks."

"Sure," I said, taking deep breaths and waiting for my heart to slow down.

Chaturvedi inspected my work. "These sutures are too close together," she said. "Next time space them out farther. But not bad." She turned to the patient. "You'll get a tetanus shot and some antibiotics. After that you can go."

I slowly cleaned the considerable mess I had made. My body was devoid of energy. I might drop dead at any moment. As I was cleaning, I felt someone poke my shoulder. I turned and saw one of the nurses.

"Doc wants you to see the new guy," she said.

"New . . . guy . . ." I said like I didn't know how to speak English.

My eyes drifted to the clock. An hour had passed. I had spent a long time doing those sutures. "Yeah, okay, just a sec," I said.

She walked away, but not before I caught a glimpse of her eyes rolling back. I surveyed the ER and saw two closed stalls. I spotted Chaturvedi's legs in one. The other must have held my patient.

I grabbed the chart from the rack. I was surprised to see orders already written for blood work and a urine drug screen. The H and P was blank. I headed behind the curtain.

The man inside looked like he was about to jump out of his skin. "The fuck are you?" he growled.

Immediately, I felt cold and shaky. "I'm a medical student."

"Whaddaya want?"

I wasn't sure how to answer. He was, after all, the one who came here. "I'm just going to get some information and do a physical exam," I said.

"You ain't gonna touch me."

"I'm sorry?"

"I said you ain't gonna fuckin' touch me!"

"Okay."

"Just ask your questions and get the fuck out."

"Sure, well, uh, what, uh, brings you in?"

"I feel like shit. My chest hurts."

"When did that start?"

"I dunno. Couple hours ago."

"How would you describe the pain?"

"I told you, it hurts."

"I understand, but is it sharp or dull or something else?"

"It just fucking hurts, all right?!"

"Okay. What were you doing when it started hurting?"

"Stop with the goddamn questions."

"I'm sorry, sir, I know these can be frustrating. But I can't help you feel better unless you help me figure out what's going on."

"*Fuck off!*"

"All right, let's skip the questions and do the physical."

I uncoiled my stethoscope. His body stiffened and his face became bright red. "What's that?" he asked, wide-eyed.

"It's a stethoscope. So I can listen to your heart and lungs."

"Don't fuckin' touch me! Get the fuck outta here, you asshole!"

I didn't need to be told again. I walked backward, afraid to turn my back on him. Once I was out of the stall, I realized why a urine drug screen had been ordered. He was obviously high on something.

After presenting the case to Chaturvedi, she told me he was probably high on meth. There wasn't much to do except let him detox. Of course, he would have to do that someplace else.

I dropped into a chair and waited for the next case to come. There wasn't another. There's a saying in the ER, that you either "feast or famine," and today had been a lean day. I liked not having much to do, but I hated it all the same.

A couple of days later, I had my last shift with Chaturvedi. It was busy again, and I saw a variety of interesting cases. Before I knew it, the end of the day had arrived. I thanked Chaturvedi for her teaching on the rotation.

"Sure," she said. She walked off, ready to see another patient.

~~~

I had a couple of days off, and I spent those trying new things. Instead of beer I drank cider, and instead of spirits I drank wine. It all went down the same, and it all did the job.

Anne called me incessantly. I let the phone go to voicemail every time. I didn't bother to check the messages. She came to check on me a couple of times, but I managed to escape to a nearby bar instead of seeing her. I'm not sure what she was doing, trying to get hold of me like that. Didn't she know I was busy?

My month in the ER was half over. The remaining shifts would be at night. The Attending was the guy who was constantly upset by Chaturvedi's tardiness. His name was Hartley.

Sort of like Chaturvedi, Hartley ignored me. With Chaturvedi, she was too frazzled to find the time to work with me. Hartley, on the other hand, found me to be an annoyance. The first few shifts were awkward at best.

Hartley wanted me to gravitate toward cases that would take a long time, like suturing or abdominal pain or vaginal bleeding. This meant I would present fewer cases to him. I was okay with that.

One night, a guy came in with a massive laceration on his right thigh. He accidentally wounded himself with a chainsaw. He cut down a tree the previous day, but he was unsatisfied that the stump was still sticking out of the ground. So, he knelt down, leveled the saw to the ground, and pressed the trigger. Once he cleared the stump, the chainsaw bit into his leg.

I looked the wound over with Hartley. He wasn't impressed. Although it was wide, it wasn't deep. He told me to staple it closed, and he moved on with his evening. I spent about an hour cleaning the wound, removing debris, snipping away ragged pieces of flesh, and closing the wound with a staple gun. There wasn't much blood.

Night patients were stranger than day patients. Half of them were drunk or high or going through withdrawals. The rest were the dregs of society.

There was a guy who came in with rectal bleeding. Hartley ordered me to stick a finger in his ass. I pulled out a small rodent. There was a teenager who broke his hand having a "punching contest" with his friends. There was a lady who swallowed her glasses. She did it because she knew would need surgery to remove them, and she would be given narcotics. She was correct.

Over the following nights we saw heart attacks, deep venous thromboses, broken bones, a pneumothorax, kidney stones, intractable vomiting, and plenty of old people getting dumped in the ER because their nursing home refused to deal with them anymore.

Throughout all this, Hartley treated me as a nuisance. My presence put him in a funk. I wanted him to like me, but no matter how hard I worked, he didn't care. By the time the final night rolled around, I gave up. I wouldn't try to impress him. I wouldn't even talk to him unless I had to. Once this stupid rotation was over, I would move on with my life.

My final shift was one of those coveted slow nights. Only two patients came in, but both were disastrous.

The first guy was wheeled in by EMTs. He had chest pain, and his face was purple. Hartley bounded over, screaming at the techs to put EKG leads on the patient.

"What's wrong?" Hartley asked, shaking the patient by his shoulder.

"Hhhnnnggg," the patient grunted, turning a darker shade of purple.

Hartley put his fingers against the patient's neck, timing the pulse. He shook his head disapprovingly.

"We're up, Dr. Hartley," the tech said.

He looked at the monitor. The EKG display was a frenzy of green lines peaking and plummeting.

"Shit!" Hartley said. "Call a code!"

A robotic voice blared overhead announcing a Code Blue in the ER. Nurses and techs rushed over.

An IV was put in. A red crash cart was wheeled over. Someone dropped a bag-mask over the patient's mouth and pressed it rhythmically, forcing air into his lungs. Someone started chest compressions. Techs, nurses, and other people in scrubs were all over the place.

Hartley studied the monitor. He barked orders: epinephrine injection, compressions, defibrillation, and more compressions. It was like the code I had seen before but more chaotic. Hartley was flummoxed.

The patient's face took on a bluish hue. He was no longer conscious. A line of people waited to give him compressions. I'm not sure why, but my legs carried me into the line. The minute hand wheeled around the clock, closing in on an hour and a half.

I was next in line. The guy in front of me was slamming the patient's chest. He had gone ninety seconds, paused for another EKG reading, and went again for another ninety seconds.

"Switch!" a nurse shouted.

I stepped to the patient's side. He already looked dead. I shot a glance at Hartley. He scowled. I wrapped my hands together and began compressions.

"Faster," Hartley said.

I sped up.

"Faster!"

I was going as fast as I could. I was pumping up and down, using the entire weight of my body. The patient's sternum had already turned to mush. I tried not to look at his face.

"*Faster!*"

I was weak, but I kept going. Hartley screamed at me to stop. He ordered something else. I couldn't hear what it was over the sound of blood thundering in my ears. After a break that only seemed like a second, he waved at me to go again.

Another ninety seconds. Another billion compressions. My body was on fire. Sweat exploded from every pore. I was delirious. How much longer could I hold out? Go, go go, I had to keep going.

"Stop!" a nurse yelled.

It was time for the next person to have their chance. As I lurched from the fray, I noticed everyone was milling around. Why did they stop? What were they doing?

"I'm calling it," Hartley spat.

The patient was dead.

As quickly as all the extra staff had materialized, they disappeared. Hartley walked away, cursing. The patient was left behind. His arms hung limply off either side of his bed. Lines and wires stuck out of him, rendered useless. His skin was the color of cement.

I teetered back to the Nurses Station and collapsed on the floor. I didn't cry. I didn't feel anything. All I knew was that guy was dead, and I was the last one to touch him.

I took my lunch break early. I left the hospital and bought a bottle of tequila. I drained a third of it before stumbling back to the ER. When I returned to the Nurses Station, Hartley said, "There's a psych patient in Bed Four. You take care of him."

I walked toward the curtain and heard a strange mumbling. I grabbed the thin fabric and pulled it aside. Looking back at me from the other side was John 3:16.

"OhheypraiseJesuslistenmanyougottagetmeouttaheremywifeisi ncahootswiththegovernmentThey'retryingtolockmeupandIprayedt oJesusforsalvationandhereyouarethankstoLordGodAlmightyLiketh eysayinJohn3:16TheLordismyshepardwhoartinHeavenhallowedbet hyname–"

"Did you stop taking your meds?" I asked.

"TheLordworksinmysteriouswayspraiseJesusamen–"

As he prattled on, I realized he had no idea who I was. It had only been a month since we last saw each other, but my face hadn't even registered. All that effort, all that time had been completely wasted. He was right back where he started.

My shoulders slumped and my limbs felt heavy. With a sigh, I pulled the curtain closed. John 3:16 kept rambling. I reported my findings to Hartley. He didn't notice my sullen expression, and he didn't bother to ask me what I wanted to do for treatment. John 3:16 got some medication and he quieted for a while.

Eventually, the sun rose and it was time to go. My buzz wore off, but the numbness remained. Hartley performed his usual theatrics when Chaturvedi didn't arrive on time to relieve him. He drew a lot of attention to himself, but I don't think anyone felt bad for him.

I left. Nobody said a word to me. I departed as I had arrived, unnoticed.

I needed to feel different. I didn't know how, but a warm touch would help. I drove to Anne's apartment and let myself in. She was gone, at work. I dropped onto the couch and slept.

~~~

I awoke to the sound of a door slamming. I sat bolt upright while she stomped toward the couch. She thrust her hands on her hips.

"What are you doing here?" she asked sternly.

"Oh, yeah, I was really tired after the rotation, so I just crashed here. I thought we could hang out after you got back from work."

"Really? That's what you thought?"

"Yeah."

"If that's the case, then why haven't I seen you in a goddamn month?"

"You know my rotations keep me really busy."

"Too busy to call me?"

"I'm sorry," I said. I tried to put on my sweetest voice, but found I didn't have the energy for it.

"Why are you avoiding me?"

"I'm not avoiding you. I've just been busy, that's all."

"I can't believe I took you back. You're just like Tony."

I didn't ask who that was. I had to plead hard, and a detour wouldn't make her forgive me. I gathered my strength. "I've been under a lot of stress lately. That and studying have eaten up all my free time. But I'm here now, so let's pick up where we left off."

"No."

"Anne, please, I'm sorry."

"Sorry isn't good enough."

I stood and turned my palms up like a beggar. I began to speak, but she cut me off. "I want you out of my house!"

I started to cry. I hadn't even felt the tears well up. Where had they come from? A moment ago I had felt nothing.

"Anne, wait, I'm sorry. Give me another chance."

"Get out," she said, pointing toward the door.

A lump was in my throat. I walked through the living room, the world a liquid blur. All colors turned to blue. I opened the door and heard her mutter, "I can't believe I wanted to marry you."

I whirled around. "Let's do it! Let's get married!" I said.

Her eyes flashed red. She stomped toward me while I stood in the doorway hopefully. She shoved me backward and slammed the door in my face.

"*Fuck you, you asshole!*" she screamed, her voice muffled through the door.

"But we love each other."

"It's over."

"Anne, please."

"Get off my porch before I call the cops."

I waited in silence, hoping to see the door reopen. It didn't.

The world was silent. Traffic was probably at a standstill. All the passersby were undoubtedly looking at me, jeering. All eyes in the city were staring. Hey, look at that jerk that just got dumped. Look at that loser, that idiot. They were all right.

I dragged myself to my car. The engine took forever to turn over. Once it did, the drive home was an eternity. Back in my apartment, I stopped crying. The numbness returned.

MAY
SURGERY

Summer had returned. The desert afforded no spring and no gentle transition out of winter. The heat was like a punch to the face. The sun burned angrily in the sky, and the days were long. Air conditioners never stopped running.

The academic year had stretched on interminably, and now it had reached the finale. Surgery was the one specialty everyone dreaded. It was a grinder, infamous for decimating young, hopeful medical students. I wished I had gotten this over with already.

Once again, I was at the county hospital. As I trudged toward the entrance, I heard the familiar crow of the rooster. I wished the damn thing would shut up.

I followed the signs toward the surgical suites. When I arrived, I found two large double doors, locked. An ID badge reader hung on the wall to my right. There was an intercom next to that. I pushed the button.

"Yeah?" asked a voice, distorted by static.

"Hi, I'm a med student. I'm supposed to start today."

". . . who are you?"

"A med student. I'm starting today."

". . . I don't have anything . . . about med students."

I didn't feel up to this. "Can you please let me in so I can explain?"

" . . . okay."

The lock clicked and the doors swung inward. The other side was an obsessive-compulsive's paradise. The floors were spotless. The halls were lined with carts, neatly organized and filled with surgical supplies. The main hallway stretched infinitely with doors on either side leading to operating rooms.

To the left was a high desk. A man in blue scrubs glared at me from behind it. "Who are you?" he asked.

I spoke slowly and evenly so someone of his intelligence could understand. "I am a third year medical student. I am starting my surgery rotation today. I need to meet whoever I am assigned to so I can get started."

"Medical student? I think we already have one of them."

"Yes," I said and paused, trying not to lose my cool. "Every month we switch over. Today is the first day of the new rotation."

"Hmm," he said, pondering this. He acted like this place was the CIA and I was trying to steal state secrets. "Lemme page someone, see what I can find out."

If this guy represented the quality of the people they hired in the Surgery Department, then I would have to make sure I never got operated on here.

The telephone rang and the guy answered it. He nodded and said "Uh-huh" a couple of times after explaining the situation. He hung up and said, "The team's already rounding. Go up to the second floor."

I hustled upstairs. I thought it was a little odd that the team was already rounding at 6:30 AM. I pushed the thought away and continued upstairs. The surgical ward looked exactly the same as the medical ward: the same cross-shaped layout and the same dated décor.

As I walked down the hall, a woman in green scrubs and a long white coat rushed out of a patient room. She crashed into me, and we flopped onto the floor. She picked herself up, and then offered me her hand.

"Sorry about that," she said, pulling me up.

"No problem," I said, wincing.

"Are you one of the med students?"

"Yeah."

"I'm Katie, one of the Residents. You are?"

I told her my name.

"I think you're working with me," she said. "They paged me a couple of minutes ago. Anyway, we're on Dr. Chang's team. And we're late."

We raced down the hall to the Nurses Station. The team had already assembled. There were two other Residents and a stern-faced man, presumably Dr. Chang.

Chang was the Attending. He also wore green scrubs and a long white coat. His black hair was cropped close to his perfectly shaped skull. He was quite tall, standing a head above everyone else. His arms were folded over his chest, and his lips were turned up in a snarl.

"Blaine!" he shouted at Katie. "Where the hell were you?"

"Sorry, Dr. Chang. I had to use an interpreter for the last two patients."

"Don't fall behind again."

"Yes, of course."

His laser eyes targeted me. I felt his death-glare burrow deep into my chest and grip my soul. "What year are you?" he asked grimly.

"Third year."

"What time did you get here this morning?"

"Just now."

"Why were you late?"

"I-I didn't realize I was. What time do we start?"

"I don't have time for your piddly shit. Either show up on time, or don't show your face at all. Got it?"

"Yes."

"Let's get started."

He led the group. We followed him silently. I leaned close to Katie to ask her what time I was supposed to arrive, but she pressed her index finger to her lips and shook her head.

Surgical rounds were unlike anything I had ever seen. The patient was the least important person in the room. The team gathered around their bed. Chang poked, prodded, and articulated them in various ways, some more excruciating than others. He barked questions at the Residents. A guess was a wrong answer. A delayed response was a wrong answer. I prayed he wouldn't ask me anything.

We rounded in about fifteen minutes. With each patient we saw, Chang grew more agitated. Once we finished, we gathered in front of the Nurses Station again. It was busier now with nurses and people from other specialties milling about.

"First case is in twenty. Blaine, you're up," Chang said.

"Yes, Dr. Chang," Katie said with a quick nod.

He began to walk away, but then stopped. He stepped back and directed his ire at me. "What arteries do the left coronary branch into?"

Shit. An anatomy question. I had to think fast. I tried to visualize the heart. The left coronary artery branched off the aorta, ran down the anterior heart, and had two more branches. There was the left anterior descending and . . . the . . . what was it called?

Chang scowled.

"Left anterior descending and, um . . ."

"Did they teach anatomy at your medical school?"

"Yes."

"I suggest you ask for your money back."

And with that, he was gone.

I looked at Katie with disbelief. She patted my shoulder. "It's not you. He's always like that," she said.

"Great."

"Come on, let's scrub in."

We went back to the surgical suite. This time Katie let us in with her ID badge. The guy behind the desk gave us a cursory glance and went back to staring off into space. Katie showed me where the men's locker room was, and instructed me to meet her in OR Twelve.

The locker room was cramped. Two narrow wooden benches sat low to the floor, surrounded by small metal lockers. A shelf to the right held fresh scrubs. I found an empty locker and began to change. I stashed my usual attire in the locker and donned a too-tight pair of green scrubs and my dress shoes. I hadn't thought to wear sneakers. I looked like a fool.

There were paper booties that could be slipped over shoes. I tried to fit them over my shoes, but they kept tearing. I decided I didn't care, and walked to OR Twelve wearing booties with holes in them.

A deep basin stood beside the entrance to the operating room. Chang and Katie were rinsing a thick lather of soap off their arms. They held their arms upright and let gravity carry the water down to clean them.

Chang caught me in his peripheral vision. "He with you, Blaine?"

"Yes, Dr. Chang."

"Don't bother scrubbing in," he said without looking at me. "You can watch, but that's it. People who don't know anatomy don't get to scrub in."

It was funny the way he said that. As if forcing me to do less work was a punishment.

I stood idly as Chang and Katie finished washing themselves. Then, just like in the movies, they walked with their arms up, and pushed backward into the operating room.

I hesitantly followed. The two surgeons were getting suited up in full gowns and gloves, but I only wore a surgical cap and mask. I stood at the patient's feet. I watched as Chang and Katie prepared the sterile field.

I didn't even know what kind of surgery they were performing. From here, I could hardly see anything. The last time I had been in an OR was during my Anesthesiology rotation, and I went through that drunk.

As they worked, Chang and the anesthesiologist spoke about their respective backyard pools. Occasionally, Chang would pimp Katie, and she answered correctly every time.

An hour crawled by. My feet were numb and my body was frigid. Why did they always keep these damn ORs so cold? I was bored out of my mind and getting frostbite at the same time.

Another hour later they began to suture the body closed. I picked my right foot up and shook it to get the blood flowing again. I did the same with the left. Eventually, they had sutured everything except the skin. Change took a step back and said, "I'll leave it to you."

Like a flash, he was gone. Katie sutured the skin, only taking about five minutes. She left in the same fashion, exiting the room without looking back. I had been forgotten.

I caught up with Katie. She asked me what I thought of the surgery. I lied and said it was really interesting. The rest of the day we rounded and admitted new patients. I was allowed to observe another surgery in the afternoon. That surgeon, whoever he was, ignored me just like everyone else.

~~~

Brad and I sat next to each other at the bar. I was halfway through my second drink. The place was fairly empty since it was a weeknight. I took a gulp and set my glass down on the bar.

"How are you and your wife doing?" I asked.

"Pretty good. The long distance thing sucks, but we see each other every chance we get."

"That's nice," I said before taking another gulp.

"What're you on now?" Brad asked.

"Surgery."

"I hated that one. All those early mornings. The surgeons yelling at you all the time. Why would anyone voluntarily subject themselves to that?"

I set my empty glass down on the bar. Above us, a TV was silently broadcasting a baseball game. Popular music blared overhead. The bartender came over and asked if I wanted another drink. I gave a single nod.

"You figure out what you want to go into?" Brad asked.

"I dunno. So far I've hated everything. You?"

"Probably IM. I liked that the most. Plus, it has the most fellowships."

"Sounds good."

The bartender set my drink in front of me. I snatched it up and downed half of it.

"Easy there, chief," Brad cautioned.

"It's one of those days."

"You got plans for the weekend?"

"Nah."

"A buddy of mine from college is getting married in Vegas. Sort of a spur of the moment thing. I'm flying out Friday. You wanna go?"

"Do I want to watch two strangers make the biggest mistake of their lives? No thanks."

Brad chuckled. "Okay. Let me know if you change your mind."

We sat in silence for the next few minutes. I guzzled the rest of my drink while Brad nursed a bottle of imported beer. My fingertips became numb and my neck loosened. I ordered a fourth drink.

"How about them?" Brad asked, looking across the room.

Opposite the bar, four cute ladies were crammed into a booth. They had perfect makeup and were dressed to the nines. "I got no chance," I croaked.

"There's nothing like getting back on the horse," Brad said.

I appreciated what he was trying to do, but it didn't matter. Getting mixed up with a woman was the last thing I needed right now. I tilted my glass on its axis. "You never tol' me what rotation yer on," I said.

"Ugh. OBGYN."

"Who you with?"

"This asshole name Ravmani."

"That guy's such a prick. I had him, too."

"What's the secret to getting him to like you?"

"He's not capable of liking anyone."

"Yeah, I had that feeling."

"I showed up ever' day, did a terr'ble job, and he still gave me a perfect score on my eval."

"Well, that's a relief," Brad said as he finished his beer.

While the bar bustled around us, we sat in silence. The longer it lasted, the more uncomfortable it became. I struggled to think of something to say, but words wouldn't come. At last, Brad spoke. "Hey, listen, I know you're bummed about Anne, but she just wasn't for you."

"She was, though. She was perfect."

"Don't you remember all that crap she pulled on you in the beginning? Going out with you and then not calling for months? She was never that interested. She only liked the attention."

"I dunno know, man."

"Don't worry, we'll find you someone better. In the meantime, if you ever want to talk or hang out, feel free to give me a call."

"Brad, you wanna know the worst Attending I had?"

"Huh? Oh, uh, sure."

"It was my FP Attending. His name was Stein, uh, Stein-something. Stein-cock."

"Really? FP? They're usually nice."

"Not this guy. He's right up there with Ravmani. And Mengele. Those guys could teach a course together. How to be a dick one-oh-one."

"I think I'm enrolled in it right now," Brad said with a laugh.

I started my fifth drink. My face was numb. Time seemed endless. Brad had a second beer, and our banter continued. We spoke about rotations, Attendings, and nothing in particular. It was the best night I ever had.

~~~

Wearing scrubs, I arrived at 5:00 AM. I learned quickly that being a medical student on a Surgery rotation was kind of like being a ghost. I added nothing to the team, the Residents got to do the procedures, and the Attending ignored me.

My head was still reeling from the night before. After I awoke, I had two shots of vodka to settle my nerves. Before I left home, I filled up my plastic water bottle with cola and whiskey. Whiskey to get me through the day, and cola for the calories.

On the second floor, I printed out my census. I was assigned four patients. Each was as uninteresting as the next.

The Liver was first. I went into his room and started examining him in his sleep. The guy was incredibly sick. His skin was neon orange. His distended abdomen had patterns of veins that looked like Medusa's head.

I put my stethoscope on the four listening posts. I heard nothing but a faint tinkle. I could have listened longer, but there wasn't much point.

Next was percussion. I tapped around the belly, one finger on top of another. The Liver started to groan as he awoke. I didn't want to talk to this guy, so I cut the percussion short.

Finally, palpation. I palpated quickly around the abdomen. When I reached the right upper quadrant, I felt the dense, enlarged liver. Everything felt the same as it had yesterday.

The Liver asked me something in Spanish. I didn't acknowledge him. I quickly walked out of the room. He called into the hallway. I made my way out of sight. As I walked, I jotted my exam findings on the back of my census paper. I burped and tasted whiskey.

Next, I went to the Hernia's room. This lady had been admitted last night. The room was dark. She was still asleep. I saw a phlebotomist hovering over her, about to steal her blood like a vampire. The phlebotomist looked up as I entered.

"Oh, I'm sorry, doctor. I was just getting her labs. Do you want me to come back?"

"No, no, go ahead. I'll come back later," I said, conjuring my most sober voice.

I exited. I had no intention of returning. I would just plagiarize the exam findings that were already in the Hernia's chart. I doubted they had changed from last night.

My water bottle bulged from the inner pocket of my white coat. Nobody was nearby. I took a drink from it. The bubbly concoction soothed me. I put the bottle away and resumed my morning rounds.

The old man in the next room, the Colectomy, was already awake. Damn. I tried to get here early enough so I wouldn't have to talk to anyone.

"Hi, doc."

"Morning. How're you feeling?"

"Oh, not so bad, considering."

"Good. I'm gonna do a quick exam and then get outta your hair, okay?"

"Sure thing, doc."

The old bastard kept trying to talk to me while I examined him. He asked where I was from, what year I was in my training, and a bunch of nonsense about his condition. I tried my best to ignore him. I gave monosyllabic answers whenever possible.

As I attempted auscultation, he asked me something muffled and unintelligible. Asking someone a question when they are using a stethoscope is like trying to talk to someone who is underwater.

"What?" I asked, annoyed.

I pointed the diaphragm of the stethoscope at him.

"Do you know what time my surgery will be?"

"Should be sometime this morning."

I resumed the examination. I did everything I could to make it clear I wasn't interested in chatting. No matter what I did, the Colectomy didn't get it. When I wrapped up, the Colectomy put his hand out and I reluctantly shook it.

I went to see the Stomach. She was a disgusting, morbidly obese woman here to have gastric bypass surgery. She needed surgery to lose weight because she was too lazy to exercise and too weak-willed to diet.

Fortunately, she was asleep. The lights in the room were off. I crept toward her bed like a stalker. She snored heavily. Her bedsheet was down around her ankles. Her hospital gown was pulled up to her breasts. She wasn't wearing underwear.

Touching an unconscious naked woman was a lawsuit waiting to happen. I scrutinized her appearance: giant belly with rolls of fat, thick legs, and pubic hair like a forest. I turned away. I knew enough about gastric bypass surgery to know a physical exam wouldn't reveal much.

It was now 5:30 AM. I had one hour to write four progress notes before rounds began. I took another swig from my water bottle and went to the Nurses Station.

I had become accustomed to writing Surgery progress notes. Unlike the other specialties, Surgery notes were incredibly brief. If any section was longer than two sentences, too much had been written.

I finished the notes and snapped them into the charts just as Chang arrived. The team assembled and we began rounds.

When he pimped me, I got most of the questions wrong. The right answers went unnoticed. Whether it was the alcohol or my attitude, this no longer bothered me. Katie should have stepped in from time to time to bail me out, but she stood quietly and did nothing. She was useless.

The first surgery of the day was the Stomach. I should have read up on the procedure last night, but I didn't bother. Chang and Katie scrubbed in, and I took up my post at the Stomach's feet.

The surgeons made four small incisions at strategic places on the abdomen. Then, they inserted a slim metal rod into each incision. Three were used for tools: cauterization, cutting, grasping, etc. The fourth was used for a camera. A flat screen TV was set up on either side of the Stomach. Each showed the image from the camera so both surgeons could watch. It was nice for me, too, because I could finally see what was going on.

Chang and Katie worked methodically, performing a Roux-en-Y gastric bypass. It took forever and was incredibly boring. Everything on the monitor looked exactly the same from the stomach to the intestine. I was totally lost.

Throughout the procedure, Chang kept commenting on how this patient was "a beast." The anesthesiologist wanted to talk about his stock portfolio. Katie kept having a nurse scratch her nose and defog her glasses. I held my post, my headache growing stronger.

The next surgery was much shorter for me. It was the Colectomy. Chang and a different Resident got started. A few minutes into the procedure, Chang realized I was in the room.

"Third year."

"Yes?"

"What is the pectinate line?"

"The line that divides the upper two-thirds and lower one-third of the anal canal."

He asked me shit-related questions as he diligently worked in the colon.

"Where does the inferior mesenteric vein drain?"

"The splenic vein."

"What about the colon's lymphatic flow?"

"Um . . ."

"Well?"

". . . the para-aortic lymph nodes."

"And where do those drain?"

"I don't know."

Chang looked annoyed. "How can you expect to do surgery if you don't know anatomy? Go to the library. I want you reading on this procedure all afternoon. I'll ask you about it tomorrow."

I was kicked out of the OR. I had a feeling he was going to keep asking questions until I got one wrong just so he could evict me. I went to the library and looked up the answer to his question: cisterna chyli. After that, I went home. Nobody would miss me.

The next day, no one knew I had left. Chang forgot to pimp me. Katie interacted with me as little as possible. All of the cases blurred together. I got through the day with help from my special water bottle.

~~~

Her hair was crazy. Streaks of pink and purple ran down either side of her head. The rest was the same dirty blonde. She had never been one to wear a lot of makeup, but today it was caked on like a clown: white powdered face, bright blue eye shadow, and ruby red lips.

We sat at a tiny round table. The room was filled with the bustle of baristas churning out countless orders of fancy coffee. It was a busy Saturday morning and the coffee shop was crammed with people.

"So? Do you have them or what?" Anne asked, perturbed.

"Yeah, right here," I said. I raised my hand, letting the key ring dangle from my finger.

She reached forward to grab it, but I pulled back. Her perturbed look turned to disgust. She narrowed her eyes and prepared to try again.

"Anne, I'll give you back your keys. Just wait a second."

"You said you wanted to meet so we could trade our keys back. What else do you want?"

Ambivalence flooded me. Looking into her clown face, I remembered the great times and horrible times. I hadn't slept well since the breakup. I needed closure.

"Anne . . ." I paused, not sure what to say. My face, which had been hardened until now, quickly turned to mush. Tears streamed down my face. "Take me back! I don't know what to do without you!"

She leaned back in her chair, crossing her arms and "harrumphing." She averted her eyes. She was slipping away. I pleaded harder, trying to keep her in my grasp.

"Anne, we love each other. Give us another chance. I'll do anything you want."

She stared at the ceiling. The noise level in the coffee shop had dropped. The other patrons gawked at me. A few of them at least pretended to mind their own business while they eavesdropped. But the majority watched intently, mocking me.

"You mean the whole world to me," I said. "I'm nothing without you. We were perfect together. I was always happiest with you. I love you so much. Please don't leave me."

"Are you done?" Anne asked, looking at me.

"What?"

"Are you finished talking?"

"Yeah, I guess."

"Good, 'cause I'm through listening."

Anne tucked the colored strands of her hair behind her ears. She leaned across the table. I could see every particle of her makeup. In a stern, even voice she said, "You had your chance, but now it's over. Deal with it."

I tried to speak, to beg her to change her mind, but no words came. She slapped my spare keys on the table. She raised the same hand and turned it over, palm up. I trembled. Her keys jingled as they slid down my finger. I felt like I was floating outside my body.

I heard a man's voice, cocky and dumb, calling, "Hey, babe. You okay?"

"Yeah," Anne said without turning around.

A man had entered the coffee shop. He wore khaki shorts, a shirt with the collar flipped up, and an orange hat on backward. "What's takin' so long?" he asked.

"Nothing," Anne said. "I'll be out in a second."

"Okay."

"Just wait in the car."

"Would you order me a–"

"Get out!"

"All right, babe."

He disappeared.

My vision began to blur. Teardrops fell onto the table. I mustered the courage to speak. "Who was that?"

"Tony."

"Y-you already m-met someone else?"

"I knew him from before you and I met."

I looked down and saw the diamond ring was back on her finger.

"Can I have my keys now?" Anne asked.

The key ring slid off my finger and dropped into her open palm. She clutched it while we stared at each other. Her countenance was icy. My image was reflected in her eyes. I wanted her to leave, and I wanted her to stay.

"Anne–"

"Goodbye."

She pushed back from the table and left.

I picked up the coffee I had ordered earlier. It had grown cold. The world around me grew bigger, and as it did, I became smaller. The person nearest to me seemed miles away.

I fumbled the lid off my flask. I dumped its entire contents, whiskey, into the coffee. I took another sip. It didn't taste any better.

I sat in a heap, waiting for the tears to stop. The people around me sent odd looks my direction. They kept a wide berth when they walked by. Slowly, the noise level returned to normal. My time as a point of interest had ended.

Once I finished my drink, I stepped outside. I took out my cell phone and navigated the menu until I found Anne's contact information. I pressed "delete."

A confirmation window popped up. "Do you want to delete contact: Anne? Yes/No."

My thumb hovered over the button. One option removed her from my life forever. The other kept hope, no matter how small, alive. I squeezed my eyes shut. I tried to think of reasons to delete her, but nothing came to mind.

I pushed "No."

~~~

I got three hours of sleep. Every night I slept less. I drank more to put me out, but the more I drank, the earlier I awoke.

I drove to the hospital still woozy. I swerved around the highway. It was hard to keep my eyes open. And when I could, the world revolved on a skewed axis. I managed to reach the hospital without incident.

I sat in the car, engine off, listening to the sound of my breath. It was dark outside. My head pounded. I wasn't sure I'd be able to make it from the parking lot to the hospital. Why was I here? Why did I keep coming back? What was the point?

The blue glow of my cell phone lit up my car. I had flipped it open, knowing there would be no missed calls or voicemails, but hopeful all the same.

The clock read 5:09 AM. I took a deep breath and got out of the car. I staggered into the hospital. The world around me was a blur. I trudged up to the second floor and began rounding.

The Liver was first. He got worse every day. He was encephalopathic now. Essentially, he was completely out of his mind. Day, night, people, food, they were all the same to him. Everything was equally incomprehensible. His belly was drained of liters of fluid every couple of days while he waited for a liver transplant.

I tried to examine him, but the Liver squirmed too much. He groaned in slurred Spanish. I gave up, putting the stethoscope back behind my neck. I went into a dark corner of the room. I pressed my back against the wall and slid to the floor.

Eyes closed, face in my hands, I could feel the world rock like the ocean. My stomach contracted suddenly, followed by a pressure in my throat. I vomited.

When I woke up, I felt a little better. The sun peeked through the window. My eyes darted to the clock on the wall: 6:11 AM. Only nineteen minutes until rounds with Chang.

My chest was wet. I looked down and saw I had vomited all over myself. I couldn't be seen like this. I could lie and say the Liver did it, but they'd probably figure out I was drunk.

I picked myself up. The world did not list quite as much as before. I staggered into the hallway and found myself face to face with Katie. Her eyes were drawn to the vomit that ran down my shirt and onto the crotch of my pants.

"What happened?" she asked.

"Uh, I threw up on myself."

"Are you sick?"

"No, I'm fine. It was breakfast."

"Are you sure? You look terrible."

"Yeah, I just need to run downstairs and change."

"Okay, but hurry up. Rounds will be starting any minute."

"No problem."

I ran downstairs. I didn't pass anyone on the way. It was late enough that everyone had already changed and gone to see their patients. This was going well. I was going to get away with it.

I burst into the locker room. I reached for a clean set of scrubs and felt my heart stop. There was someone else in the room. Chang.

He was in the middle of changing. He had his scrub pants on, but was shirtless. Every muscle in his body was perfectly defined. He looked like a sculpture.

"What the hell happened to you?" Chang asked.

"I threw up."

"You sick? You can't be here if you're sick."

"No, Dr. Chang, I'm not sick. It was breakfast."

"Breakfast?" He looked me up and down, inspecting the vomit stains. "It was one of the cafeteria burritos, wasn't it?"

"Yeah. How did you know?"

"Same thing happened to me last week."

I couldn't believe it. Was I going to escape this situation?

Chang put his scrub top on. "Hurry and get changed. I'll see you upstairs."

When the locker room door closed, I dropped to the floor. My legs were like noodles. I sat on the floor a while, waiting for my strength to return.

Upstairs, I wore my white coat and a fresh pair of scrubs. When the team assembled, Chang gave me the slightest nod. When we rounded, he didn't pimp me. When he asked where the Liver's progress note was, I apologized and told him I didn't have time to write it. Amazingly, he told me to get it done soon, and he didn't look agitated. Chang and I had bonded. We had our own little secret, never mind that my part was a lie.

When rounds ended, I jotted down sloppy progress notes. There was no point in being thorough. Nobody would bother to read them.

Once finished, I returned to the surgical suites. Katie was there, studying the big dry erase board that served as a schedule for the day's procedures. She and Chang were set to work on the Gallbladder in half an hour.

"We've got a cholecystectomy coming up?" I asked.

"Have you seen one before?" Katie asked.

"Last week. From the back of the room. Well, I didn't get to see the whole thing. Dr. Chang kicked me out because he pointed to the cystic duct and I didn't know what it was."

"Hopefully, you'll get to see the whole thing this time."

"I won't hold my breath."

Katie snorted and turned away. I had twenty-five minutes to kill before the procedure. My stomach growled and my head pounded. I needed to get some protein, otherwise I'd be going through the day with a hangover.

I traversed a silent hallway to the cafeteria. The walls were painted a putrid yellow only found in institutions. A zig-zagging orange stripe ran horizontally along the wall. I passed the Radiology Reading Room. I smirked, remembering the anguish the old man had put me through.

At the far end of the hall, a man rounded the corner and approached me. He was ancient, and had a slight hunchback and bushy white eyebrows. He was the old radiology Attending!

I raised my hand and waved. "Oh, hi!" I said.

The old man furrowed his brow. He grumbled, "Hello," and kept on walking. He entered the Reading Room without losing a step.

He hadn't remembered me. It had only been a few months. I didn't expect him to recall my name or for us to have a conversation, but I thought he'd at least recognize my face. It was like he had seen me for the first time. Maybe I wasn't worth remembering?

My shoulders drooped and my feet became leaden. I dragged myself the rest of the way to the cafeteria. I picked out some slop that tasted like glue. The food sat like a rock in my stomach. I picked at it for a while, and then returned to the surgical suites.

Just inside, I passed a series of storage cabinets with thick translucent doors. Some housed tools, others sterile gowns and gloves, and others various medications. The cabinets were kept locked so people wouldn't steal from them. Mindlessly, I attempted to open one.

It opened. The lock must have been broken. I looked left and right. Nobody was nearby. I reached inside and grabbed a syringe and a bag of clear fluid. The label on the front read, "K+ Cl-." I wasn't sure why I took it, only that the impulse felt right. If narcotics were missing, they would investigate, but they wouldn't miss a bag of potassium chloride.

I ducked into the locker room. I stashed the items in my locker, hiding them underneath my white coat. I guzzled down half my cola and whiskey. If anything would get me through the next surgery, this would.

I took up my usual position at the rear of the frigid room. Chang and Katie hovered over the abdomen, instruments already sliding inside. They worked for a while until Chang remembered I was present. "Third year," he said brusquely, "what's this structure?"

I looked at one of the screens. His instrument pointed to a small vessel joining the gallbladder and the common bile duct.

"The cystic duct," I answered triumphantly. I wasn't sure if it was fortuitous or if he asked me again on purpose. Either way, I was glad to get it right. After that, Chang resumed talking about the convertible he planned to buy.

The surgeons clipped the gallbladder away, stuffed it into a small bag, and removed it through a laparoscopic port. When the surgery ended, Chang disappeared like he usually did. Katie wrapped up. I wandered back to the locker room.

A couple of guys were changing clothes and talking about their golf game. I smiled at them and hovered around my locker. I pretended to take my shoes off, as slowly as possible, while they finished. They exited the room, talking about the sand trap on the ninth hole.

Once they were gone, I grabbed my water bottle from my locker. I drained it in three massive gulps. With it now empty, I wondered if I would manage to get through the rest of the day. Tomorrow I would bring a second bottle as a backup.

I was reeling. My equilibrium was shot. I teetered backward. I caught myself for an instant, but then gravity got the better of me. I toppled over the wooden bench and landed head first on the floor.

I gasped and watched the ceiling spin above me.

I picked myself up and walked back into the hallway. Chang was nowhere to be found. Katie was absorbed in a dictation. I stood there with the world falling into silence. I decided to leave. No one would notice.

~ ~ ~

The stench of liquor filled my car. My hands were wrapped around the steering wheel, the keys were in the ignition, but the engine was off. Even so, as I stared out the windshield, the world looked like it was moving one hundred miles per hour.

I must have sat there for half an hour, waiting for my brain to settle. If not for finishing the water bottle, I might have been able to drive away safely. If I left now, I'd probably crash.

I started the engine.

Before pulling out, I licked the pad of my thumb and marked a large cross in the windshield with saliva. If I could keep the road aligned with my crosshairs, I might make it home.

I didn't drive home. I drove around the city, making a full loop on the Interstate bypass. When I saw the hospital again, I exited to the surface streets and continued to drive aimlessly. It was the middle of the day, so traffic was relatively light. I passed a couple of police cars which took no notice of me.

My bladder was on the verge of bursting. I looked around for someplace to stop. On the left I saw a familiar building: Panthers. Its tacky sign proclaimed, "Finest Girls in the State!" Just beneath that a smaller sign read, "$5 Prime Rib Lunch!"

It must have been my lucky day.

No one manned the entryway, so I didn't have to pay a cover charge. I blew into the main room. The place was deserted. There were two disheveled men, each sitting alone at their own tables. They watched a single girl dance lethargically on the main stage. I found the bathroom and relieved myself.

When I finished, I decided I was still too drunk to drive home. I found an open chair as far away from the other men as possible. A couple of minutes later a waitress took my drink order. I ordered a gin and tonic. When she brought it, I gave her a generous tip.

"Thanks, doc," she said with a wink.

I was still wearing scrubs. I looked like a buffoon. The other sad sacks didn't notice, though. One was watching the lazy dancer, and the other was staring into his beer. I sipped my drink. It was so watered down it wouldn't prolong my drunken state.

The music eventually ended and the dancer stepped off the stage. Another girl appeared and a new song started. She danced with more effort than the first girl. She was short, thin, and had closely cropped dark hair. Already topless, it was easy to tell her breasts were natural. There was something familiar about her.

I finished my drink. The waitress reappeared. "Can I get you another?" she asked, startling me.

"No, thanks. I'm good."

"There's a two drink minimum."

"Yeah. Sure. Another one."

I resumed watching the dancer. I liked her. She had a nice girl-next-door quality. I decided to tip her, but I was too far from the stage. The song concluded, and I pulled a five dollar bill out of my wallet and waved to her. She waved back and smiled.

As she approached, the waitress brought my second drink. I didn't tip her this time. What was so hard about delivering watered down gin?

I tried to look casual as the cute dancer walked over. I arranged myself with one arm stretched across the table and my posture slouched. She reached me and plucked the bill from my hand.

"Thanks," she said.

Strange, even her voice sounded familiar.

"Pull up a seat," I said.

"Sorry, babe, but I gotta work."

"You can't stay for a minute?"

"I could if you wanted a dance."

"Sounds good."

As the next song played, she gave me a lap dance. Despite the dim lighting, I could tell she was hot. Perfect ass. Flawless skin. Youthful. As she grinded on me, my mind went blank. Unfortunately, she was feeling chatty.

"How you doin', babe?" she asked.

"Fine."

"You a doctor?"

"No. Med student."

"That's nice. You like it?"

Her tits were in my face now, muffling my voice. "Not really."

"Too bad."

She continued writhing on me, turning her back to me, gyrating her butt up and down. She turned her head to the side and said, "You look familiar. You come here a lot?"

"No."

"Where you from?"

"Nowheresville."

"I could swear we met before."

This bordered on surreal. She and I had both felt it. I racked my brain, trying to recall where we had met. She wasn't one of Anne's friends, she certainly wasn't a fellow student or a nurse. But she was–

The song ended. She turned around with a smile of recognition. "Now I remember!" she exclaimed. "You gave me a ride that one time! Me and my daughter!"

–a doctor's wife.

"Cat," I said.

"It's great to see you again."

That was a surprise. I figured she would have completely forgotten me. Stranger still, she was talking like we were old friends. "I really wanna catch up with you," she said. "I have a break in about forty-five minutes. Why don't you hang out for a while, and I'll come find you later?"

"Okay," I said with a confused smile.

Forty-five minutes passed at an agonizingly slow pace. The two other patrons left and a few others trickled in. I ordered the prime rib. It was a flat, bland, dry piece of meat unceremoniously slapped between two pieces of bread.

The girls were on a rotation. As far as I could tell, there were only four working. It didn't really matter. Cat was all I could think about. When the time was finally up, she returned, wearing clothes. "You wanna go talk somewhere?" she asked.

"Yeah. My car's outside," I said.

We walked out. My head pounded. If I hadn't felt so awful, I would have felt like a rock star, having picked up a stripper.

Cat told me to pull around to the back of the building. I did, perplexed yet hopeful about what was going to happen.

"You know, it's really good to see you again," she said.

"Thanks. You, too."

There was a long pause. I tried to act cool, but it was hard being so drunk. Eventually, I cut through the silence. "I didn't know you still worked here."

"I quit when I married Bob. But I've been back for about a month."

"He's okay with this?"

"I don't give a shit what he's okay with."

"Oh."

"We're getting divorced," she said solemnly. She let out a long sigh. She stared vacantly through the windshield. "I caught that son of a bitch cheating on me. I walked right in on him fucking some slut."

I remembered him saying something similar about her.

"Cat, I'm sorry."

"It's okay. Things weren't great between us, anyway. We only got married because of Jocelyn."

"How'd you end up back here?"

"I need to make a living. Bob, that prick, is fighting me every step of the way. But I got a good lawyer. He was happy to help when I told him Bob was a big-shot doctor."

Another pause.

Cat's eyes grew wide and sparkled deviously. "You were one of his students. It would piss him off if he found out I banged you," she said.

My stomach started doing backflips. "A-are you sure that's a—"

"Yeah, he would hate that," she said with a grin. "Whaddaya say? You wanna go for it?"

"Well, Cat, I dunno."

"It's okay, don't worry, I'm on the pill now."

"It's not that. I just—"

"What? You have a girlfriend?"

I struggled to find the right thing to say. "Cat, I, no. It's just, I . . ."

"Come on, don't you want me?"

I looked her over. She wore faded pink track pants and a tight gray t-shirt. The curves of her hips and swell of her breasts were enticing. I reached over and squeezed her left breast. It was big and soft. I thought about Anne, with her small chest, clown hair, and haggard face. And then, there was nothing I wanted more than to fuck Cat. She smiled and rubbed her hand over my crotch.

We relocated to the back of the car. It was tight, with barely any room to maneuver. Still, we managed to take off our pants, and she mounted me. I pulled her shirt up and buried my face in her tits. She was hot and wet as she rocked on top of me.

My mind clouded by desire, I lost track of the world around me. The only thing I felt was her warmth. I wanted this to last forever. She moved harder and faster. I felt a mounting urge in my groin, and I climaxed.

Afterward, Cat tried to get off, but I wrapped my arms around her, pulling her close. She tolerated this for a few seconds and tried again. I resisted. "Let me off," she said.

Cat broke free, and flopped onto the seat next to me. She pulled up her pants. "Whew, hit my head on the roof a couple of times," she said.

". . . yeah."

"That oughtta show that bastard. Don't you think?"

She got out of the car. "Come back again sometime. I'll let you know how the divorce is going," she said. She closed the door and walked off, headed toward the club.

Fisher was a bastard. He treated his wife like crap. He gave me a bad evaluation, and I had just gotten revenge. Plus, I had sex with a beautiful woman. I should have been thrilled. Wasn't it normal to be excited about something like this?

I didn't feel excited. I didn't feel disgusting or cheap. I didn't feel worried about herpes or gonorrhea. I didn't feel anything.

~~~

The rest of the month passed in a haze. Chang forgot about our bond, and resumed screaming at me and kicking me out of the OR. The patients rotated in and out, but they were all the same. The only one who remained was the Liver, glowing electric orange every day.

I had fine-tuned the amount of booze I needed to drink so I got through the day numb, but not so drunk as to arouse suspicion.

The early mornings didn't affect me anymore. My sleep had gotten so bad that I awoke every few hours throughout the night. I looked like a wreck, but nobody noticed. I could have come to work with a hand missing and no one would have said a word.

On my final day of the rotation, Katie was absent. Chang met us all, stern-faced as ever. "We've got a lot of cases and Blaine's out sick," he said. "We're going to move at double speed. Got it?"

The faceless Interns and Residents answered in the affirmative. Chang set his eyes on me and said, "Third year, I'm putting you to work today. Understand?"

"Yes, Dr. Chang," I said robotically.

Six months ago, that kind of order would have given me diarrhea. Today, nothing. And so, we rounded. Chang was in rare form today.

"What's the sensitivity and specificity of right upper quadrant ultrasound for gallbladder disease?"

"What's the resting pressure of the Sphincter of Oddi?"

"What are the possible causes of pancreatitis?"

"What's the most common EKG finding in pulmonary embolism?"

"What are the steps of the clotting cascade?"

"What are the most common causes of post-surgical infection, and on which days do they occur?"

Chang was obviously pissed off about something. Maybe his wife told him he wouldn't be able to buy that new sports car? I got two of his questions right, the first two. He didn't like that, so he went all out, pimping me into submission. Of course, a strategy like that only worked if the person being pimped actually cared. His questions bounced off of me like gnats.

When we finished rounds, we were sixteen minutes behind schedule. Chang fumed. He barked orders at the Residents. He cursed at the nurses. He told an old man hobbling down the hallway, "Get the fuck out of my way!"

Later, Chang was outside OR Four, scrubbing in. I stood a couple of yards to the side as usual. He rinsed his arms under the flowing water and asked, "You gonna scrub in or just stand there?"

This month I had never scrubbed in. My job was to stand back and watch. I was shaken awake by the proposal. Chances were I wasn't going to become a surgeon, so this might be my only opportunity to participate.

Without replying, I stepped up to the basin. I pressed the hot and cold floor levers down with my foot, and the faucet spurted water. I rinsed my hands and arms to the elbows, then opened a soap-filled sponge from a sterile package.

One wrong move and Chang could change his mind. So, I washed carefully, thoroughly scouring every millimeter from my fingernails to my elbows.

Chang finished and entered the OR. I hurried, rinsing the soap off, careful not to touch the faucet or basin. Even the slightest contact would mean starting over from the beginning. It felt like I was taking forever. Chang was probably cursing up a storm, wondering what I was doing.

Quickly, I rotated away and brushed my finger against the faucet. I was no longer sterile. I would have to do it all over again. I looked around. No one had seen. I didn't want to waste any more time. I entered the OR.

Chang stood on the Gallbladder's left side. I stood directly across from him. We would be removing the diseased organ laparoscopically.

Chang made the four incisions while I stood idly. He inserted the instruments while I observed. He maneuvered the camera until it was in position while I kept my hands folded high up against my chest.

"Hold this," Chang said.

I took hold of the camera. I held it steady while he began to cut and cauterize within the abdominal cavity. Every so often he would ask me to move the camera one way or another. They were small adjustments. It was tricky, though, because the picture on the TV screens was inverted. To see right, I had to move the camera left. To see up, move the camera down, and so on. I wasn't getting the hang of it, and Chang was getting irritated.

"Left," he said.

I jostled the image into position.

"Too far."

Back just a bit.

"Up."

Another minor correction.

"Down!"

Chang grabbed my hand. He jerked the camera into the exact spot he wanted. "There! Don't move!" he barked.

He shouted all kinds of orders. He screamed at the Scrub Nurse to hand him things, and he yelled at the anesthesiologist to reposition the table's degree of incline. When he wasn't shouting, the OR was deathly silent.

I craved a drink. I could have one if I somehow got kicked out. But it would be better for everyone, the Gallbladder included, if I stayed quiet and did as I was told.

Chang's frustration grew. Copious fatty tissue made visualization difficult, and there was a rare anatomical variant to deal with. Chang cursed loudly. Every time fat obscured the camera, Chang grumbled, "Goddamn monster."

As the procedure dragged on, Chang's face grew redder. He bagged the gallbladder and withdrew it from the abdomen. "Finally!" he shouted.

The rest of the case went much faster. He sutured and cauterized and restored everything to working order.

Once the laparoscopic tools were removed, all that remained was to suture the four small abdominal incisions. He pointed to two of them. "You take those two," he said.

Chang quickly sutured the other two in a flurry of precision. Meanwhile, I clumsily worked on mine. I wanted this ordeal to come to an end.

Changed stepped back from the table. I was still working on closing my first incision. I tied it off and went to the second. My body was on fire. Chang didn't say a word. He stared intensely as I struggled.

I had the manual dexterity of a toddler. The needle fell out of my hemostat, and I pulled the suture out because I failed to tie it properly. Seconds turned into minutes. My breaths were shallow and I felt lightheaded. I felt like an imbecile, taking so long to do something so simple.

When I finished, Chang turned away. He grabbed the tray of surgical instruments and flung it across the room. He roared. He ripped off his gown and stormed out.

The Scrub Nurse put her hand over my forearm and squeezed. "Don't worry," she said. "He gets that way sometimes. You did fine."

I nodded. I wanted to thank her but couldn't. My mouth was too dry to speak.

I helped clean the Gallbladder and prep them for the trip down to the Post-Anesthesia Care Unit. Eventually, the anesthesiologist wheeled them away. I slowly removed my gown and gloves and sullenly exited the OR.

Outside, Chang was completing his dictation. The moment he finished, he slammed the telephone down. His pager blared. "We've got an emergent appy coming from the ER," he said. "You've got ten minutes to eat something."

I raced to the cafeteria. They weren't set up for lunch yet and breakfast had already been put away. I grabbed a bottle of water, two bags of chips, and a candy bar. I inhaled the food and then ran back. Chang stalked down the hallway.

"OR Two. Get ready."

I went to the basin and started to scrub. Chang followed and scrubbed beside me. He didn't say a word. He scrubbed fast and was in the OR as I started my final rinse. I hurried after him, moving as fast as I could.

The Appendix was being transferred to the operating table. They groaned deliriously, and rolled their head side to side. Their abdomen bulged like they had swallowed a grapefruit whole.

A gaggle of people were in the room. I recognized a couple of the Interns. In the far corner of the room was No-Name. Oh great, an audience.

The anesthesiologist sedated the Appendix and intubated him. He was quickly prepped for surgery. A nurse helped me suit up.

"The CT showed the appendix has ruptured. So, we're gonna move fast. Got it?" Chang said.

"Yes, Dr. Chang."

"Where do we make the incision?"

"McBurney's point."

"Where's that?"

"One third of the distance between the ASIS and the umbilicus."

For needing to move fast, he was wasting a lot of time asking me questions. I had gotten them right, but he didn't acknowledge that. He worked silently. He sliced through skin with his scalpel. Beneath was a layer of skeletal muscle. The striations ran diagonally downward and inward.

"Which layer is this?"

I paused for a second to think, and then said, "External oblique."

He looked at the Scrub Nurse. "Give him the retractor."

She slapped it into my hand, and I pulled the incision wide. Just then, one of the Residents barged into the OR. They were freshly scrubbed. One of the nurses helped him into his gown and gloves. "Sorry I'm late, Dr. Chang. That hernia wound up being strangulated," he said.

Changed grunted.

The Resident was given a retractor, and he pulled the side opposite mine. Meanwhile, Chang cut through the musculature. Beneath that were fibers running the other direction. He continued cutting. Each layer deeper, he asked me to identify a structure. Somehow, I got each question right.

The peritoneum was a mess. Greenish-yellow pus was splattered about. The smell of feces wafted upward. Fecal matter had spread throughout the cavity.

"Shit," Chang grumbled.

"You said it," the Resident replied.

Chang swept his fingers around the perforated appendix to make certain it was clear from adhesions. "Babcock," he said, still looking at the mess in front of him.

The Scrub Nurse handed him a clamp. He attached it and continued. He cut methodically. The Resident irrigated with water and applied cauterization or suction whenever instructed. Meanwhile, I held my retractor.

My arm ached and began to tremble. I had been stuck in the same position for nearly thirty minutes. I flexed harder, but as I did, my muscles slackened. I had an irresistible itch on my nose, but I couldn't scratch it. Sweat trickled down my face, but I couldn't wipe it. My legs tingled numbly, but I couldn't move them. I felt like one of those tortured characters in the underworld of Greek mythology.

Chang removed the burst appendix. He and the Resident cleaned the abdominal cavity. They flushed it with irrigation and drained it with suction. They wiped with four-by-fours. It was an arduous and meticulous process. It seemed like it would never end.

With the exciting part over, the crowd left the OR. I still couldn't move. I tried to hold on, but I was losing my grip. My body's quivering progressed to shuddering.

"Hold still!" Chang shouted.

I regripped the handle and pulled back as hard as I could.

Chang and the Resident began to suture the Appendix's body closed. Each layer of muscle was rejoined. Soon, all that remained was the three-inch incision Chang had first made.

"Third year, close him up," Chang said.

The Resident vanished. Chang removed his gear. I took a moment to compose myself. I put the retractor on the instrument tray and let my arm go limp for a minute. I stamped my legs to get my blood circulating.

With all traces of booze clear from my brain, the pressure was on. My anxiety had rebounded stronger than ever. Chang was burning to get out of here.

I started flawlessly. I placed the sutures evenly and approximated the skin perfectly. When I was halfway through, Chang left the OR without a word. He couldn't have been more casual.

My anxiety reached greater heights than I thought possible. My hands shook. My vision faded. I was breathing so fast I thought I was going to pass out.

"It's all right. Take your time," the Scrub Nurse said reassuringly.

Color returned to the world. I looked at her and nodded. Although my hands shook, I kept them steady enough to continue. I dropped the needle twice, but I kept working. When I tied off the final suture, my body flooded with relief.

"Good job," she said.

"Thanks," I replied wearily.

Back in the hallway, I found someone waiting for me. It was No-Name. He perked up when I appeared. "Hey," he said.

"What are you doing here?"

"I wanted to hang around for a minute, just to say you did a great job in there."

"Oh, thanks. Too bad we couldn't trade places since you love this stuff."

No-Name looked doleful. "Eh, I don't think I'm gonna do Surgery, after all."

"Why not?"

"It's just . . . not my thing."

"What are you going into?"

"Probably FP or IM."

So much for his plan of solving all of the world's problems with the stroke of a knife. He was the latest in a long line of people who had been humbled by the actual work.

"Anyway," he said as he started to walk away, "see ya 'round."

I walked the opposite direction and found Chang writing orders. A clock hung on the wall above him. It was only noon. There was no way I'd get through the rest of this day.

"How'd it go?" he asked.

"That was intense."

"Hmm," he said, expressionless. "I just found out I've got a family emergency. I have to leave. I want you to follow Dr. Jones the rest of the day."

"Sure, Dr. Chang. Uh, before you go, uh, it's my last day. Would you mind filling out my evaluation?"

As much as I knew Chang disliked me, I needed him to complete the form. Katie wasn't here and I couldn't give it to an Attending I didn't know. Chang would pass me. It wouldn't be a great score, but at least I wouldn't have to repeat the rotation.

I handed it to him and looked away as he filled it out. I couldn't bear to watch him tally up whatever wretched score awaited me.

"Here," he said.

I reluctantly took the paper and looked it over. Chang had given me a score of five in every category except one. "Technical Skills" was marked a three.

"As the year goes on, students get more experience, and my expectations get higher," Chang said. "You did extremely well. In fact, you are one of the smartest students I had all year. You're the only one to get that external oblique question right. Unfortunately, your technical skills are quite average."

I had answered the vast majority of his questions incorrectly. But getting the one right that everybody else got wrong had left him with a good impression. That was fine with me.

"Thanks a lot, Dr. Chang," I said, offering my hand.

He gave it a quick shake, and then he was gone. He was straight and to the point. A true surgeon.

Of course, I had no intention of working with Dr. Jones. At this point, evaluation in hand, there would be no repercussions. I waited about twenty minutes in the locker room, just long enough to make sure Chang was gone. Then, I gathered my things and headed home.

JUNE
BREAK

I spent the next three days in a stupor. When I wasn't blacked out I was just sober enough to go to the store to buy more booze. Seventy-two hours were spent either drinking or unconscious.

I checked my voicemail ritualistically. No one ever called. The one person I wanted to hear from the most had forsaken me. I contemplated calling Brad, but decided against it. He was probably enjoying his vacation with his wife.

June was a month-long holiday between the third and fourth years. We were supposed to use this time as an opportunity to study for the second part of the medical licensing exam. I felt better studying the bottom of a bottle.

Once July rolled around, it would be back to rotations. I was supposed to choose electives. I hadn't started. The rotation approval forms sat in a pile on my desk, blank.

On Tuesday afternoon my phone rang. I was sprawled on the couch, disheveled. I had just enough strength to lift my head up. It took several seconds for the phone to come into focus. The display read, "Home."

I reached for the phone, moving in slow-motion. As I grasped it, the phone fell silent. I turned onto my back. I closed my eyes and tried to let sleep come.

The phone sprang to life again, buzzing on my chest. Why were my parents calling me so incessantly? What the hell did they want?

I pressed the phone to my ear. I tried to speak but found my mouth glued shut. I swiped my tongue around for moisture. "Hello?" I croaked.

Mom was hysterical. I understood every other word between her sobs. I tried to talk, to tell her something comforting, but she wouldn't listen. She told me the funeral was two days from now. I agreed to fly home first thing tomorrow morning.

Dad was dead.

~~~

It wasn't a good idea to go through the afternoon sober. My refrigerator was empty. I stumbled around my apartment, tripping over empty bottles and cans. I was too drunk to walk to my car, let alone drive to the store. In the cabinet under the sink was a nearly full bottle of rubbing alcohol. I drank that. Miraculously, it got me through the rest of the day.

The next morning I woke up with a horrendous hangover. I put on a pot of coffee and checked the Internet for flights home. The cost to fly out today would be astronomical, but I had no choice. After searching for an hour, I settled on a flight that I could afford, and left at a reasonable time. I didn't want to get home too soon and have to deal with all those people.

This left me with four hours to pack and get to the airport. I drank three cups of coffee and the headache diminished. By the time I finished packing, I still had two hours before I had to be at the airport. That was enough time for a drink.

There was a little convenience store about a mile away. I went there and bought a couple of six-packs of beer and a bottle of vodka. Back at my apartment, I stashed the vodka in my suitcase and drank one of the six-packs. The other went into the fridge.

I managed to keep it together well enough to get through airport security. I got a funny look when I banged my shoulder against the metal detector, but nothing more. I hauled myself down to the gate.

Having a mid-day flight meant the airport wasn't busy. I still had forty-five minutes before my plane boarded. Fortunately, the airport bar was in sight. The bartender, a balding guy in his forties, nodded to me.

"Whiskey sour," I said.

He poured me a drink.

I sat on a bar stool, feeling odd. In front of me was a bar with all the familiar trappings. Behind me was the airport terminal with screaming kids, sleepy commuters, and various other upstanding citizens.

I looked down at my glass. I couldn't believe I was going home. I wished I could take the train again, but there wasn't time for it. I liked how long it took to travel by train.

The bartender noticed my head hanging. "Your drink okay?"

I pulled my head up with some effort. I hadn't tried it yet. I took a sip. "Yeah, it's fine."

"Where you headed?"

"Home."

"Ah, home. Good place to go."

My eyes wandered past him, down the bar. There was only one other customer, a pathetic guy in a wrinkled suit. With business this slow, I guess the bartender had time to chat.

"Eh, not really," I said.

"Trouble at home?" he asked. He had a strange accent I couldn't quite place.

"Funeral."

"Sorry to hear it."

I took another sip.

"Someone you were close to?"

"No, it was my dad."

He took a few seconds to process that. "My condolences," he said.

I shrugged and finished my drink. I didn't want to sit here any longer with this nosy bartender. "How much do I owe you?" I asked, standing up.

"It's on the house."

"Thanks."

I headed for the gate. There was still a lot of time until takeoff. I slouched in one of those uncomfortable airport chairs and closed my eyes.

I woke up in time to board the plane, only to fall asleep again immediately. I slept through the entire four-hour flight. I awoke when my seat was jostled as passengers departed single-file. Everyone was in such a hurry to disembark, the faster they tried to move, the slower they went.

Summer in the Midwest was exactly as I remembered. The trees were full of vibrant green leaves, and the green lawns of the homes I passed were meticulously trimmed. The last time I was here, the landscape was blanketed with snow, the plants dormant. Now, life bloomed everywhere.

I pulled into the front driveway. Another rental car was already there. I got out and dragged my suitcase behind me. The thing weighed a thousand pounds.

Just before I entered the house, I hesitated. I had traveled so far and done it automatically, but why? To watch a bunch of people sob and carry on? I was better off on the other side of the country.

I turned around. The car's engine hissed and popped as it cooled. The expanse of the world in this direction was vast. I turned back toward the house. It was a closed space of misery.

There was no way I could go through with this. I spun around and staggered off the front porch. I heard the front door open behind me. Someone called my name. I was too late. I slowly turned back. Eve stood in the doorway.

"Oh, hey, Evie," I said meekly.

"Come on in."

I entered the house. It was so quiet. When Dad was alive, he would always have the TV or stereo on. There was always some level of background noise. Without it, the place seemed like a stranger's house.

"Where's Mom?" I asked.

"She's lying down in the bedroom. She's exhausted from all the funeral arrangements, so I told her to take a nap."

"Oh."

"Why don't you put your stuff away? I'll fix us a drink."

"Sure."

I went to my old room. It looked just as I had left it. The thing was practically a shrine. I put my suitcase on the bed and unzipped it. I rummaged around a bit, not looking for anything in particular, just wasting time. If I took too long, Eve would come get me. So, I took a deep breath and headed for the kitchen.

"Here," she said, handing me a tumbler of soda.

I took a sip. It was a rum and cola. Coconut flavored rum. It tasted all right.

The two of us sat in the breakfast nook. I wasn't in the mood to talk to her. I wasn't in the mood to look at her face. But that didn't matter. Eve wanted to talk, and Eve always got what she wanted.

"How's school going?" she asked.

"How's California?"

"It's fine. The weather's nice."

"You didn't bring the kid?"

"No, I left her with Rick. I thought it would be better."

"Are you doing okay?"

"I'm not sure. I mean, not really. It doesn't feel like Dad's gone. It hasn't hit me yet."

"Yeah. Me neither."

I sipped my drink. Eve eased back into her chair and stared out the window. The only sound was the ticking of the clock's second hand. One minute elapsed. One turned into two. Two turned into five. Eve was mentally somewhere else, and I couldn't handle any more of this. I finished the drink and walked back to my bedroom.

I locked the door and pulled the vodka from my suitcase. I drank straight from the bottle. The liquid burned down my throat. I flopped onto the bed with my back against the headboard. I gazed out the window opposite me.

Suburbia sprawled out on the other side. The houses all looked the same. I heard the distant shouts of children playing. A few birds twittered in the nearby trees. Everything out there was alive. Everything in this house was dead.

I continued to drink as the sun began its descent. I watched the world beyond, separated by a pane of glass.

~~~

The next morning I awoke to a pounding on my door. The doorknob rattled. Eve shouted from the other side. "Come on! You gotta wake up and get ready!"

"Okay, I'm awake," I said hoarsely.

"You've got two hours, and then we've gotta go."

"Fine."

I picked myself off the bed, but quickly fell back onto it. The world was spinning around me. My stomach was queasy, and I resisted the urge to vomit. I ran my hands through my greasy hair. I pushed on either side of my head, hoping the pressure would somehow make me feel better.

I was still drunk.

I got up, and nearly tripped when I kicked the empty vodka bottle across the floor. Being drunk, my foot didn't hurt much. I unlocked the door and went to take a shower.

The shower helped a little. Wearing only a towel, and still dripping water, I headed back into the hallway. "You want some coffee?" Eve called from the kitchen.

"Definitely."

If I was going to be drunk, I might as well be awake and drunk.

I dressed slowly, mostly from lack of coordination. Getting my tie on was the hardest part. I grappled with it over and over again. When I finished, I looked clean and put together except for the dark circles under my eyes. I could probably get away with it, citing immense grief for why I looked so terrible.

I lumbered into the kitchen.

"Jesus, you look terrible," Eve said.

". . . yeah."

I grabbed a mug out of the cabinet and filled it with coffee. "Where's Mom?"

"She's redoing her makeup. We already ate breakfast. I think we've got some cereal, though."

I filled a bowl and sat down to eat. Eve kept clattering around the kitchen, putting away plates, washing pans, and drying glasses. I wished she would leave. I needed peace and quiet.

Eventually, she did leave so she could finish getting ready. My solace lasted only a moment before I saw Mom coming down the hallway.

"Hi, sweetheart," she said with a wan smile.

We hugged.

"I'm glad you're home."

"Me too, Mom."

She took a step back but kept one hand on each of my arms. She looked me up and down. "You look nice," she said.

"Thanks."

"But you're so thin. Haven't you been eating?"

"I was just now," I said, nodding toward my breakfast.

Mom smiled and released me. We both sat at the table, and I resumed eating.

"How's school?"

"It's okay. I finished third year."

"I'm so proud of you. Your father was too, you know?"

"Sure, Mom."

"Do you know what kind of doctor you're going to be?"

"I'm still not sure. It's hard to pick," I said between crunches of cereal. I spoke carefully, trying not to slur my words. The coffee helped mask the ethanol fumes I emitted.

"How long will you be staying?"

"Just until tomorrow."

"Oh," she said, disappointed.

"I'm sorry, Mom, but I've got to get back to school."

"I know, sweetheart. It's just that I don't see you very often. You know, Eve is staying a whole week."

It took nearly five minutes before Eve's infallibility was brought up. I supposed that was some kind of a record. I crunched my cereal a bit longer and washed it down with the rest of the coffee.

Mom and I continued with the small talk. I didn't want to talk about Dad and I couldn't tell if Mom did. So, I skirted the topic. When Eve reappeared, the pressure released. She took charge of the conversation. Being constantly doted upon by my parents always made her a good buffer.

When 1:00 PM finally hit, we drove to the funeral home.

I had seen a couple of dead bodies in medical school. They looked like shit, with wires attached to their chests and tubes sticking out of their throats, naked and prostrate on hospital beds.

Dad didn't look anything like that. He was dressed in a suit, hands folded over his chest, with his hair perfectly straight and weird makeup caking his face. He looked like a fake dead person.

And now a mass of voyeurs took turns gawking at him. It was disgusting. I couldn't believe someone would want to have their rotting corpse on display for the world to see.

People lined up to give condolences to Mom and Eve. A lot of them were Dad's friends from the VFW. Only a few of them trickled over to speak with me. My father was dead, and I was invisible to the majority of people here.

The memorial service went quickly. A few people reminisced fondly about Dad. A few others read Bible verses. Dad hadn't been particularly religious, so those seemed out of place. I remained in my seat, counting the minutes as they passed. Fortunately, by the time we adjourned to the cemetery, I was still drunk.

It was cloudy. On the horizon, gray clouds mixed with the hazy ground, creating an otherworldly illusion. There was no longer a division between Earth and sky.

Mom and Eve bawled uncontrollably. I didn't cry. I felt nothing. I was transfixed on the casket. Someone sang Amazing Grace. Everyone said the Lord's Prayer in unison. I knew the words, but I didn't see the point in joining in.

A lifeless husk was in the casket. It would be lowered into the ground and covered with dirt. It was best to keep the dead where they couldn't be seen. Nobody wanted to be reminded of them. Forgetting them was easier. And someday, when the rest of us die, we'll all be forgotten, too. It was best to be forgotten.

Everything Dad had worked for: money, family, possessions, it was all pointless. He was dead and all his effort had been wasted. If the end point for every person was death, then what was the point of trying?

There certainly wasn't a point in having a family. No matter how long you hold on, everyone dies alone.

I felt a hand reaching for mine. The fingers worked their way in and wrapped around my palm. It was Mom. She squeezed hard, and she sobbed louder. I limply squeezed back.

The ceremony concluded, and we returned to our car in silence. Eve drove us home. Nobody felt like cooking, so we ordered a pizza. Mom and Eve had no appetite. I ate almost the entire thing. Mom went to bed early. Eve and I sat in the living room staring at each other.

"How are you holding up, little brother?"

"I'm okay."

"Are you sure? It's all right to be sad, you know?"

"I'm fine."

"But you had this stone face the whole day. You looked like you wanted to let something out. And believe me, if you did, you'd feel a lot better."

"Evie, really."

"I won't tell anyone if you cry."

She was starting to get on my nerves. "I don't need to cry," I said.

"You don't have to *cry*. But it would be good if you felt *something*."

"And what exactly should I feel?"

"I don't know. Sad, angry, depressed, anything. Come on. Dad's gone."

Her eyes were getting watery again. Her makeup was already smudged from all the tears she had shed today.

"Yeah? So what?" I asked, throwing my hands up.

"I know you weren't close, but he was your father," she said with tears rolling down her cheeks.

I stood up. I had enough. "He was a shitty father to me. He hardly said more than three words to me at a time. And when he did, it was to tell me how disappointing I was compared to you. Who does that to their own kid? An asshole, that's who. Dad never gave a shit about me, Mom only talks to me twice year, and you set a standard that's impossible to live up to."

"I-I'm so sorry," she said, rising out of her chair. She wrapped her arms around me.

I stood there, letting her hug me, but wishing she would leave. I didn't have the strength to push her away. "I'm so sorry. I'm so sorry," Eve sniveled.

I stepped back and broke free from her. "It's not your fault," I said.

"But if had known that's how you felt, I–"

"I told you, it's not your fault. It's theirs," I said. My gaze dropped to the floor. "I'm tired. I'm going to bed."

She reached out and tried to grab my arm, but I blew past her. She didn't come after me.

In the bedroom, I turned the vodka bottle over and a few drops fell on my tongue. I wished I hadn't wasted it all last night.

I sat on the bed, and stared out the window. It was nearly dark. The world was cast a dusky blue. I sat there, trying not to think, focusing on my breaths. An hour passed. I heard the door on the far end of the hall close. Eve had gone to bed.

I ventured into the kitchen. I rummaged through the cabinets as quietly as possible. I found the bottle of coconut rum. I took it back to my room. I also took a tumbler and a bottle of cola. I didn't use either. By the time I finished the rum, I was tired enough to sleep.

~ ~ ~

The next morning Eve was in the kitchen frying bacon and mixing pancake batter. Mom was pouring orange juice.

"Good morning," Mom said.

"Morning!" Eve said, more cheerfully than I expected.

"Morning," I replied wearily.

"I'm making pancakes. You want some?" Eve asked.

"Sure."

"Pancakes were always your father's favorite. I used to joke that he loved pancakes more than me," Mom said with a forlorn smile.

I slumped into a chair. I tilted my head back as far as it would go. For some reason, this position eased my hangover.

"What time are you leaving today?" Mom asked.

"Six, I think."

She came over, set a glass of orange juice in front of me, and kissed my forehead. "I'm glad you came. It meant a lot to me," she said.

Good old Mom. She thought a glass of juice and a kiss constituted good parenting. The words were nice, I suppose, but they were hollow. She stepped away to start a pot of coffee. I brought my head back up and chugged the orange juice. It relieved my cotton mouth.

Mom and Eve talked about the baby. It was older now, already grown out of its clothes, and crawling all over the place. This mindless dreck continued for the rest of the morning. How could anyone talk about a baby for hours? I've had them throw up on me. They aren't all that special.

When we finished breakfast, Eve and Mom adjourned to the living room, still chatting. "Can you please clean up?" Mom asked. She was giving me orders again. She was resilient.

I washed the dishes slowly. Dishes were another of life's fruitless battles. Still, it afforded me plenty of time alone. I didn't have to sit and make small talk. That would have been worse.

I swallowed a handful of Tylenol and went back to my room. I managed to get a few more hours of sleep. When I awoke, it was midday. I was eager to get out of this house, so I packed my things and rolled my suitcase to the entryway. Mom and Eve were both there, watching TV and laughing at its twaddle.

Mom's eyes widened at my sight. "Are you leaving already?"

Eve checked her watch. "You don't need to leave for a couple of hours."

"I need to get some alone time. Clear my head, you know?" I said.

Mom got up and hugged me. "I know. It's been hard on all of us," she said.

Eve frowned but didn't say anything. I had expected them to try a little harder to get me to stay, but no more words of protest came. I took that as my chance to escape.

"Well, bye, Evie," I said.

"Later."

"Bye, Mom."

"Goodbye, sweetheart."

Mom kissed me and walked me to my car. Eve stayed inside. I loaded up, and gave Mom another silent hug before starting the engine.

Unshowered, unshaved, I drove to the airport. I ran a hand through my unkempt hair. It stood up on its own. I looked like a wreck. At least I looked better than a corpse.

~~~

My apartment smelled musty. It looked like a hurricane had hit it. The trash can overflowed. Dirty plates were stashed on any surface that would hold them. Clothes were rumpled on the floor. A legion of empty bottles and cans stood on the kitchen table.

I grabbed the six-pack from the fridge and cracked the first beer open. I drank and flipped through the paperwork for next year's rotations. I leaned back in my chair, balancing it on its back legs. Which specialties had I actually liked?

Family Medicine? Ugh, no. Internal Medicine? It was too busy. Radiology? Too boring. OB/GYN? Not a chance. Anesthesiology? Too boring. Pediatrics? I had fun, but I wasn't crazy about kids. Neurology? I learned nothing. Psychiatry? It was the most interesting. Emergency Medicine? It was the same as Family Medicine with emergencies thrown in. Surgery? Only if I wanted to be miserable.

There were several other specialties that weren't core rotations that I hadn't tried. But what if I hated those, too? Would I have to choose a career based on process of elimination?

I hated Medicine, but I couldn't quit. If I did, I would never be able to pay off the two hundred thousand dollars I owed in student loans. And those weren't forgiven if you declared bankruptcy. There was no way out. I was screwed.

I dropped the forms back on the desk and took a shower. Afterward, I checked out a new bar in the area. It seemed like a good way to spend the rest of the day.

The place was bursting with people. Friends, couples, college kids, it was popular. The bar itself was L-shaped. I sat at the far corner. From here I could see the crush of people, but no one saw me.

My cell phone buzzed. I dug it out of my pocket. The number on the front panel wasn't familiar. "Hello?" I answered.

"Oh, hi. My name's Becky. You probably don't remember me. I'm one of Anne's friends."

I knew who she was. She was Anne's cute friend who wasn't as attractive as her friend Sabrina. Having spent the entire day drinking, I wasn't in the mood to be polite.

"Whaddaya want?"

"I wanted to talk to you. To talk about Anne."

"What about her?"

"She's making a big mistake."

"And why should I care?"

"You were the best guy she ever dated. And now, well, she got engaged again to this guy Tony. But he's not right for her, and she knows it."

"Who's this Tony, anyway?"

"They've been on and off for a while. They had a big falling out a ways back. She wanted to get married and he didn't. She broke it off. That was before she started dating you."

An image flashed in my mind. On our first date, Anne had seemed preoccupied. She kept looking around the bar. Had she been looking for him? That was when she still wore the diamond ring.

"He's prob'ly the right guy for her," I said.

"I'm not sure. Just yesterday she said she wondered what you were doing."

My back stiffened.

"I think she still has feelings for you. I think you can win her back."

"But she's engaged to this other guy."

"I know, but she was always happiest with you. If you really let her know how you feel, I know you can get back together."

"She won't even answer my calls."

"She's stubborn. But if you tell her in person, she'll have to listen."

"And how will I ever have the chance to do that?"

Becky paused. She held something back, but then nervously spat it out. "On Sunday she and Tony are having their engagement photos taken. Out at Pinefield Ranch. One o'clock."

"Hmm, I dunno. The way things ended . . ."

"You've gotta try. She can't end up with Tony. She just can't."

"I'll think about it."

"Okay. I wanted to let you know."

A new thought entered my mind. "Hey, Becky?"

"Yeah?"

"If it doesn't work with Anne, how 'bout you and I go out?"

"Ugh, creep," she said before disconnecting.

It had been worth a shot.

How could I win Anne back? I couldn't inundate her with mere words. I would have to do something bold.

She was all I could think about now. What could I do? How could I make her remember how much she loved me? My time to devise a plan was limited.

I wasn't sure how much I had left on my tab, so I tossed the contents of my wallet on the bar. As I walked out, my memory surged with Anne's beautiful face, her golden hair, her flawless skin, and her soft eyes. I could do this, I could win her back!

~ ~ ~

I had grown accustomed to hangovers, so the one I had the next morning hardly registered. Last night, I spent hours agonizing over what I should do. And then, like a man having a religious epiphany, an idea came to me.

Anne had told me once how she dreamed of a knight in shining armor whisking her away. She wanted a fairy tale. She wanted Prince Charming.

I called the Ranch. It was a large acreage, a holdover from cattle days. As the city aged and expanded, it grew around the Ranch. These days, it operated more as a tourist attraction than anything else.

I found the telephone number on their website. The phone rang once, twice. I became nervous. Maybe I shouldn't go through with this? Too late, someone answered.

"Hello?" a female voice asked.

"Yeah, hi. My name's Tony, and my fiancé and I are scheduled for photos today," I said, putting on a meathead accent, trying to sound believably dumb. "Only thing is, I forgot where we are supposed to do it. Can you help me out?"

"Just a moment, sir. Ah, here it is. You are set up with the house photographer at Rosewood Gable."

"Thanks a lot. Bye."

The website also had the number for the horse stables listed. The phone was picked up almost instantly. "Hi, how much to rent a horse?" I asked.

"We don't rent horses," the guy on the phone said, sounding annoyed.

He thought I was stupid. My meathead routine was working.

"Sure, sure. How much for a riding lesson?"

"Fifty dollars for one hour. Eighty for two hours."

"And can I ride it anywhere? Like over to Rosewood Gable?"

"Sorry, pal, but you can only ride within the fenced riding area."

"Oh, I see. Thanks."

I hung up. I could make this happen. It would just be a little complicated. I checked the time. I had four hours to get ready.

I quickly showered and prepared to leave. As I walked out the door, I noticed the tremor in my hands had returned. I would need to make an extra stop.

This early in the morning, the only place selling alcohol was the grocery store. I bought a bottle of vodka. Inside my car, I transferred as much as I could into my flask. I took a couple of heavy swigs from the bottle. My nerves calmed.

Next, I hit the ATM. With the horse guy at the Ranch stonewalling me, I was going to need extra cash. At least my student loans were being put to good use. After that, I drove to the tuxedo shop. They didn't open until 10:30 AM. So, I waited in the car and finished the vodka.

~~~

Gravel crunched under my feet as I approached the stable.

I wore an ill-fitting tuxedo. The sleeves were too long, coming to rest halfway down my hands. The pants were also too long, and caught beneath my heels several times. The store clerk couldn't fathom why I didn't want to make alterations. Yes, I told him, I knew it didn't fit right. No, I told him, I couldn't wait for adjustments. At least he cut me a break on the price.

There was a small building connected to the stable. It was labeled "Business Office." I entered and drew a perplexed look from the clerk inside.

"Can I help you?" he asked.

"I'd like a one-hour lesson."

"Sure thing," he said. I recognized his voice from the phone. He brought out a day planner and flipped it open. "What time did you want?"

"Right now."

"Now? There aren't any instructors are available."

"I don't need one."

"Huh?"

"Listen," I said, resting my arm on the counter. I was trying to act suave. I pulled my wallet out and removed two crisp fifty dollar bills. "One's for the lesson and one's for you. I just need the horse for an hour."

He greedily took the bills. "Let's go see if we can find you a nice horse."

We walked into the stable. There were rows of horses paddocked on either side. The smell of manure was pungent. We walked on dirt and straw. The man stopped and pointed at a brown horse. "This is Whisper. She's perfect for a beginner like you," he said.

I'm sure he was right, but Whisper was plain. I needed something flashy. Directly across from Whisper stood an all-black horse. Light shimmered off its coat. "What about this one?" I asked.

"That's Johnny Come Lately. He's fairly new. A little temperamental. You wouldn't want to ride him."

"Why not?"

"I'd only put an experienced rider on him."

"I want him."

"I don't know—"

I pulled out another fifty dollar bill. In an instant, the money was gone and the guy was saddling the horse. "I'll show you to the riding area. Take as much time as you like."

"I was thinking of riding out to Rosewood Gable."

The man shook his head. "I can't let you do that. This here is an expensive animal. If anything happened to him, it would be my ass."

"I'm doing this for my fiancé. We're having our picture taken there in a few minutes. I want to surprise her."

He finished preparing the horse, opened its stall, and walked it out to me. "Sorry, pal, it's a nice sentiment, but I can't let you," he said.

I pulled every bill out of my wallet, four hundred dollars. He snatched them away.

"Okay," he said. "Just bring him back as soon as you're done."

"Great, thanks. How do I get there?"

He gave me directions. After that, he helped me into the saddle and sent me on my way.

I rode slowly. Above, the sky was looking grim. The light gray had given way to dark thunderclouds. I hoped it wouldn't rain. After all this, I couldn't have my big chance ruined by inclement weather.

The gravel turned to packed dirt, which turned to grass. In the distance was a clump of tall green trees surrounded by pink rose bushes.

Cold sweat sprang to my forehead. I wiped it away and took several breaths. My hands shook. I gripped the reins and waited for the shaking to subside. My chance had finally come.

Johnny Come Lately cantered past the rose bushes, through the line of trees, and bore me into a small grassy enclosure. More rose bushes formed a circle around a white gazebo. I pulled back on the reins. The horse slowed to a stop.

Anne was in the gazebo. She looked radiant. Her breasts practically spilled out of her yellow sundress. Her hair fell over her shoulders. The guy, Tony, was there, too. They kissed while the photographer snapped pictures.

"Anne!" I called out.

The three faces inside the gazebo turned around.

"Anne!"

I gave the horse a kick and he trotted forward. Anne squinted. "What the hell are you doing here?" she asked.

"I'm here for you!"

"What?"

"I came for you! For us!"

She walked toward me. I pulled the reins again and the horse stopped. Anne shoved her fists onto her hips. Her eyes blazed the way they had the last time I saw her. She tried to keep her voice subdued, but struggled to do so. "Why are you here?"

"I came here for us, Anne."

"You keep saying that, but I don't know what *the fuck* it means."

"We were meant to be together. I know that now. I was stupid. I was afraid to give you what you wanted. But now I'm here. Come with me, Anne."

"Why are you dressed like that?"

"I'm your Prince Charming."

She guffawed.

I felt like I was sinking.

"I know you want to get married," I said. "So, let's do it. Let's ride away and start a new life together."

I was laying the clichés on a thickly as possible. I sounded like a fool, but it was the kind of thing Anne liked.

Apparently, I was wrong. Anne's face turned bright red. A thick vein popped out of the center of her skull. Her restraint was gone. "That's exactly the fucking problem!" she bellowed. "I didn't just want to get married! I wanted you to want to marry me!"

"Oh, Anne, I'm so—"

"Don't sorry me! You always do that! Be a goddamn man for once!"

"I-I am. That's why I'm here."

"You aren't here for that! You're here to ruin this for me!" she said, pointing to the gazebo where Tony and the photographer stared at us.

Johnny Come Lately decided he was bored with all this. He turned around. Anne was hurling a torrent of obscenities at me, and my horse was showing her its ass.

I craned my torso, trying to keep her in view. I pulled on the reins to turn the horse back, but he didn't obey.

"You bastard! I hate you! Get out of here before Tony breaks your neck!"

Tony stayed in the gazebo. He looked at the floor, embarrassed.

A peculiar thing happened. I heard a rumble. It was a gurgle from deep within the horse. I'd heard bowel sounds a thousand times before on humans. It sounded like that only much bigger.

"You get the hell out of here right now, or I'll—"

Johnny Come Lately unleashed a mighty fart followed by a spray of diarrhea. Anne was splashed head-on. She was covered from face to feet with liquid feces. A little bit splattered on me, too. When the horse finished, the rumbling in its stomach ceased.

Her yellow sun dress had turned brown. Flecks of shit speckled her face and hair. She stood in a small brown puddle. She was too shocked to do anything.

It was time for me to go.

I kicked the horse hard and it raced forward. My body jerked back, but I grabbed the saddle horn before I flew off. As we galloped away, I heard Anne roar, "You son of a bitch! If I ever see you again, I'll kill you!"

I pulled the reins left. The horse went right. I pulled back to slow him down. He sped up. I bounced violently in the saddle. No matter what I did, the horse didn't obey. Johnny Come Lately was in charge.

We galloped at full speed. Pinefield Ranch grew smaller behind us, and the city grew larger before us. We were about to reach the demarcation between ranch and city. I gripped the saddle hard between my thighs.

The horse leaped over a split-rail fence and landed on concrete. It raced across four lanes of traffic. Cars on either side of the road slammed on their brakes. Their horns blared.

We made it to the sidewalk on the other side. Confronted with a building, the horse made a sharp right turn and galloped down the sidewalk.

There were few pedestrians, but the ones nearby yelped and dove out of the way. The last thing I needed right now was to trample someone.

Still holding tight, I looked back. The Ranch was completely out of sight. I had no idea how far we'd traveled.

The horse breathed hard and began to tire. It slowed to a canter. It covered more ground before it slowed to a trot. And then, finally, it stopped. Johnny Come Lately had worn himself out.

I dismounted and managed to turn the horse around. There was no way in hell I was going to get back on him. He was done taking me for a ride. We began the slow trudge back to the ranch.

As we walked, thunder boomed. The gloom of the oncoming storm had cast midday into darkness.

I pulled the stupid horse behind me. It wasn't long before he started to fight. People on the street gaped. My heart sunk low in my chest. It was finally over. My last chance at happiness was gone.

It didn't really matter what happened next. Happy or unhappy, married or single, loved or unloved. Despite the circumstances, we all share the same fate in the end. Alone in a box with nothing to show for it.

Rain started to fall.

PRESENT

Everything was hazy. My throat burned. It felt raw inside. It hurt to talk. It hurt to breathe. I felt like I had aged a thousand years, and all my muscles had atrophied.

A guy in gray scrubs and a long white coat asked me questions. I shook my head "no" even though I couldn't understand him. He shined a light in one of my eyes, and then the other. I didn't have the energy to squeeze my eyes shut.

Two other people entered the room, a woman, smartly dressed, and a man in business-casual attire. They spoke with the guy in scrubs, but their voices were muffled. They pointed at me and then at a machine next to my bed.

The business-casual man, with round glasses and a perfectly shaved head, came over. He shined his own light at me, hit my limbs with a reflex hammer, and talked to me. What was he saying? I tried to speak but could only gasp.

Another woman, dressed in burgundy scrubs, entered the room. She held a syringe. She grabbed my hand and inspected a strip of plastic looped around my wrist. It bore three words. They were fuzzy. They might have been my name.

Satisfied I was the right patient, she inserted the syringe into a port in my arm. She pushed the plunger and clear liquid raced into my veins.

My body flushed hot. My vision got hazier, dimmer. The voices of the people in the room grew more distorted. I struggled to stay awake, but fighting was impossible. I gave in and slept.

~~~

Two days passed. I had been admitted to the ICU of a private hospital. Once I had my senses back, I recognized everything. So far, I hadn't seen anyone I knew.

I sat up in bed. The tiny hospital TV was on, but there was nothing good to watch. A tray of bland food was placed in front of me. I tried to feed myself gelatin, but I wasn't hungry.

As I swallowed the slimy cherry substance, the guy in gray scrubs entered my room. "Hey there, how're you feeling today?" he asked, approaching my bed.

It was eerie. I had always been on his side of things. Now, all the attention was on me. I felt like a zoo animal.

"Tired, but okay, I guess," I croaked.

"How's your throat?"

"Scratchy."

"We had you intubated. That's when we put a tube down your throat to help you breathe."

I knew what it meant.

He went on, "It should feel better in a day or two. Now, can you tell me what happened?"

I wasn't sure how to answer. He was staring at me intently. His demeanor was upbeat. He didn't seem judgmental. I looked down. "I injected potassium," I said.

"Were you trying to kill yourself?"

". . . yeah."

"Where did you get that stuff?"

"I'm a . . . medical student."

"Oh, okay. It's a good thing you called nine-one-one. When they got to your place, you were dead."

I set the spoon down on the tray. My minuscule appetite was obliterated. My head drooped and my shoulders slumped.

The guy, still friendly, asked me a few questions about where I was from, what school I went to, did I use drugs or alcohol, mixing the history and physical exam with some chit chat. By the end, I felt marginally better.

"Any time someone tries to harm themselves, we order a Psych consult. It's standard procedure. Someone will come and talk to you, and see if you need any additional treatment. All right?" he said.

"Sure," I said. As if I had a choice.

"Great. Have a good day."

He was up and out of the room. I looked back at my tray of food. Everything still looked disgusting, but I gave the gelatin a second try.

Later that day, a psychiatrist came to evaluate me. I gave him an expanded version of my story. I was ashamed about what I had done. He asked me if I wanted to spend a few days on the psych unit. Honestly, I didn't mind.

~ ~ ~

The hospital didn't have an inpatient psychiatric unit, so I was sent to the county hospital via ambulance. When I arrived, the metal double doors looked more imposing than I remembered. When I heard them lock behind me, they did so with deafening finality. I was trapped.

I swung my head around a few times, wondering if I would see an Attending or Resident I knew. So far, I didn't recognize anyone.

The techs took my clothes and draped a fashionable hospital gown and cordless sweat pants on me. I had to hold the gown closed with a fist to keep it from billowing open. The techs walked me down to one of the interview rooms where I met the Resident.

She asked me questions I had heard a hundred times before. Ones I had asked when I was here a few months ago. It was surreal. I tried to expand my story further, but she kept interrupting me. Any time I deviated from her questions, she was no longer interested in what I had to say.

When she finished, she told me she would talk to the Attending about what medication to start me on. After that, she would get back to me. I didn't care.

I shuffled out to the Day Room. The patients were huddled around the TV, watching the news. I sat down at the back of the room and watched.

Another patient, a chipper-looking guy, sat down next to me and said, "Hey, man. You just get here?"

"Yeah."

"Name's David. What's yours?"

I told him.

"Cool. It's nice to meet you."

We shook hands. He radiated unexpected friendliness.

"Have you been here long?" I asked.

"About five days."

"So, you might be getting out soon?"

"I sure hope so. My social worker's helping me find a halfway house."

I turned my attention back to the TV.

"Where you from?" David asked.

"Uh, the Midwest. You?"

"Here. Born and raised. Which do you like better, here or the Midwest?"

"I'm not sure."

"What brought you all the way out here?"

"What time do they serve dinner around here, anyway?"

"At five-thirty. About an hour."

David was still glowing with a familiar smile. He was nice, but I didn't feel like talking anymore. I stood up and said, "It's nice to meet you. I think I might take a nap until dinner."

"Cool. See you later."

I shuffled down to my room. It was a shared room, but my roommate wasn't there. I laid down, and stared up at the smooth white ceiling. I went over the event again and again. Why did I do it? What had I been thinking? I had no answers. I had just done it, like I was someone else.

There was a knock at the door. The Resident stepped into the room. "I'm here to talk to you about meds," she said.

"Okay," I said, sitting up.

She took a second step into the room but kept her distance. She was still visible to anyone in the hallway. "We'd like to start you on Citalopram. It's an antidepressant. It should be really helpful at getting you to feel better."

"Okay."

"Great. I just need you to sign this," she said, holding out a single sheet of paper. It was a medication informed consent document. I took the paper, signed it sloppily, and handed it back.

"Thanks. You'll start tomorrow morning. Do you have any questions?"

"No."

"All right, then. Have a good evening."

I dropped back onto the bed. So, this was how it felt to be a patient.

~~~

Life had become an endless string of groups. In the morning we had Goals Group, then Process Group, and then Art Therapy. In the afternoon we had Music Therapy, Pet Therapy, Family Group, and CBT. In the evening we concluded with Wrap-Up Group. The groups were fine, I suppose. They kept us busy all day so we wouldn't go crazy.

Goals Group was my favorite. A Borderline lady made her goal, "To not get mad if someone takes my seat in the Day Room." A PTSD guy said his goal was, "Not spend all day in my room." One of the Schizophrenics' was, "Take my meds." They were not exactly the highest achievers. Although, who was I to judge? The first two days I couldn't even think of a goal. On the third, I said, "I want to call my family."

The doctors appeared briefly. They talked to me for ten minutes, and then moved on to the next poor sap. The rest of the day they were off doing other things. I knew they were busy because I had been on their side. But from over here, it didn't seem that way.

I made an ally in David. We chatted about a lot of things. Politics, religion, philosophy, art, music, etc. He was a smart guy, and more well-rounded than I could ever hope to be. For some odd reason, he took an interest in me.

It was mid-afternoon. We were between groups, the only time we were allowed to use the telephone. Cell phones weren't allowed. The Day Room had an old corded phone that hung on the wall. It had been white at one point in its life, but had browned with the passage of time. I stared at it. It stared back, taunting me, daring me to use it.

Should I call Mom? Tell her what I had done? I would never hear the end of it. The only other choice I had was Eve, and this would permanently cement my loser status in her mind. And yet, it was today's goal. If I didn't show any effort, any progress, I would never go home.

I walked over to the phone and lifted the handset. As I placed the receiver to my ear, the hum of the dial tone was drowned out by a horrendous shriek. I jumped and dropped the handset. Everyone in the room turned toward the sound.

The new patient, a woman about my age, who had just come in a few hours ago, was being dragged to the Quiet Room. She shrieked again. Everyone returned to their books and board games. They had hoped to see something more exciting.

The handset swung back and forth. I picked it up and dialed.

"Hello?" my sister said, sounding sleepy.

"E-Evie."

She perked up a bit. "Hey. I wasn't expecting to hear from you. What's up?"

"Am I . . . calling at a bad time?"

"No, not at," she paused to yawn, ". . . all."

"That's good."

"How are you?"

"Well, um, Evie, the truth is, um, not good."

"What's wrong?" she asked with a crisper voice.

". . . you see, uh, well, I'm . . . in the hospital."

"What happened?!"

"I'm fine now. I made a full recovery, so don't worry."

"Did you call Mom? What happened?"

"Evie, this is something I can't call Mom about. Not yet."

My evasiveness only worried her more. I had to be honest. If I didn't, this entire phone call would be pointless. I felt my throat catch. I felt like I was on a stage, a spectacle for everyone around me to see and judge.

I shifted my eyes back toward the room. The other patients were absorbed in their own activities. Nobody was interested in my phone call. I tried again, this time finding the words. "I'm in the psych hospital. I tried to kill myself."

The words hung there for a moment. And then, they drifted away, taking with them the heavy weight that had clung to me for so long.

"I'm so sorry. Are you okay?"

"Yeah. The doctors have me on a medication, and I'm going to groups. I'll be fine."

"What happened?"

"I injected myself with potassium. I hadn't planned it. It was impulsive."

"No, not that. I mean, what happened?" Eve asked, sounding like she was on the verge of tears.

My vision flooded and my face felt wet. I lost the strength in my knees. "It's just – just – with everything. School. This girl. Dad. And this city. Just everything, Evie," I said.

I collapsed. Fat tears streamed down my face. My breaths came in big, rolling heaves. On the other end of the phone Eve was crying, too.

Later that night, we had Wrap-Up Group. The Day Room's TV was off, and the chairs were arranged in a circle. We took turns, one by one, discussing how the day went.

When it was my turn, I said, "I had a pretty good day. My goal was to call my family, and I did. I called my sister. I told her why I was here."

"That's great," David said with a smile. "How'd it go?"

"Surprisingly well. It was the first time she ever listened to what I had to say."

The group leader, a social worker, congratulated me on accomplishing my goal. Then it was the next person's turn. I didn't hear what they had to say. I replayed the conversation with Eve in my mind. For the first time in my life, I didn't hate her.

~~~

The coffee in this place was terrible. Nevertheless, I always had a cup first thing in the morning. It helped keep life somewhat normal. Not that it was so strange here, but reminders of regular life helped.

The other reminder of regular life was a set of normal clothes. The techs presented me with some clothes that I could wear while on the unit. It was nice to wear a t-shirt and jeans. I didn't feel so exposed.

I sat down in one of two perpendicular couches so I could watch the morning news. A couple of talking heads blathered on about a celebrity donating their time to charity. It must have been a slow news day.

David walked around the couch with an enormous smile.

"Hey," I said sleepily, still waiting for the caffeine to work its magic.

David dropped onto the opposite couch. "Morning," he said.

"What are you so happy about?"

"Just met with my doc."

"And?"

"And I'm going home today!"

I smiled. "That's great. Congrats."

"You know what the first thing I'm going to do is?"

"What?"

"Go down to this dive diner and get the biggest, greasiest burger they've got. Mmm-mmm, I can taste it now."

My smile grew larger. David's moods were infectious. "Sounds nice," I said.

"When are you going home?" he asked.

"I don't know. They aren't saying much about it. Probably a few more days."

"You just hang tight, buddy. You'll be home sooner than you think."

"I hope so."

"I had a thought, though, if you don't mind."

"What's that?"

"Maybe you should think about going to AA."

"Why would I go there?"

"I'm an alcoholic, too. I can see it in your face."

"So?"

"So, I'm six years sober now. I go to AA all the time. Best thing for me."

"Eh, I don't know."

"Just give it a try."

"But listening to all those drunks will just make me feel worse."

"I guarantee it won't. What have you got to lose?"

"Okay, David, I'll think about it."

"That's all I'm asking."

"Anyway, I'm really happy for you."

"Thanks. I'd better start packing. See you around."

David left to pack his belongings. He skipped Goals Group. There wasn't much point in him attending. That delicious burger was his goal today.

One thing we had to do while we were hospitalized was set up our own psychiatric follow-up appointment. We weren't allowed to discharge without one. I made that my goal for the day. I got a list of potential clinics from my social worker and started to call around. On the second attempt, I had something set up. It was easy, and it wasn't even noon yet. Feeling rather accomplished, I sauntered from the phone to the center of the Day Room.

The new girl was sulking at a table. Her arms were crossed and pressed against the tabletop. Her head rested on her arms. Her dirty brown hair was splayed out in disarray. She wore a grim look on her face.

I sat down next to her. I stared off at nothing in particular. "Good morning," I said with casual interest.

"What's good about it?" she grumbled.

"There's that turd on TV," I said, nodding toward the self-righteous newscaster.

She gave a restrained chuckle. "I'm Tanya."

"Nice to meet you."

". . . same."

"Where are you from?"

". . . here. The city."

"Born and raised, huh?"

". . . I guess so."

I peeked at her. She kept her head buried in the folds of her arms. I'm not sure why, but I felt like I could help her. She needed someone to be nice to her, but I didn't want to push it.

"Lunch will be in about thirty minutes," I said.

"How is it?"

"Didn't you eat yesterday?"

"No."

"Oh, well, it could be worse."

"How's that?"

"It could be dog food."

She raised her head and gave a slightly less subdued chuckle.

"Well, Tanya, it's nice to meet you. I'll see you around."

I got up and walked laps. The unit was shaped like a giant rectangle. It was open on either end, forming a makeshift track. The staff told us not to run, but if we walked six laps, it was a mile. And so, I walked.

I walked lap after lap. I nodded hello to my fellow patients. I waved goodbye to David as he was escorted out. I excused myself when I bumped into a Resident who was exiting an interview room. I walked until lunch was served. By then I had worked up an appetite.

My tray held a plate of congealed macaroni and cheese. It tasted like glue with a flavor mildly reminiscent of cheddar. Another tray slid onto the table. Tanya sat in the chair opposite me. She was still disheveled.

"They'll get you some regular clothes soon," I said.

She readjusted her gown, pulling the loose shoulder loops tight. She slicked her matted hair back in an attempt to tame it. "I hope so," she replied. She took a bite of food, considered it, and then took a second. "How long you been here?"

"Four days."

"They got you on meds?"

"Just one."

"They want me to take three."

"So many?"

"Yeah. One for my mood, one for my voices, and one for the side effects I get from the one for my voices."

"If that's what they think will help."

"I don't think it will. I'm not sure about those doctors."

I tried to act nonchalant. "I think the ones here are pretty good. As far as I can tell, they just want to help us."

"Hmm," she said, mulling over my words as she chewed unidentified gray meat.

We ate the rest of our meals without speaking again. The people around us talked and laughed. The TV glowed although no one watched it. One person vomited. That made someone else have a pseudo-seizure. A third person ran off to the Nurses Station hollering about needing Valium for a panic attack. It was amazing how hospital food could set off such a chain reaction.

Tanya and I finished eating at the same time. She quickly stood up. "You sure these doctors really want to help?" she asked.

"Yeah, I think they're on the up and up."

"Okay."

She zipped out of the room. I bussed both our trays. I didn't feel like going to any more groups today, so I returned to doing laps.

~~~

It was my sixth day of admission. I felt better. I couldn't be certain how much was due to medication and how much was due to me being in here. I was cut off from all the stress of the world, and I was finally able to think clearly.

I poured coffee into a cup. It looked like motor oil. I tasted it and grimaced. When I got out of here, the first thing I was going to do was get a good cup of coffee. I tossed the cup and grabbed yesterday's newspaper.

A woman approached me. At first I didn't recognize her, but a moment later she registered. It was Tanya, only she was showered, her hair was straight, and she wore regular clothes.

"Hi," she said.

"How are you?"

"I'm good."

"You're looking a lot better these days."

"Thanks."

"Good thing you started taking the meds."

"Yeah, I guess. But I don't like having to take pills. Seems weird putting stuff in your body, you know?"

"The main thing is you're feeling better. Keep it up."

"Yeah, okay."

Something in her peripheral vision caught her attention, and she walked away.

Some of the other patients did whatever they could to get out of here as fast as possible, like they had something really important to do. I didn't mind sticking around. For the first time since before medical school, I felt at ease.

The day passed quickly, and the clock now read 3:59 PM. People filed into the Day Room. It had become a reflex for me to vanish every day at this time. I stood up as the patients circled the chairs. I headed for the exit, but stopped abruptly. I had done everything else since I was here, so why not do this one last thing?

The other patients sat in a circle, murmuring, waiting for the group to begin. I thought about what David said to me before he left.

I grabbed a chair and found a place in the circle. The group leader arrived and welcomed us to Alcoholics Anonymous.

~~~

The female Resident shuffled through a dozen loose sheets of paper. Her hair stuck out in every direction. Dark circles underlined her eyes. Her scrubs were wrinkled.

"How are you this morning?" I asked.

"Tired," she replied, yawning.

"Post-call?"

She looked up at me, not expecting a patient to use that term. She looked back at the papers. "It was a long night. Ah, here we are. How are you doing?" she asked as she pulled out a particular document.

"Fine."

She scribbled my response on the paper. "Any suicidal thoughts?"

"No."

She rattled through the questions quickly. We had been through them every morning since my admission. She knew what the answers would be. Asking them was a formality at this point. "How do you feel about going home?" she asked

"I feel great about it."

"Would you be safe from harming yourself outside the hospital?"

"Absolutely."

"Good. My Attending still has to sign off, but I think you're ready to leave. Let's go over your discharge plan."

We reviewed the safety plan, my upcoming psychiatric appointment, and how to take my medication. After that, she wished me luck. She had some paperwork to do, but I would be out of here in a few hours.

I went back to the Day Room. I found Tanya playing a card game with three other people. I sat down beside her.

"Good morning," she said, slapping a card on the table.

"Morning."

"What's up?"

"I just found out I'm leaving today."

Tanya put her cards down on the table. "That's great! I'm so happy for you!"

The other card players gave me a round of subdued congratulations. Tanya hugged me tightly. "What are you gonna do once you're out?"

It was funny how we talked like prison inmates. "I haven't thought that far ahead yet. I imagine my apartment needs a good cleaning," I said.

"I'm sure gonna miss you."

"Me, too."

"Thanks for everything."

"Anytime," I said with a smile.

I packed up my belongings, which only took about five minutes. I spent the rest of my time reading, and trying not to get too excited about discharging. And when the time finally came, one of the techs walked me out.

The two monolithic metal doors slammed shut behind us. The tech took me downstairs where an arranged taxi waited for me. Instead of giving the driver my address, I told him to take me to a coffee shop.

~~~

My fingers twitched at my sides. The volume of the room seemed to be turned up to an abnormal level. I could hear every word, every syllable of the people around me. The influx of noise was near deafening.

Above me, the lights shone brightly. They were too bright. I had to squint just so I didn't feel like I was under an array of heat lamps.

The floor was dirty and disgusting. Hair and gum and trash littered the place. Why didn't they keep it cleaner? What the hell was wrong with the staff? The psychiatric unit had been better than this place in every single way.

I stepped up to the counter and ordered a drink. As the barista made it, I felt the eyes of every patron crawling over my back. They were all looking at me, waiting for me to screw up. Why couldn't people just mind their own business?

My coffee appeared on the counter. I grabbed it and turned so I could leave. I stopped short, face to face with Brad.

His face lit up when he saw me. We hadn't spoken in a long time. "Wow! Great to see you!" he said.

A beautiful woman stood beside him. She wore a long dress which did little to conceal the swell of her belly. She smiled and looked at Brad while he spoke.

"What have you been up to?" he asked.

"Uh, not much."

"How's your vacation going?"

"Fine," I said with a shrug. "How's yours?"

"Studying a lot for the big test."

He looked at the woman and then back at me. "I'm sorry, I didn't introduce you. This is my wife, Heather."

We shook hands and exchanged the usual pleasantries. "We did an Internal Medicine rotation together," Brad said to his wife. "It was hell, but somehow we got through it."

I smiled wanly.

"So, how's it going, you know, with everything?" Brad asked. I was getting irritated with how much he was digging. Why didn't he mind his own business?

"How far along are you?" I asked Heather.

"Seven months," she said.

"That's great. Boy or girl?"

"Girl. We're really excited."

Brad wrapped an arm around her shoulders and squeezed. "Yeah, this has been a great month. I was in California for most of it. But Heather decided to come back with me for the last week."

"I never get to see him, so I've got to spend as much time with him as I can," she said.

The two of them were infatuated with one another. I couldn't decide what was more annoying, this or all of Brad's questions.

"Why don't we get together for dinner tonight?" Brad asked.

"I can't, I'm busy," I said.

"Then how about tomorrow?"

"I'll get back to you. Listen, I've got to run."

"All right, well, it was great seeing you again."

"Nice to meet you," Heather said.

I repeated the empty sentiment and scurried away.

~~~

I mounted the stairs to my apartment. I paused at the door. The last time I was here I had done something stupid. On the psychiatric unit, I was certain it would never happen again. But now I wasn't entirely convinced.

I opened the door and stepped inside. As I did, I heard someone call my name. I turned back.

"Eve?"

She wore jeans and a green blouse. Her hair was pulled up. A look of uncertainty was on her face. "Hi," was all she managed to say. It was enough.

We embraced in the hallway forever. She emitted true warmth. We both pulled back and looked at one another. Eve gave a nod, and I smiled.

We went inside the apartment. Bottles, papers, and trash were strewn about. Almost everything in the refrigerator had spoiled. The foul stench of rotten food filled the air.

"Did a bomb go off in here?" Eve quipped.

"I swear it was clean when I left," I said.

"There's no time like the present," she said. "Let's get started."

Our epic cleaning project commenced. We picked up the debris, tossed out the garbage, and collected the seemingly endless supply of empty liquor bottles and beer cans. I thought Eve would make some remark, but she didn't. She helped clean, scrub, and vacuum right alongside me.

As we cleaned, I told her what happened. The whole story. She listened, and by the time we finished cleaning, I reached the present day of my tale.

Surveying the apartment, Eve said, "The place looks good. What do you say we get some fresh air?"

We stepped onto the balcony. The sun was setting. The balcony was cast in an orange glow. I put my elbows against the railing and leaned forward. Eve leaned the opposite direction. Below, busy commuters fought with traffic to get home.

"Thanks for coming, Eve," I said.

"No problem."

"You didn't have trouble getting off work, huh?"

"It's easy when you're the boss."

"Yeah, I suppose so."

"So, did you call Mom yet?"

"No, not yet. But I will."

"She'd love to hear from you."

"I know."

Eve turned around and adopted the same position as me. The sun was a huge ball of fire now. It started to dip below the horizon.

"It's so hot out here. How do you stand it?" she asked.

"I can't. But I have to put up with it for one more year. When Residency rolls around, I'll get out of this town."

"You know, California is nice this time of year."

"And I suppose you want me to live with you?"

"Oh, God no."

We laughed together.

"I think it's great you're gonna stay here and finish school. And when you move to California, be sure you live in driving distance from me. How else are you gonna get a home-cooked meal?"

"Hmm, good point."

The sun dipped lower. The orange gave way to the gray of dusk. Eve stretched her back. I did the same.

"In any case, wherever you go, you'll be a good doctor. I'm proud of you."

"Thanks, Eve."

"And when you're ready, I know a couple of really cute girls who work at the office."

"You're not serious."

"What? Sure I am. We girls aren't all bad. You just have to stay away from the crazy ones."

"All right, that's enough, let's go back inside."

I ushered her back inside the apartment while she laughed hysterically.

~~~

My last week of break flew by. Eve stayed for two more days. I slept on the couch while she took the bed. I scrambled to set up my rotations for fourth year. I wasn't sure what I wanted to do, so I included electives to supplement Pediatrics and Psychiatry, the only two rotations I liked. Maybe that would steer me in the right direction.

When it was time for Eve to go, we said a much longer goodbye than ever before. Our interaction still had a snarky undercurrent, but there was mutual respect.

When Monday morning came, I awoke and got ready to begin my final year of medical school. My first rotation was Pediatric Internal Medicine. If it was anything like the adult version, I was sure to have a wild time.

I stood near the side entrance of the hospital. People filed in and out. Someone I didn't know walked past me. He wore a short white coat and a mystified expression. He looked so young. Without a doubt he was a fresh third year student. Poor bastard.

And then I saw another, and another. All the medical students looked the same. Nameless, faceless, forgettable, just like me. I shook that thought away and entered the hospital.

ACKNOWLEDGEMENTS

This book would not have been possible without the contributions of many people. My family, who are supportive of my writing and all my various endeavours. Fairley Neal, who graciously gave me the "Prince Charming" idea. Cathy Ulrich for helping me write the book's synopsis. And James at GoOnWrite.com who created my cover art. Thank you all.